T0022373

Praise for Alexander McCall Smith's

NO. 1 LADIES' DETECTIVE AGENCY

"There is no end to the pleasure that may be extracted from these . . . books."   —*The New York Times Book Review*

"McCall Smith's plots offer wit, charm, and intrigue in equal doses."   —*Richmond Times-Dispatch*

"Enthralling. . . . [Mma Ramotswe] is someone readers can't help but love."   —*USA Today*

"Charming and hilarious. . . . Sweet and timeless."
     —*The Seattle Times*

"These gentle stories of manners and morality have a clarity that . . . seems far harder to discern in our own rushed, deadline-driven lives."   —*The Scotsman*

"Radiant. . . . Calling Precious Ramotswe . . . a detective doesn't do her justice. 'Problem solver extraordinaire' would be much better."   —*Booklist* (starred review)

Alexander McCall Smith

TO THE LAND OF LONG LOST FRIENDS

Alexander McCall Smith is the author of the No. 1 Ladies' Detective Agency novels and a number of other series and stand-alone books. His works have been translated into more than forty languages and have been bestsellers throughout the world. He lives in Scotland.

www.alexandermccallsmith.com

**BOOKS BY
ALEXANDER McCALL SMITH**

TO THE LAND OF LONG LOST FRIENDS

A THOUSAND DRAGON SWEATERS

TO THE LAND OF

LONG LOST FRIENDS

Alexander McCall Smith

Anchor Books

A DIVISION OF PENGUIN RANDOM HOUSE LLC

NEW YORK

FIRST ANCHOR BOOKS EDITION, SEPTEMBER 2020

The Library of Congress has cataloged the Pantheon edition as follows:
Names: McCall Smith, Alexander, 1948– author.
Title: To the land of long lost friends / Alexander McCall Smith.
Description: First United States Edition. | New York : Pantheon, 2019.
Identifiers: LCCN 2019023510 (print) | LCCN 2019023511 (ebook)
Subjects: LCSH: Ramotswe, Precious (Fictitious character)—Fiction. | Women
private investigators—Botswana—Fiction. | No. 1 Ladies' Detective Agency
(Imaginary organization)—Fiction. | Botswana—Fiction.
Classification: LCC PR6063.C326 (ebook) | LCC PR6063.C326 T6 2019 (print) |
DDC 823/.914—dc23
LC record available at https://lccn.loc.gov/2019023510

Anchor Books Trade Paperback ISBN: 978-0-525-56427-0
eBook ISBN: 978-1-524-74783-1

Book design by Anna B. Knighton

www.anchorbooks.com

Printed in the United States of America
10 9 8 7 6 5

This book is for Sue and Neil Douglas.

TO THE LAND OF LONG LOST FRIENDS

CHAPTER ONE

INSIDE PEOPLE, OUTSIDE PEOPLE

PRECIOUS RAMOTSWE, founder of the No. 1 Ladies' Detective Agency, doyenne of private investigators in Botswana (not that there were any others, apart from her assistant, Grace Makutsi), wife of Mr. J.L.B. Matekoni (*garagiste* and past chairman of the Botswana Motor Trades Association), citizen of Botswana—that same Precious Ramotswe was sitting in the second row of chairs at the open-air wedding of Mr. Seemo Outule to Ms. Thato Kgwadi. The chairs were lined up under a large awning protecting the guests from the sun, which, since the wedding ceremony was taking place at eleven-thirty, was almost at its highest point in the echoing, empty sky. It was a hot day in October, a month of heat and unremitting thirst for the land and all that lived upon the land: the cattle, the wild animals, the small, almost invisible creatures that conducted their lives in the undergrowth or among the rocks, creatures whose very names had been forgotten now. They were all waiting for the rains, which would come, of course, in greater or smaller measure at a time when they were ready. And that was a time nobody could predict, even if they hoped against hope that it was not long off.

The land was waiting for that first rain, and the people too, but this did not mean that life did not go on as normal in spite of the dryness. Those who planned to move house or change their job, or start studying for something, or paint their kitchen, or turn over a new leaf—all of these people would go ahead with these things even though many of their waking hours were spent waiting for the relief of rain. You had to, because otherwise life would grind to a halt, and nobody would be ready for the rains once they came. And of course this applied to those who wanted to get married and get on with family life. Their weddings would take place in the heat, but that was probably better than getting married in the cold season—such as it was—and shivering before the preacher because you couldn't wear an overcoat at your own wedding.

The two young people now taking their vows were well known to Mma Ramotswe, who was friendly with the families on both sides. The engagement of Seemo and his long-time girlfriend, Thato, had given her particular pleasure, as it seemed to her that the two families were ideally suited to one another. This was not only because both fathers were interested in cattle-breeding—although who wasn't, in Botswana, a famous cattle-owning democracy?—but also because the mothers on both sides were passionate picklers and bottlers, preserving all sorts of fruits and vegetables in pickling jars of one shape or another. A shared interest in cattle and pickling may seem to be peripheral and not all that important in the overall scheme of things, but to take that view would be wrong, thought Mma Ramotswe, because these everyday things were often much more important to people than matters of politics or principle, or tribal affiliation. Cattle, Mr. J.L.B. Matekoni once remarked, bring people together. Mma Ramotswe fully agreed with this observation, and felt that the same could be said of pickled marulas and kumquat jam, which also brought people together, in their own particular way.

Of course those were parental interests rather than the interests of the bride and groom themselves, but it was of the utmost importance, Mma Ramotswe had always maintained, that families should get on in any prospective marriage. The reason for that was that you did not just marry a man, you married his father and grandfather, his grandmother and, most important, you married his mother. That last relationship was weightier than any of the others, because a mother-in-law could make or break a marriage, sometimes even without saying anything at all. Sometimes body language was quite sufficient.

So she had no reservations when she heard that Seemo and Thato were going to marry on the fifteenth of October, in the grounds of Tlokweng Orphan Farm, courtesy of Mma Potokwane, who was a cousin of the bride's family and who arranged with the house-mothers to do the catering at a special cut-price rate. The Kgwadis had been generous to the Orphan Farm in the past, donating a used tractor and paying for the renewal of several bathrooms in which the concrete floor had cracked beyond repair. These were things that fell beyond the scope of Mma Potokwane's normal budget, and the munificence of donors was the only way in which they would ever be done. If she could repay by hosting a family wedding in the Orphan Farm's low-walled *kgotla,* or meeting-place enclosure, near the vegetable fields, then that was what she would do. And from the point of view of the housemothers, this was an opportunity to show off their culinary skills and make a small amount of pin money into the bargain. The children themselves, of course, would love it. They would be happy were a wedding to take place every weekend; weddings gave the older children the chance to act as waiters and plate-washers, while the smaller children could help by fetching and carrying all the things that needed to be fetched and carried at such an occasion.

Mma Ramotswe knew Seemo a bit better than she knew his bride. She had first become acquainted with him when he was in his late teens, and doing well at Gaborone Secondary School. He had occasionally washed and polished her tiny white van on Saturday mornings to raise money for his boy-scout troop, and this had impressed her. Then he had gone off to do a course in dental mechanics, and had recently returned to be one of the few people in the country who could assemble and fix a set of false teeth or a complicated dental plate. This profession paid well, and within a few months of his return he was able to afford to propose marriage to his girlfriend, and pay her family every single pula agreed to in the bride-price negotiations. As both families were traditionalists, this price was expressed in head of cattle, and, although money equivalents were broadly acceptable, in this case there had been an actual transfer from the herd of one father to that of the other. Few people saw that transfer other than the cattlemen and herd boys retained by both at their remote cattle posts, who carried out the transaction at the behest of their employers. A new brand was burned into fifteen head of cattle—a substantial dowry, when eight was more normal—and that sealed the bargain. Now all that remained was for the bride and groom to exchange their vows and for the assembled guests to fall with enthusiasm upon the beef and *boervors* already sizzling over the cooking pits dug in the Orphan Farm grounds for this very occasion. The smells that accompanied this wafted over to where the congregation was sitting, causing more than one set of nostrils to turn slightly to savour the delectable odour of Botswana beef being prepared for an imminent wedding feast.

As at most Botswana weddings, the guest list had been drawn up in a spirit of generosity. A wedding was a very significant event for the entire community, and the general expectation was that anybody who had the slightest dealings with the families or with the bride and groom themselves was entitled to be at least considered for an invitation. Of course, limits had to be set, as this circle of acquaintanceship could be a very wide one, in some cases involving thousands, and a line had to be drawn somewhere. The drawing of that line was a difficult task, and not always was it described in just the right place. Nor was it always expressed in a sufficiently tactful way—as was the case, Mma Ramotswe feared, with this particular wedding. Here, the invitation, which was in all other respects normal, created a new precedent by disclosing whether the invitee could expect a seat or not. Mma Ramotswe had received one that stated unambiguously, *Seats available for two persons,* while less fortunate guests received an invitation saying, *In view of the fact that seating is limited by the venue, we regret that you will not be able to sit down for the actual ceremony. Please bring a blanket to sit upon, if required.*

Looking about her, Mma Ramotswe understood why it had been necessary to distinguish between guests in this way. The *kgotla* was not large, essentially being a well-swept circle of packed earth surrounded by a waist-high, whitewashed wall. Within this space twelve rows of folding chairs had been set out, enough to accommodate just over one hundred and twenty people. The other guests, who numbered at least two hundred, were expected to stand around the *kgotla* walls, looking in on the ceremony. Once assembled, these guests made up a crowd five or six persons deep all the way round, unprotected by the shade afforded by the awning and consequently relying on umbrellas for protection against the hammer blows of the sun. It was not ideal, particularly if you were Mma Makutsi and her husband, Phuti Radiphuti, who had received standing-only invitations, and who were now surveying the rows of seated guests and wondering about the criteria upon which selection for that privileged group had been made. It was not moral merit, thought Mma Makutsi, as her eye fell on a well-known Gaborone businessman, seated near the front, who had only the previous week been exposed as having not only one but two mistresses, and three children by each of them. Nor was it good looks or fashion, as there, she noted, was that woman whom she sometimes saw at the supermarket who looked, she decided, remarkably like a hippo and had a voice that sounded like a hippo's too. She was there, and they might even be able to pick her voice out once they started to sing hymns. She would sing exactly as a hippo would sing, thought Mma Makutsi, who smiled at the rather uncharitable thought.

And then Mma Makutsi spotted Mma Ramotswe and Mr. J.L.B. Matekoni, firmly and comfortably seated, and thought, Why should Mma Ramotswe receive a better invitation than mine? Was it because they thought she was more important, being the managing director of the agency, whereas she, Mma Makutsi, was only an ordinary director? Was it because Mma Ramotswe had been written about occasionally in the *Botswana Daily News* and was therefore, in the view of people who did not know any better, a local celebrity of some sort? Was that it? The possibility was an uncomfortable one for Mma Makutsi; after all, who was the Botswana Secretarial College's most distinguished graduate (with ninety-seven per cent) of her year—and indeed of all years, before and after? She was that person, and she had a certificate to prove it. Mma Ramotswe had many merits—Mma Makutsi would never dispute that—but she had no paper qualifications to speak of, other than some small and insignificant certificate from that school at Mochudi to the effect that she had completed three years or so of secondary education. If there were any justice in the world, people would be more aware of these things and not need to be given a reminder, as Mma Makutsi had to provide from time to time, of who got what in which examinations.

Of course, a more innocent, less provocative explanation for Mma Ramotswe having the superior invitation was possible, and this would be cousinage with one of the families. In Botswana everybody was related to everybody one way or another, and it was perfectly possible that this was the basis on which Mma Ramotswe and Mr. J.L.B. Matekoni had been preferred. That made relegation to the outside a little easier to bear, although it was still an annoyance.

"I see that Mma Ramotswe is sitting down," Mma Makutsi remarked to Phuti Radiphuti.

Phuti glanced over the wall. "Yes, I see that, Mma. She is very lucky to be in the shade."

"And sitting on a chair," said Mma Makutsi, "while ordinary people are having to stand in this heat."

"It will not be for hours," said Phuti. "This part of the wedding is usually short enough, isn't it? As long as they don't sing for too long. Or make endless speeches."

"Endless speeches are not a problem if you have a chair," muttered Mma Makutsi. "Provided the chair is strong enough."

Phuti gave her a puzzled look.

"Strong enough," whispered Mma Makutsi. "There are some very traditionally built people over there. Those chairs do not look too strong, Rra. It would be a big pity if some of them gave way."

Phuti made a silencing gesture. "We should be happy when people have chairs," he admonished. "We should be happy, even if we do not have a chair ourselves."

Mma Makutsi looked down at the ground. Her husband was right, of course, and his gentle reproach made her feel guilty. She should be pleased for Mma Ramotswe and Mr. J.L.B. Matekoni— they were older than she was and they had a much greater claim to shade, and to chairs. Phuti was right.

By now the bride had arrived and was standing with the groom at the front of the congregation. A photographer crouched and darted about to get the best angle for his shots; necks craned in an effort to see the bride's finery; several women ululated, the traditional way of expressing joy. There would be more ululations, shrill and exultant, when the business of the ceremony was concluded.

The preacher, a tall, bespectacled man whom Mma Ramotswe knew vaguely through some distant Mochudi connection, now raised a hand to silence the congregation.

"My brothers and my sisters," he began, "we are gathered together in the sight of God."

My brothers and my sisters. Those words, as simple and direct as they were, never failed to resonate with her. They were words that said so much about how people should feel about one another. When you addressed others as your brothers or your sisters, you professed something deep and essential about how you felt towards them. You were saying *We are not strangers to one another*. You were reminding them, and yourself as well, of your shared humanity. You were not claiming to be anything more than they were; you were not claiming any advantage or chance of advantage. You were saying: Here I am, as I am, and I am speaking to you, as you are, as a brother or a sister must speak to one with whom he or she was brought up, from whom no secrets would be hidden, to whom no untruths would be told.

"We are gathered here," the preacher went on, "to witness the coming together in holy matrimony of this man and this woman, as at that wedding in Cana of Galilee . . ."

She looked at Mr. J.L.B. Matekoni and remembered how, not all that many years ago, she had stood next to him not far from here, at their own wedding, and they had been addressed in similar terms, and how, when she had looked up, as she had done during that ceremony, she had seen a Cape dove watching them from a bough in the tree above their heads. And the dove had stayed there until, a few minutes later, it launched itself into the air and disappeared, and she realised she had not been paying attention to what was being said to her and had to be nudged to give the necessary response.

Now as those same questions were put to Seemo and Thato, and as each uttered the appropriate response, Mma Ramotswe noticed that Mr. J.L.B. Matekoni was nodding at each answer, as if he agreed with the proposition behind the question, or as if he were himself echoing the couple's words. It occurred to her that he was thinking back to their own wedding, and was, in a sense, renewing the promises he had made on that occasion. And how faithfully he had carried out those vows—observing them to the letter, she thought, in a way that some husbands, perhaps even many husbands, found so difficult to do. So, yes, he had honoured and cherished her, just as he had promised to do at the altar; and yes, he had shared all his worldly goods with her, asking for very little for himself; and yes, he had forsaken all others for her, even though there were always husband-stealers on the prowl—people like Violet Sephotho—who were constantly circling round, looking for opportunities to take advantage of men in all their weakness.

She looked at Mr. J.L.B. Matekoni with pride—and gratitude that he had been delivered into her care, and thanked whatever, or whomever, it was that kept watch over her life. God, perhaps, or God acting in concert, so to speak, with a committee of ancestors—her mother, her grandmother, and ladies going back a long time to the early days of her people. And Africa, too, she was there somewhere in those protective forces; wise and nurturing, Mother Africa had arms wide enough to embrace all her children.

Mr. J.L.B. Matekoni nudged her gently. "You're dreaming about something, Mma," he whispered.

She brought herself back to reality. "I was remembering," she whispered back. "I was remembering our own wedding, Rra. Not far away from where we are."

He smiled. "You said yes," he said. "You said yes, just like Thato's just done."

"Good. It would be too late to say no at the altar. Far too late."

Mr. J.L.B. Matekoni looked concerned. "I hope that has never happened, Mma."

"I'm afraid that it has," said Mma Ramotswe. "There was a wedding in Gaborone a few years back when they both said no, apparently."

"Ow!" exclaimed Mr. J.L.B. Matekoni. And then, "Ow!" once more.

"Yes, they said that they had both been persuaded by their families to get married, and they decided to refuse right at the last moment."

Mr. J.L.B. Matekoni rolled his eyes. "Their poor families."

"Yes. And I heard that they had already cooked the roasts and so the guests just went on and ate all the food."

"It would not have helped anybody if they had wasted the food," said Mr. J.L.B. Matekoni. "That never helps."

Mma Ramotswe remembered another detail. "The groom didn't go to the feast," she said. "I think he felt too embarrassed."

"I'm not surprised," said Mr. J.L.B. Matekoni.

"But the bride—or the almost bride—wasn't embarrassed. I heard that she stayed for the feast and met another man there—one she had not met before. He was a guest of the groom's family. She married him, I was told."

Mr. J.L.B. Matekoni's eyes opened wide. "There and then? At the same wedding?"

"No, later, Rra. A few months later, I think."

"Then something good came of it," said Mr. J.L.B. Matekoni.

THE VOWS HAVING BEEN EXCHANGED, the preacher pronounced the couple man and wife. There was applause from the congregation, and ululating cries, too. The couple turned around and smiled, and the applause became louder. Mma Ramotswe tried not to cry, but failed. She always cried at a wedding, no matter how hard she tried to remain dry-eyed. Mr. J.L.B. Matekoni passed her a handkerchief that he extracted from the top pocket of his suit. The man standing next to him caught his eye and smiled, as if the two of them were exchanging some secret man's message: women cry. Mma Ramotswe intercepted this as she wiped her eyes, and thought, Yes, we may cry, but you should do so too.

She returned the handkerchief as the congregation rose to its feet to sing. *Shall we gather at the river, the beautiful river, the beautiful river . . .* It had been a favourite of hers as a girl, when she had thought that the river must be the Limpopo, that rose very near to Mochudi, and that would always be her river. As a young girl she had felt proud that her local river should have been referred to in this hymn, so clearly crafted somewhere else, as most things were. They wrote hymns in England, she thought, and then sent them out into the world for people to sing them in all sorts of places, even here, on the very edge of the Kalahari.

The bride and groom left. Friends stopped to talk. Clothes were admired. Children ran about, laughing, playing little games of their own devising.

"Mma Ramotswe, so there you are!"

She looked up and saw Mma Makutsi waiting outside the gate of the *kgotla*. Behind her, Phuti Radiphuti, wearing a light grey suit and a bright red tie, smiled nervously.

"And you, Phuti," said Mma Ramotswe. "There you are too."

"It was a very good service," said Mma Makutsi, "even if Phuti and I couldn't see very well . . ."

"Oh, I don't know," said Phuti. "We were not too far away."

Mma Makutsi gave him a discouraging glance. "That's a matter of opinion, Rra," she said. "Who would have thought in advance that this would be a wedding with inside people and outside people? Who would have thought that, Mma?"

Mma Ramotswe sighed. "Numbers are always a problem when you have a wedding, Mma. You can't invite the whole world, I think."

"Oh, I know that," said Mma Makutsi. "I'm not saying that you should invite the whole world—or even all of Gaborone, for instance. I am not saying that."

Phuti Radiphuti made a valiant effort to move the conversation on. "And the bride was very pretty," he said loudly. "I sell furniture to her father, you know. He has a shop somewhere up north, and it stocks some of our furniture."

"That is all very interesting, Rra," said Mma Makutsi sharply. "Perhaps we can talk about sofas and dining-room tables later on. What I was talking about now-now was the idea of dividing your guests into inside people and outside people. That sometimes doesn't make the outside people feel very happy. They may sit there—or stand there, shall I say—and ask themselves: Are we not good enough to be inside people? That is what they might think, Mma. I'm just reporting it. I'm just saying what I believe they might be thinking."

"Oh well," said Mma Ramotswe. "The important thing is that the bride and groom are happy. This is their day, after all, not ours."

Mr. J.L.B. Matekoni shifted awkwardly on his feet. "There is a very fine smell of beef," he said. "That is one way of being happy—having some beef to eat."

Phuti seized the opportunity. "That is very funny, Rra. But it is also very true. If you have a good slice of beef on your plate, then you are happy. Many studies have shown that, I think."

Mma Ramotswe pointed to the large tent on the other side of the garden. "That is where we will find some lunch," she said. "And then we can talk more about some other things."

While Phuti and Grace went off to greet other friends in the crowd, Mma Ramotswe and Mr. J.L.B. Matekoni made their way through the throng of guests towards the catering tent, where already the outside people, having enjoyed a head start, were making inroads on the meat. And it was on the way that Mma Ramotswe suddenly gripped Mr. J.L.B. Matekoni's arm.

"I have seen a ghost, Rra," she said, her voice filled with alarm.

He looked at her in astonishment, uncertain whether to laugh.

"There," hissed Mma Ramotswe. "There, Rra—right over there."

He looked where she was pointing. There was a group of four women and two men, each dressed in their wedding best. One of the women wore an elaborate, broad-brimmed hat—one of those hats that is more umbrella, perhaps, than headgear.

"Those are people, Mma," he said. "They are not ghosts, as far as I can see."

She shook her head. Lowering her voice, she said, "One of them is late, Rra. That one over there—she is late."

CHAPTER TWO

A VERY UNOFFICIAL ENGAGEMENT

MR. J.L.B. MATEKONI WAITED for an explanation as Mma Ramotswe stared intently at the small group of wedding guests. If her husband was confused, then she herself was wondering whether her eyesight was playing tricks on her. Yet the woman in the large hat, who had just turned her back on her, now turned around again, affording Mma Ramotswe an even better view of her face. And now there was no doubt.

"That is definitely her, Rra," she said, her voice still uneven with shock. "That woman over there. That's Calviniah. And she's late. She's definitely late."

Mr. J.L.B. Matekoni frowned. "Who is this Calviniah, Mma Ramotswe? I really don't know what you're talking about. There are no late people here, Mma." He shrugged helplessly. The sun was hot. At such times, if you weren't careful, it could make you say nonsensical things. Heatstroke was a dangerous thing.

He reached out to shelter her head from the sun with a handkerchief. It gave scant protection, but it would have to do until he could get her back into the shade.

But Mma Ramotswe brushed the inadequate shelter away. "Calviniah Ramoroka," she said. "That's her, standing over there."

"That lady with the big hat?" asked Mr. J.L.B. Matekoni. "That one, Mma? The one who is clearly not late?"

She said nothing for a moment. Then she turned to him. "I know you think it's the sun. I know you think I've gone mad, Mr. J.L.B. Matekoni."

He stuttered an apology. "I was not accusing you of that, Mma. I was just pointing out—"

She cut him short. "I have not taken leave of my senses, Rra. All that has happened is that I have seen a very old friend—somebody I knew a long time ago, from schooldays. She went off to live up in Francistown and I lost touch with her, and with her family too. Then . . ." She trailed off. The woman was coming towards them now, still talking to the group around her.

"Then?" asked Mr. J.L.B. Matekoni.

"Then I read in the papers that she had been killed in a road accident. There was a picture of her in the press. I couldn't get to the funeral because it was up north and . . . well, something or other prevented me from going—work, I think . . ."

Mma Ramotswe put a hand to her mouth, in a gesture of profound shock. The woman in the hat had suddenly stopped, and was staring at her. Then, very quickly, she ran forwards towards Mma Ramotswe, stopping just short of her. Mr. J.L.B. Matekoni stood quite still. Things had happened so quickly, and he was uncertain what to do.

"Precious Ramotswe?" The woman spoke loudly.

Mma Ramotswe nodded. "Calviniah . . ."

Calviniah took a step forward, her arms wide. "I thought it was you," she said. "And it is you, isn't it?" She glanced at Mr. J.L.B. Matekoni. "And this is . . . ?"

"This is my husband," said Mma Ramotswe, her voice still faltering. "This is Mr. J.L.B. Matekoni."

They exchanged the polite, traditional greetings. Then Calviniah turned back to Mma Ramotswe and embraced her friend. "It is so long," she said. "It is so very long."

"I thought you were late," Mma Ramotswe struggled to say. "I couldn't believe my eyes."

Calviniah drew back and laughed. "Oh, that? That was very unfortunate."

Mr. J.L.B. Matekoni's eyes widened. That was one way of putting it, he thought.

"But you are not," concluded Mma Ramotswe.

Calviniah let out an amused shriek. "No! I am definitely not late, as I hope you can see. No, that was a big mistake by the newspaper. There was another Calviniah Ramoroka, you see. She lived up in Francistown too. You knew I went to Francistown?"

Mma Ramotswe nodded. "I'd heard that."

"Well, this other Calviniah Ramoroka had a very bad road accident. There was a truck driver who was drunk, and her car was very small when this big, big truck came over onto her side of the road. It was very sad, Mma."

Mma Ramotswe nodded. It happened only too often. Whatever the authorities tried to do, there were still people who would drink and drive.

"Anyway," Calviniah continued, "the newspaper printed the right facts about the accident, but they somehow got hold of a photograph of me, rather than the other Calviniah, the late one. Many people were misled, I think, Mma. For ages afterwards they came up to me and told me that they thought I was late. Some people even came up and said, 'We're sorry to hear about your death, Mma—our condolences.' And they meant it, Mma. Can you believe that people would be so . . ."

"So stupid?" suggested Mr. J.L.B. Matekoni.

"Yes, Rra," Calviniah agreed. "One doesn't like to say it, but people can be really stupid at times." She paused. "They can be very nice, of course, Mma. I'm not saying they can't be nice. It's just that while they're being nice, they're also being stupid."

"You must have been very embarrassed," said Mma Ramotswe.

Calviniah laughed. "Yes, it can be embarrassing to be late," she said. "Or to be late and not late at the same time, if you see what I mean, Mma. Anyway, they printed a correction, and an apology. But these were on the back page near the sporting news, and many people did not see them. Who wants to read about football, Mma? Only men want to read that sort of thing."

Mma Ramotswe relaxed. "I was thinking exactly the same thing, Mma. When I saw you, I had a big shock. But . . . but it is such good news, Mma, that you are alive after all."

"And we should go and have something to eat," Calviniah said, steering Mma Ramotswe towards the food tent. "People think that late people don't feel hungry . . ."

Mr. J.L.B. Matekoni smiled. "That is very funny, Mma."

Calviniah smiled at him, and to Mma Ramotswe she said, "You have a very nice husband, Mma. I have some friends who are keen to get married. Can you tell me about the place where you found him so that they can have a look too?"

They both laughed. "This is a very happy day in so many ways," said Mma Ramotswe.

THAT WAS ON A SATURDAY. On the Monday after the wedding, Mma Ramotswe was at her desk early, catching up with correspondence. Mma Makutsi was slightly late in coming in, and when she did, Mma Ramotswe had already made the first cup of tea.

"I am sorry I'm a bit behind this morning, Mma," Mma Makutsi said. "Phuti lost his car keys and we had to search every corner of the house before he found them."

"Men," sighed Mma Ramotswe. And then, realising how unfair this was, she said, "Well, I suppose women lose their keys too." It was wrong to speak like that of men, she thought. It was very tempting sometimes to do so—to blame men for everything—but there were too many women doing it and it was not right. Men could take the blame for many things, but not *everything*.

Mma Makutsi sat down at her desk and polished her large round spectacles. "You know what they taught us at the Botswana Secretarial College, Mma? You know what? They said: Make a key board. Put your office keys on hooks. A key that is on a hook is never lost, Mma. I have never forgotten that. A key that is on a hook is never lost."

Mma Ramotswe agreed. "I'm sure that is right, Mma."

"And the same goes for other things," went on Mma Makutsi. "Hooks are the answer."

Mma Ramotswe had a momentary vision of Mma Makutsi's house covered in hooks. Even her baby, Itumelang, would be suspended in a basket from a hook; and Phuti would have a hook too, a large, solid one, from which he would dangle by his collar, awaiting instructions from his wife.

Unware of this vision, of course, Mma Makutsi continued to expound on the merits of hooks. "It's a good idea to have hooks for men's clothes, in my view. You know how untidy they are, Mma. You know how they leave their things lying around on the floor."

Mma Ramotswe, in spite of her commitment to fairness, had to agree. Men were very untidy, for the most part. They could not help it, she knew, and one could not blame them for it, as neither could they help being men. It was just the way things were.

"You're right about clothes on the floor, Mma Makutsi," she said, a tinge of resignation in her voice. "I'm always picking up clothes. Mr. J.L.B. Matekoni does it, and so does Puso. They just leave them on the floor. And then . . ." She remembered something with a shudder. "It can be dangerous too. Puso left his trousers on the floor one night and the next morning, when he put them on, a scorpion was hiding in one of the legs."

Mma Makutsi winced. "That would have been very sore, Mma."

"It was," said Mma Ramotswe. "Those creatures give a very bad sting. Very bad."

Mma Makutsi winced again. "Ow!"

"He yelled and yelled," Mma Ramotswe continued. "Poor little boy."

"If he had put the trousers up on a hook, then it would not have happened."

Mma Ramotswe nodded. "No, it would not." She decided to change the subject. Hooks were useful, but there was a limit to what one could say about them. "That was a good wedding, I think, Mma. We enjoyed it."

"A very good wedding," Mma Makutsi agreed. "Unfortunately, Phuti developed a headache and we didn't stay all that long. It was being out in the sun, you see. He doesn't like that very much and it gives him a headache sometimes. The sun makes the brain swell and then it presses on the skull, which cannot expand very much, if at all."

She looked at Mma Ramotswe while she continued to polish the lenses of her spectacles. "The skull is the same size all the time," she said. "Once you're fully grown, your head doesn't get any bigger. Even if you become quite fat, Mma—even then. Your body gets bigger, but your head stays the same size."

"I think I know that, Mma," said Mma Ramotswe. "You don't hear many people say, 'Oh, my head is getting so big, I must go on a diet.'"

Mma Makutsi put on her spectacles. "That's true. And there's another thing I've thought about, Mma, and that is the relationship between the size of the head and intelligence. You'd think there'd be a connection, wouldn't you?"

Mma Ramotswe was doubtful. Any such connection would be far too obvious, she thought, and one thing she had learned in her profession was that that which is obvious frequently turns out to be false. Except sometimes, of course, as Clovis Andersen himself pointed out in *The Principles of Private Detection*. He advised his readers to look at the most likely possibilities first because a cunning malefactor might assume—incorrectly, it was to be hoped—that the obvious solution would be discounted in any search or enquiry. *If I were a thief trying to conceal the things I had stolen,* he wrote, *I would put them behind a door marked "Storeroom for Stolen Items." That would be the safest place, as everybody would think that was far too obvious. People would look everywhere but behind that door. It is all a question of psychology.*

Mma Makutsi recalled one of the instructors at the Botswana Secretarial College. "I remember one of my professors . . . ," she began.

Mma Ramotswe raised an eyebrow. She had heard Mma Makutsi refer to her teachers as professors, but it was completely unjustified. Whatever the merits of the Botswana Secretarial College might be, it was still just that—a secretarial college. It was not a branch of the University of Botswana, as were places like the Botswana College of Agriculture. It did not award degrees, and its staff were definitely not professors.

When she first heard mention of these so-called professors, she had felt inclined to stop Mma Makutsi and say, "But who are these professors, Mma? I didn't know that the Botswana Secretarial College was part of the University of Botswana, where all the professors work. This is very interesting news, Mma." She had not said this, though; kindness prevented her, as it always did. If Mma Makutsi wanted to promote her teachers in this way, then there was no real reason why she should not do so. It evidently gave her pleasure to think of her instructors in these terms, and it was a harmless enough promotion. The real professors, those erudite men and women at the University of Botswana who knew so much about such a wide range of subjects, might perhaps object if they heard of it, but even they would turn a blind eye, she imagined, to this innocent piece of wishful thinking.

"This professor," Mma Makutsi continued, "taught us book-keeping. He was not very tall—normal height, I think, for a man—but he was very well built. In fact, Mma, he was a bit round in shape, a bit like a pumpkin, you know."

Mma Ramotswe listened. Mma Makutsi had a habit of referring to fruit and vegetables when describing people. She had recently referred to a man as being "banana-shaped," and indeed, when Mma Ramotswe saw the person in question, she could see what she meant. The man in question did have a curve to his back, with the result that the tip of his nose lined up with his toes; but the front of his stomach was some inches behind both of those points. And then there had been a man she referred to as having a face "a bit like a cauliflower," a description that, once again, seemed strikingly accurate, even if it was, Mma Ramotswe felt, somewhat unkind. Of course, such terms could not be used publicly, for fear of giving offence: the police, for example, could not issue them in their descriptions of wanted persons—*We are looking for a tall, string-bean-shaped man*—helpful though such descriptions might be.

"So, he looked like a pumpkin?" Mma Ramotswe prompted.

"Yes, he did," came the reply. But then Mma Makutsi frowned. "I don't want to sound disrespectful, Mma. I would never be rude about my professors."

"Of course not." And Mma Ramotswe knew that Mma Makutsi meant that. That college, for all she went on about it, and for all Mma Ramotswe was fed up with hearing of it, had given Mma Makutsi everything. It meant the world to her, and there was nothing wrong with that. A good teacher could mean the world.

Mma Makutsi gazed out of the window. "I'm not saying that he was altogether like a pumpkin, Mma. If you saw him standing next to a pumpkin, you'd be able to tell the difference, of course."

"Of course," said Mma Ramotswe. "You wouldn't make that mistake easily."

"Anyway, that was his general shape, but when it came to his head . . ." Mma Makutsi brought her gaze back into the room. "Oh, Mma, it was very, very small. You really had to strain to see it at all."

"Surely not. Surely . . ."

"No, Mma Ramotswe, I am not exaggerating. It was that small—it really was. The ears were quite big, though. You saw those easily enough. But the head . . . ow, it was tiny. Yet—and this is the amazing thing, Mma—and yet he knew just about everything. That tiny head was full of information about everything you wanted to know. It was all there. And not just book-keeping—there was a lot of book-keeping in his head, but other things too. History of Botswana—it was there. Geography—names of rivers, foreign places, North Pole, height of Kilimanjaro—it was all there. He could tell you."

"Kilimanjaro," mused Mma Ramotswe. "When I was a young girl

I saw a picture of Kilimanjaro in a book. I wanted to go there. I said to my auntie who was looking after me at the time, *I want to go to a very high hill called Kilimanjaro,* and she said, *We cannot go today, I am too busy.* I remember my disappointment, because when you are a child you want to do everything immediately, don't you? Now-now. You don't want to wait because at that age you think that even tomorrow is a very long time away."

"That is true, Mma," said Mma Makutsi. "So if you asked this professor how high Kilimanjaro was, he'd say . . ." She trailed off.

"What would he say, Mma?"

"He would give you the height," Mma Makutsi said quickly.

She doesn't know, thought Mma Ramotswe. But then she thought, Neither do I.

Mma Makutsi returned to headaches. "That is why Phuti got a headache." She paused. "The heat must have made his brain expand until it hit the side of his head. We didn't have an awning, Mma. We were outside people, you see."

She looked reproachfully at Mma Ramotswe, as if the lack of an awning had been her fault. Mma Ramotswe, impervious to this, rose to her feet. "I have made tea, Mma," she said. "Let me pour you a cup."

While they drank their tea, Mma Ramotswe told Mma Makutsi about the meeting with Calviniah, and the shock of recognition that had preceded it. Mma Makutsi listened intently. "Newspapers," she muttered at the end, shaking her head. "They should be more careful."

CHARLIE ARRIVED TEN MINUTES LATER, while they were still drinking their tea and Mma Ramotswe was reminiscing about her early friendship with Calviniah. Charlie was now dividing his time between the No. 1 Ladies' Detective Agency and Tlokweng Road Speedy Motors, Mr. J.L.B. Matekoni's business, which adjoined the agency office. Neither was in a position to pay him a full wage, but, put together, the two jobs came up with just enough. On Mma Ramotswe's side of the arrangement, Charlie probably did not generate sufficient fee income to justify his being employed at all, but she had nonetheless taken him on out of sympathy when Mr. J.L.B. Matekoni had been obliged to retrench. Nothing specific had been said about his status: in her eyes, he was a general assistant, not quite an office helper, but close to it, one whose responsibilities included anything that needed doing at the time, from collecting the mail to taking part in the less skilled parts of an investigation. For all his impetuosity, Charlie was an observer, and noticed details that others might miss. On several occasions, too, he had shown a talent for surveillance, standing on street corners without being noticed, or following a suspected errant husband into a bar without attracting suspicion. That he would eventually make a competent detective she was in no doubt, although she was not sure when that would be. If Charlie was lacking anything, she felt, it was judgement, and that was something that only came with time.

Mma Makutsi had a different view of the situation. Her relationship with Charlie had not been easy, at least to begin with, although it had improved greatly in recent times. The two were fond of one another—in an odd sort of way, observed Mma Ramotswe; Charlie had recently come across the word *chutzpah,* and had decided that Mma Makutsi was the embodiment of that particular quality. If only she would stop boasting about her ninety-seven per cent, he thought. That was achieved ages ago, and you'd think she would have something else to talk about. And if only she would stop challenging the views he expressed on just about any subject. If that happened, then there would be nothing to take exception to in her. Indeed, he would go further, and say that he could imagine rather enjoying her feisty company.

Mma Makutsi was happy enough to have Charlie working in the office—provided he remembered that he was not to describe himself as an assistant detective. She had heard him doing that over the telephone one day, and she had shouted out from the other side of the room, "Excuse me, *not* assistant detective, if you don't mind. Office assistant, please." She accepted that he might one day be able to shoulder wider responsibilities, but that day, she emphasised, was yet to come.

"Charlie is still just a boy," she said to Mma Ramotswe. "He may be twenty-whatever, but there are many men who are still boys until they are in the early thirties, and beyond. In some cases, they remain boys until they are very old. They become old boys. I'm not saying that Charlie is that sort of man, all I am saying is that he has a bit more growing up to do."

Now, coming into the office on a day that would see him working with Mma Ramotswe and Mma Makutsi rather than with Mr. J.L.B. Matekoni and Fanwell, the junior mechanic, Charlie poured himself a mug of tea and perched on one of Mma Makutsi's filing cabinets while he drank it.

"So, you ladies went to a wedding on Saturday. How did it go?"

"Very well, thank you, Charlie," Mma Ramotswe replied. "There were many people there."

"There always are at weddings," said Charlie. "Not that I go to many myself."

"Are your friends not settling down yet?" asked Mma Makutsi. "Maybe you should set them an example. Maybe you should marry that girlfriend of yours. What's she called? Queenie-Queenie?"

Charlie nodded. "That's her name, Mma."

"Strange name," mused Mma Makutsi. "Why would anybody want to be called Queenie-Queenie?, I ask myself. Still, there's no accounting for taste."

"It's a very nice name," said Charlie loyally.

"There is nothing wrong with it," said Mma Ramotswe. "The important thing about a name is that the person who has that name should like it."

"Well, she does like it, Mma," said Charlie. "And so do I." He paused. "And you say I should marry her, Mma Makutsi. Well, maybe I will. What if I told you we are unofficially engaged."

This was greeted with complete silence. Mma Makutsi and Mma Ramotswe glanced at one another. Then Mma Ramotswe said, "And if you did tell us that, Charlie, would it be true?"

Charlie, sipping on his tea, seemed to bask in their attention. "You could say so, Mma."

For a moment the two women were silent. Charlie smiled with all the satisfaction of one who has dropped a bombshell. Then Mma Ramotswe clapped her hands together. "That is very good news, Charlie," she said. "You will both be very happy, I'm sure."

Charlie acknowledged the sentiments with a small bow. He looked across the room at Mma Makutsi, clearly waiting for her to follow Mma Ramotswe's lead.

"Yes," said Mma Makutsi, a note of reluctance in her voice. "This is very good news." She paused before continuing, "But what is the difference between being officially engaged and being unofficially engaged? Can you tell me, Rra?"

Charlie finished his tea and placed his mug down on the filing cabinet. "There are many differences," he began. "If you are unofficially engaged—"

Mma Makutsi interrupted him. "There is no ring?"

"That is one difference," said Charlie. "If you have a ring, then everybody will know. Most people don't know if it's unofficial."

"Does she know?" asked Mma Makutsi. "Does Queenie-Queenie know?"

Charlie looked hurt. "Of course she knows, Mma. She is my fiancée. How could a fiancée *not* know that she was engaged?"

Mma Makutsi laughed. "Oh, I can think of many cases of that. I can think of cases where a man *thinks* that the woman has said that she will marry him, but she hasn't agreed at all. Maybe she said yes when he asked her to go to the cinema with him or something like that. And then he thinks, She's said yes! She's going to marry me. Such a man can be very stupid."

Charlie looked defiant. "And women too, Mma Makutsi? What about women? You're always going on about men being stupid and thinking all sorts of things, but what about women? There are many stupid women too, you know—not just stupid men. There are stupid men and stupid women. Lots of them, if you ask me, all over the place, even Bobonong . . ."

Mma Ramotswe knew at once that sensitive territory was being entered. Mma Makutsi came from Bobonong, and would not hear a word against it. She gave Charlie a look of discouragement, hoping that he would not say anything more about Bobonong, or indeed about anything very much.

But it was too late. "Bobonong?" Mma Makutsi challenged. "Are you saying that people from Bobonong are stupid? Is that what you're saying, Charlie?"

Charlie was a picture of injured innocence. "Certainly not, Mma. I would never say that. I am just saying that there are stupid people everywhere. That's all. But I was also saying that people shouldn't pick just on men. There are many ladies who do that, Mma Makutsi.

They think that they can be rude about men, but when a man is rude about women, then big trouble for him. Big, big trouble these days. Too much. Bang! That man's finished. End of story. Gone. Big-time."

Mma Ramotswe decided to steer the conversation away from these difficult waters. "I am very happy for you, Charlie. It is very good news that you and Queenie-Queenie will be getting married. You will be a very good husband, I think."

She looked pointedly at Mma Makutsi, who knew what the look meant. Yet it took a few moments before Mma Makutsi said, "Yes, congratulations, Charlie. This is a very good bit of news—just as Mma Ramotswe has said."

"Thank you," said Charlie, beaming with pleasure.

"When will you get married?" asked Mma Ramotswe.

Charlie's face fell. "Not very soon. I'd like to get married tomorrow, if I could. But Queenie-Queenie's uncle . . ."

Mma Ramotswe gave an involuntary groan. Uncles. This was the bride-price negotiations, often carried out by an uncle or other relative. Queenie-Queenie came from a well-off family—Mma Ramotswe had already heard about her father's fleet of trucks—and that meant Charlie would be expected to come up with a considerable sum for the *bogadi,* the bridal payment. Sometimes, in modern circles, that was unnecessary, but when it was necessary, then, as Mr. J.L.B. Matekoni sometimes said of a crucial engine part, it was three hundred per cent necessary.

Mma Ramotswe would have been tactful in what was said next; not so, Mma Makutsi. "You've got no money, then. They'll have worked that out, you know. People like that uncle of hers—whoever he is—he won't be stupid, you know, unlike some men."

Charlie looked miserable. "I've been saving. I've been trying. But you know how hard it is. I have to give money to my own uncle, because I am staying in his house, and there are many children . . ."

Mma Ramotswe felt a pang of sympathy for the young man. She knew how hard it was for him: sharing a room in that shack in Old Naledi, struggling to get by, counting every pula, walking long distances in the heat in order to save the minibus fare—all the humiliations of penury. "Have you managed to save anything?" she asked.

He looked up. "I have been saving, yes. I have, Mma."

"How much?" asked Mma Makutsi. "How much have you got, Charlie?"

"I have got almost six hundred pula, Mma."

Mma Ramotswe and Mma Makutsi exchanged glances. That would get him nowhere. Queenie-Queenie's uncles would be expecting a substantial amount, reckoned in head of cattle. One head of cattle cost over five thousand pula. They would be thinking of ten to twelve cattle, at the least.

Mma Makutsi brought the discussion to a close. "I'm very sorry, Charlie, but it sounds as if your engagement is *very* unofficial. Maybe you should wait."

Charlie put down his mug. "Wait, Mma? You're telling me to wait? So that I'm an old man by the time I get married? Fifty, maybe?"

Mma Makutsi shook her head. "Fifty is not old, Charlie."

Charlie slipped off the filing cabinet and onto his feet. "Fifty is finished, Mma. Even when you're forty, you're finished." He paused, and looked apologetically at Mma Ramotswe. "Except you, Mma Ramotswe. I didn't mean you, Mma. You're not finished."

"That's good of you to say that, Charlie," said Mma Ramotswe. "It is a great relief to hear that."

The comment reminded Mma Makutsi of something. "You know, there was a man in Bobonong once. He was quite an old man—not too old, but quite old. One day he said to his daughter, 'I am finished now,' and then he lay down on his bed and became late. He had not been ill or anything—he just decided that he was finished, and that was that."

Mma Ramotswe and Charlie listened to this in silence. Then Mma Ramotswe said, "One should always be careful about what one says. I think that is very well known."

CHAPTER THREE

MOST MEN ARE UP TO SOMETHING

"MY HUSBAND," Mma Ramotswe sometimes remarked, "is very good at getting the children up and sending them off to school. Many men are not so good at that, but he is."

She was the least boastful of women, but she felt it important to proclaim the merits of Mr. J.L.B. Matekoni, a man of great modesty who would never draw attention to any of his domestic achievements. She was proud of his helpfulness around the house—of his willingness to tackle the washing-up and of his diligent, if rudimentary, attempts to cook. Some men, she realised, were just not suited to cooking, and Mr. J.L.B. Matekoni was one of them. The main problem was salt, which he added in excessive quantities to any dish he prepared, but there were other culinary shortcomings, including a tendency to fry everything, including the desserts to which he was inordinately attached. She was not sure where that came from, whether it was a widespread male failing or whether some misguided person had taught him that in the past—it was difficult to say. But there was no doubt that it was what she had once seen tactfully referred to as a "kitchen shortcoming."

On that morning, she was relieved when Mr. J.L.B. Matekoni offered her the chance to get into the office early. The previous day had been a frustrating one, beginning with that rather bleak conversation with Charlie over his seemingly ill-fated engagement, and then continuing with a series of interruptions and setbacks. There had been a difficult letter from a vexatious client who was refusing to pay a bill in spite of Mma Makutsi's having sent four reminders; there had been a circular from the city authorities warning of an increase in the level of property tax to be paid by businesses; and there had been a lost file that contained important documents, the birth and marriage certificates of a woman in Mozambique who was claiming inheritance rights to a deceased estate in Botswana. The file had eventually turned up—having been inserted, back to front, in the wrong drawer. That had been the occasion of considerable relief, as a registry fire in Maputo had made the birth certificate irreplaceable, but for the most part the day seemed to have been one of damage limitation rather than achievement.

Mma Ramotswe hoped that making an early start that morning would stamp a different tone on the day, and, as she sat at her desk at seven o'clock that morning, listening to a cock still crowing outside, it seemed to her that the day was getting off to a much better start. Everything was going smoothly. The children had been well behaved and uncomplaining of their father's chivvying. They had got out of bed without the usual complaints of missing clothes and last-minute deadlines with homework. The bath she had taken had been just the right temperature, and when she came to clean her teeth, there was still a good amount of toothpaste in the tube, and she was not obliged to do what she seemed to have to do so often—to squeeze the last morsel out of a tube that was clearly empty. That was a good sign, as was the absence of traffic on the journey from the house to the office. She had the road more or less to herself, although there were already a few cars coming in from Tlokweng as she made her way to the office. It would get so much worse later on, with overloaded minibuses crawling their way into town, bringing people in for their day's work.

How different was the traffic from what it used to be, she said to herself. And then she thought: Everybody must think that, wherever they live, because gradually we are drowning ourselves in cars. That was happening everywhere. People were drowning themselves in machinery, to the point that there would be no room left for anything else. The world would be covered in cars and there would be nowhere left to go in those cars because there would already be too many vehicles at your destination.

When she was a girl in Mochudi there had been very few local cars, and there was a boy in her class who knew every one of them, and their numbers too. She herself recognised the cars of all the teachers, as well as that of the doctor at the hospital, and of the hospital matron, and of the man from the Department of Water Affairs. Now such familiarity would be impossible, and cars would all be strangers to her.

She sighed. The old world was slipping away, it seemed . . . or . . . or, a disturbing thought occurred. Was *she* slipping away? Perhaps the world was just carrying on as usual and we, all the people thinking about how it had changed, were really just changing ourselves. No, surely not. The world *had* changed—you only had to look about you to see that. And yet, many of those changes were good ones, and not things to fret over, or lament, or bemoan in the way in which people who are slipping away often complain about everything going past them.

She rose from her desk. She had already had a cup of tea at home, before she left for the office, but that was no reason not to have one now. A cup of tea usually restored perspective on things, and that was what she needed now, rather than to sit and think about the ways in which the modern world was ordered. And she was right: a steaming cup of red bush tea was sufficient to banish thoughts of change and decay and to restore the spirits. This was going to be a good day—she was determined to make that so—and she was going to work steadily and efficiently through the list of tasks she had written out for herself.

By the time that Mma Makutsi arrived, she had already achieved a considerable amount. Three items on the list were neatly ticked off, and she had made a good start on the fourth, a particularly sensitive letter in which she had to inform a client who was hoping to expose—and leave—her husband that the husband under suspicion was *not* meeting a lover, but was actually having mathematics lessons. The secret meetings she suspected him of having were indeed meetings, but were far from the assignations she suspected. They were visits to the teacher's house, where he was being prepared for a forthcoming public examination in advanced mathematics.

The letter took a long time to write, and was still unfinished by the time Mma Makutsi arrived in the office.

"Well, Mma Ramotswe," said Mma Makutsi. "I didn't expect to find you hard at work so early."

It was an innocent remark, but Mma Ramotswe felt slightly annoyed at the inference that she was not the type to arrive early. Did Mma Makutsi think that she just sat around in the mornings?

"I am often up very early, Mma Makutsi," she said. "You should try it, perhaps."

The retort came quickly. "But I am also up early, Mma. Every day. When you have a baby, as I do, then you cannot lie about in bed.

You are up early because the baby wants his breakfast. You are also up early because you have a husband to get going. There are many things for women to do in the morning."

Mma Makutsi peered at Mma Ramotswe's desk. "You're writing a letter, Mma?"

Mma Ramotswe sat back in her chair. "It's not an easy letter, this one. You remember that woman who came to see us about her husband?"

Mma Makutsi frowned. There were so many women who came to see them about their husbands—husbands, it seemed, were the main reason why women went to private detectives.

"The one we had followed by Charlie," Mma Ramotswe prompted.

Mma Makutsi smiled. "Of course. And Charlie saw him going to the house of that teacher. That one?"

Mma Ramotswe nodded. "I have to tell her that her husband is not seeing another woman," said Mma Ramotswe. "But I think that she will not like to hear that news, Mma. When she spoke to me about it at the beginning, she said she was looking forward to divorcing him. I think she has her own lover, you see."

"Ha!" said Mma Makutsi. "She will be very disappointed then. But tell me, Mma, how can you be sure about that—about her having a lover?"

"Because I saw her," said Mma Ramotswe. "I saw her in the supermarket with another man. They were buying food together."

Mma Makutsi looked thoughtful. "But he could have been a relative, Mma. A brother, perhaps. Or a cousin. You know how many cousins there are about the place. The whole city is full of cousins. Everywhere there are cousins." She paused. "I think there are far more cousins than lovers, Mma."

"That's true enough," said Mma Ramotswe. "But I saw him pinch her, Mma. That lady is very large from the back view, Mma. And that man pinched her there. I saw it."

Mma Makutsi absorbed this information. "That is not the sort of thing a cousin does," she said at last. "Nor a brother."

"Definitely not."

"Except when you are very cross with somebody," Mma Makutsi went on. "If you are very cross, you may pinch somebody. But you do not pinch them there. That is not the place for such a pinch."

"No, I wouldn't have thought it was."

"The place to pinch another person when you are cross with them is on the arm," pronounced Mma Makutsi. She tapped her upper arm. "There, Mma. That is where you pinch people."

Mma Ramotswe went on to tell Mma Makutsi how the woman had seen her and had pretended not to have anything to do with the man. "She walked away, leaving him there," she said. "He looked very puzzled. That made it even clearer to me that he was her boyfriend. That—and the pinch. These were two pieces of evidence."

"Well," said Mma Makutsi. "She will not be able to claim that she's the wronged party." She leaned further over Mma Ramotswe's desk. "May I see the letter, Mma?"

Mma Ramotswe handed it over.

"Dear Mma Mogorosi," Mma Makutsi began. "In the matter of your husband, I am pleased to inform you that we have now completed our investigations and have come to a preliminary conclusion."

Mma Makutsi looked over her spectacles at Mma Ramotswe. "I wouldn't write *pleased,* Mma. You are not pleased about this, and nor will be, if what you say is correct. And as for calling the conclusion *preliminary,* that suggests that you might change your mind. But I do not think you will. You have decided, and so you should call it a *firm* conclusion." She paused, fixing Mma Ramotswe with a slightly reproachful stare. The inference, thought Mma Ramotswe, was that if she, like Mma Makutsi, had been to the Botswana Secretarial College then she would have understood these things and not misused the word *preliminary* and been altogether more decisive and concise.

Mma Ramotswe said nothing. Mma Makutsi had firm views on the wording of letters.

"I would say something like this," Mma Makutsi continued. "I would say: I am sorry to say that we have come to a firm conclusion about your husband."

"But I am not sorry, Mma Makutsi."

"Yet you haven't found out what the client wants you to find out," countered Mma Makutsi. "So she will hope that you are feeling sorry."

"Just continue," said Mma Ramotswe. "These small things about which word to use are not always that important."

"We have had one of our detectives observe your husband over time . . ."

Mma Makutsi stared again at Mma Ramotswe. "Detective?" she said. "Charlie is not a qualified detective, Mma. It is wrong to mislead the client like that."

"Oh, really, Mma Makutsi. Does it matter what we call Charlie?"

"It does matter, Mma," said Mma Makutsi, her voice now full of reproach. "All over the place, people are falsely claiming to be something they aren't. All over the place there are people telling lies about this, that and the next thing. It is very important to be accurate."

This was not a battle that Mma Ramotswe chose to fight. "Very well, Mma. Change that. Say *assistant,* if you think that better."

"It's more accurate," said Mma Makutsi.

Mma Ramotswe waited while Mma Makutsi scribbled her correction on the page, uttering the words as she wrote. "This *assistant* has now filed his report."

Mma Makutsi stopped again. "I do not wish to be obstructive, Mma."

"No, of course not, Mma Makutsi."

"It's just that *I* do the filing. All the filing—that's me, not this . . . this mysterious assistant we mention." Mma Ramotswe sighed. "Filing a report just means putting a report in. It doesn't mean actually filing it in the filing cabinet."

"*Submitting* would be better, Mma."

There were some battles simply not worth fighting, thought Mma Ramotswe. And then there were battles that should not be battles anyway; this, she thought, was one of those.

"Submitting, then, Mma Makutsi."

"Good," said Mma Makutsi. "Now then. Let's see." She returned to the letter. "The report indicates . . . That's very good wording, Mma. It is very professional. The report indicates that your husband is not seeing a lover but is seeing another woman—" She broke off. "No, Mma, you cannot say that. That will give quite the wrong impression."

"Read on, Mma Makutsi."

"Seeing another woman who is a teacher. Oh, I see, Mma. I see what you're saying. We could investigate further, but we think that any man who is studying for a mathematics examination is unlikely to be having an affair at the same time. For this reason, we do not recommend further surveillance."

Mma Makutsi put down the letter. "That is a very good letter, Mma."

Mma Ramotswe reached out to recover the piece of paper. "I'm glad you approve of it, Mma," she said.

"But why is he studying mathematics?" asked Mma Makutsi.

"People do, Mma. They are always studying things. You can never tell what people will get up to." People took up entirely innocent pursuits, she pointed out. She remembered a similar case, where a husband suspected of conducting an affair was in fact receiving instruction in the Roman Catholic faith. She now reminded Mma Makutsi of that case. "Remember that man who lived near the hospital, Mma? He was not having an affair at all but was thinking of becoming a Roman Catholic."

Mma Makutsi remembered the case. "People are always joining churches," she said. "This church, that church. They like the singing in one place and they go there. Then they hear there is better singing in another place, and off they go to that one. Or there is a better preacher—one with a louder voice—and they say, 'He is the one now.' And off they go to listen to him. That's how it works, Mma."

Mma Makutsi could see the wisdom of all that. Phuti had a cousin who was a good example of that, having been, in the space of a single year, a Baptist as well as an Anglican, and had now joined a small congregation of people who believed not that the end was coming—as some people did—but that it had actually come, and we had simply failed to notice it. But this situation had a particular *smell* to it, she thought. It was the smell, and that was something that was sometimes difficult to put into words. "There's one thing worrying me here, Mma," she mused. "Why has he not told his wife? She obviously doesn't know where he is going—he can't have told her, Mma."

"Perhaps he wants her to think he's going somewhere else," said Mma Ramotswe. "But does it matter? It's nothing to do with us why he should want to study mathematics."

"Oh, I know that," said Mma Makutsi. "It's just that I think there's something odd going on, Mma Ramotswe. We're not seeing everything there is to be seen. Something else is happening."

Mma Ramotswe raised an eyebrow. "Possibly. But I don't see what it has to do with us."

Mma Makutsi went to her desk and sat down, and at that

moment, from down at floor level, almost inaudible, but just to be made out, came a tiny voice. *Mathematics, Mma? Do you believe that?*

Mma Makutsi looked up sharply.

"Did you say something, Mma Ramotswe?"

Mma Ramotswe shook her head. "No, Mma. I did not. I thought I heard something, though. I thought it was you."

"It was not me," said Mma Makutsi. She looked down at her shoes. There was silence. If there had been a voice, and if it had said something about mathematics, it had nothing more to say now. She transferred her gaze to Mma Ramotswe.

"Mma Ramotswe," she said. "I have been thinking. Would you mind if I took over that case—if you've finished with it, of course."

Mma Ramotswe was surprised. "I don't think there's much else to be done," she said. "We've told her that her suspicions as to her husband—or her hopes, perhaps—are unfounded. What else is there to do?"

"I think that man is up to something," said Mma Makutsi.

"But that's got nothing to do with us. All we were asked to do was to find out whether he was having an affair. We have said that we do not think that he is."

"I still think that man is up to something. And all I'm asking is to be allowed to do a bit more digging about."

Mma Ramotswe was doubtful. "But we can't bill the client any longer," she said. "She paid for the answer to a single question. Now she has that, and there can't be any more bills. The case is closed, Mma."

Mma Makutsi shook her head. "This is nothing to do with billing anybody. This is just to find out for the sake of getting to the truth." She paused, reaching for a small pile of papers on her desk. She shuffled these, putting the larger ones on the bottom of the pile and the smaller on the top. Mma Ramotswe wondered whether this was some system of filing that had yet to be explained to her—some system advocated, for all she knew, by the Botswana Secretarial College, and faithfully implemented by that college's most faithful graduate and disciple. Or was it the simple desire for order that many of us had, in greater or smaller measure? Although there were some people, of course, who did not have it at all, and who lived their lives with small things and big things jumbled up and who were, when all was said and done, happy . . . She looked at Mma Makutsi across the room and smiled. We were all different, she thought, and it was important to remind oneself of that. It was important, too, to imagine what it must be like to be another person. That was a simple thing to do, and its effect could be salutary. Mma Makutsi came from Bobonong; she had battled to get where she had got; she saw things in a way that somebody who came from Bobonong and who had struggled against the odds would see them. And she did all of that rather well; she performed the task of being Mma Makutsi with considerable distinction—with ninety-seven per cent, really.

And now she was saying something, and Mma Ramotswe had to concentrate.

"Sometimes the truth can't be put on anybody's bill," Mma Makutsi pronounced, and then continued, "but it's still important to get to it, Mma—to get to the truth behind all the . . . all the things that cover up the truth." She moved the papers again, and then put them to the side of her desk.

Now Mma Ramotswe did not hesitate. "If that's what you want to do, Mma, I can't see any harm in it, although I must say I don't think you are going to find anything. I don't want to discourage you, but . . ."

"I shall find what I shall find," said Mma Makutsi. "Clovis Ander-

sen says that, you know. He says: *You will find what you will find.*
I can show it to you, if you like, Mma. It's in chapter eight, if my
memory serves me correctly."

Mma Ramotswe did not argue. There was no reason why Mma
Makutsi should not spend her time pursuing any issue she chose.
Since her marriage to Phuti Radiphuti, she had been financially
independent and drew only a very small salary, no more than a
nominal one, from the agency. This meant that her time was effec-
tively at her own disposal, and if she wanted to spend it pursuing a
private investigation, even one that would probably lead nowhere,
then that was her prerogative.

"It will be interesting," Mma Ramotswe said. "We shall see."

Mma Makutsi nodded. "Most men are up to something, Mma.
That is something I have learned as a woman. Most men are up to
something—and it is the job of us women to find out what that is."

Mma Ramotswe's eyes widened. Could that possibly be true?
Was Mr. J.L.B. Matekoni up to something? Was Phuti Radiphuti?
And what about Mr. Polopetsi—the most unassuming and innocent
of men, whose demeanour reminded her so much of a frightened
rabbit's—was he up to something? And rabbits—were they up to
something too?

THE HEAD OF STEAM that Mma Ramotswe had built up with her
early and productive start lasted all morning, and was still there when
the telephone call came from Calviniah. They had exchanged telephone numbers at the wedding, and had agreed to meet at some
point, but Mma Ramotswe had not expected her long lost friend to
contact her quite so quickly.

"I know that this is not much notice," Calviniah said. "But I'm going for lunch at that Sanitas place—you know, the garden place—and I wondered if you'd join me."

Mma Ramotswe accepted immediately. She had earned lunch, she felt, having started at seven, and it was now almost twelve. That was five hours, of which a good four had been spent working, once one deducted tea time and conversations with Mma Makutsi and Charlie.

"That was that old friend," she explained to Mma Makutsi. "The one I told you about."

Mma Makutsi looked up from her desk. "The one you thought was late?"

"Yes, that one."

Mma Makutsi looked thoughtful. "It must be very strange to be thought to be late, and then not to be late," she said. "But very interesting, of course. You'd hear what people had to say about you."

Mma Ramotswe reflected on that. Mma Makutsi was right: it would be extremely interesting, she thought. In fact, for some, it might even be a revelation. And, of course, for those who said things, it could be very embarrassing. Late people don't talk back, but those who were never *properly* late might take issue with what was said about them. That could be awkward. You could gladly say, as an excuse, "But I thought you were late," but that would not be a real justification. No, on the whole it was better to say kind things of late people, even if they did not fully deserve them. Kindness, after all, did not distinguish between those who merited it and those who did not. It was like rain, she thought. It fell everywhere and made everything green and new and alive once more. That is what it did.

CHAPTER FOUR

GOOD ADVICE FROM THE GOVERNMENT

CALVINIAH HAD ALREADY ARRIVED when Mma Ramotswe drove into the car park at the Sanitas Garden. Sanitas was an oasis of green in the dryness that reached into Gaborone from the Kalahari beyond. The car park benefited from the shade of the trees that had been planted and nurtured through seasons of drought. Now these trees, leafy African hardwoods, provided pools of shade for the cars of those who came to the garden to lunch or buy plants. Cars in Botswana, Mma Ramotswe had often thought, had an inbuilt sense as to where the most sheltered parking spots would be, requiring, it seemed, very little steering to guide them to such places. Her own van, she thought, understood these things, as it did now, turning sharply, almost with no guidance from her, between two larger vehicles into a space protected by a large jacaranda tree. When she came back after lunch, the van would not be an oven, as it would be were no shade to be available. That meant she would be able to grasp the steering wheel without wincing, and position herself to drive without a message of pain from the hot surface of the seat beneath her thighs.

She loved the Sanitas Garden, as anybody would who lived in a dry land. Here was proof that the earth was never too parched to respond to the encouragement of a few drops of carefully husbanded water. This water, sucked up from deep boreholes, would have started its journey in the north of the country, or even beyond, having fallen as rain in the Angola Highlands aeons ago and gradually seeped down through fissures and channels deep below the country's dry heart. That journey ended here, where the water was claimed, and carefully parcelled out to the thirsty plants in their growing troughs, allocated cup by cup to ferns, to seedlings, to vegetables—to everything that people would want to buy for their garden plots. That nurturing of plants, that desire to cultivate, to sow and reap, lay at the heart of the culture, along with the deep-seated desire to tend cattle. This was what marked people out as being from this culture, from this place.

Ask anybody what their idea of heaven is, and the answer will reveal that person's soul. Mma Ramotswe had always thought that, and if that question were to be put to her, she knew exactly how she would respond. Heaven, to her, was not unlike this place, this peaceful garden. There would be trees very much like these ones and there would be shade, not just when the sun was at a particular point in the sky, but all day. On the other side of the shade there would be warmth, and light, and the colours of the sun, and there would be land where cattle would graze, great herds of them, sleek and contented, beyond the reach of those trials that mar the life of cattle on earth, and try them so sorely: persistent flies, brittle, sparse grazing, depleted water troughs that sent cattle away unwatered and ready to die. There would be none of that in heaven—just greenery and concord between those who walked amidst the greenery, all acrimoniousness forgotten, all human arguments put away, seen for the pettiness that they were; all wrongs forgiven. She wanted it to be like that; she so wanted that, and part of her believed that it would be—the larger part, as it happened, while the smaller part told her that such things could not be and that people would always need them, if only to make up for the emptiness they would otherwise feel. She did not agree with that view, of course, because she could not see where it led you. To unhappiness, she suspected; to a feeling of horror at the grubbiness of it all; to a paralysis of will and intent that she had occasionally seen in others and that she would never want for herself. There were flowers, she said to herself; there were flowers that covered the land in the spring, tiny flowers that you might not notice unless you got down on your hands and knees and looked for them; and these flowers were in themselves a sign of the goodness that was still in the world, and in people's hearts, no matter what was happening on the outside.

She stepped out of the van and made her way towards the cluster of buildings in the centre of the large gardens. One of these was the kitchen; it was surrounded by an awning of shade netting, its mesh calculated to provide protection from the sun while allowing some light to penetrate. Calviniah was at one of these tables, and waved to Mma Ramotswe when she saw her. A waitress with whom she had been in conversation stood behind her and drew up a chair for Mma Ramotswe as she approached.

"Here, Mma," said the waitress. "This one is a strong chair."

Mma Ramotswe thanked her, but gave her a sideways look at the same time. It was not polite, she thought, for a waitress to suggest to a customer that she might need a chair that was stronger than normal, just because she was traditionally built. That was rude, she began to say to herself, but then stopped. Was it really rude, or was it no more than caution? It was the duty, surely, of a waitress to warn of the weakness of the furniture and fittings when a generously sized person was about to put them under an excessive load. A failure to warn, in such cases, might even be culpable, particularly these days, when it seemed that we were all responsible for the safety of those around us. It was better to warn than to remain silent, although there were discreet and not-so-discreet ways of issuing a warning.

There had been several occasions when Mma Ramotswe's traditional build had led to difficulty. Perhaps the most embarrassing of these had occurred when she had been visiting Mma Potokwane at the Orphan Farm and had found it necessary to use the small bathroom off the matron's office. Mma Potokwane was inordinately proud of this bathroom, which had recently been completely refitted and redecorated, and which now boasted a modern toilet in avocado green. Mma Ramotswe had broken the seat of this, although she could not see how it had happened. She had just sat down when the seat had given a loud report, as of cracking plastic, and she had jumped up, frightened and then appalled to see what damage she had done.

Mma Potokwane had been as understanding as one would expect of an experienced matron who had, in her job, seen all the indignities to which humanity was subject. "That is nothing, Mma," she had reassured her. "The important thing is that you are not hurt." But then she had added, "I thought they made those things stronger than that. If they still used wood, as they used to, then people would be able to sit down in confidence. Even an elephant wouldn't break some of those old wooden seats, Mma—even an elephant!"

Mma Ramotswe had taken this well, but had remembered the embarrassment she felt, compounded when, weeks later, on a subsequent visit to her friend, she had seen an *Out of Order* sign still displayed on the bathroom door.

Now she was seated on a strong chair and the waitress was showing her the menu of that day's specials. Three main courses were on offer—the Bombay Curry, listed as such but then with *Bombay* scored out and *Mumbai* substituted, only to be scored out again by another hand and restored to *Bombay*. Then there was a vegetable lasagne, offered with green salad, and battered fish accompanied by French fries. Once again, an anonymous hand had amended the menu, the word *French* being struck through and *Botswana* written in neatly above.

Mma Ramotswe pointed to the fish. "Botswana fries come with that one, Mma?" she said to the waitress.

The waitress smiled. "All chips are the same, Mma. It does not matter what you call them—they are just potato. Potato, potato, potato—that is all they are."

"You are right, Mma," said Mma Ramotswe.

"Although I think maybe you'd be better having salad," said the waitress. "I don't want to tell you what to eat, but maybe salad would be best, Mma."

Mma Ramotswe frowned. "Is there something wrong with the chips, Mma?"

"No," said the waitress. "There is nothing wrong with them. They are very fresh. We fry them every day, and then we dry them on paper towels so that there is not too much fat. They are very delicious—but they are not for everybody, Mma. That is all I am saying."

Calviniah intervened. She appeared to know the waitress, and told her that she thought Mma Ramotswe would like fish and chips and that should be what was fetched for her. "I do not think we need to discuss it any further," she said. "And I will have the same thing—to keep my friend company."

The two old friends settled down to lunch. There was much ground to cover and they were obliged to compress the years into a few sentences, skating over the details of family events, of work, of home, of parents and siblings and husbands, to give each other a broad picture of what had happened to them since those early years of girlhood in Mochudi. Calviniah had heard about Mma Ramotswe's marriage to Note Mokoti, although she had never met him. She remembered what people had said about his cruelty. "Men like that, Mma," she sighed, "are not made for being husbands."

Mma Ramotswe agreed. "That is very true, Mma. They are not."

"And yet," Calviniah continued, "we still marry them because we think we are going to be the one who will change them. We think that other women may have failed, but we will succeed because . . . well, because we do not think straight at such times—we do not think straight, Mma, when it comes to the heart." She put a hand on her chest, above her heart, and said, "The heart thinks differently, Mma. That is the problem."

The waitress arrived with their order. "Here are your chips, Mma," she said to Mma Ramotswe. "Do not feel that you have to finish them. If you would like to leave some, that will be all right."

Calviniah gave the waitress a discouraging look. "You are very kind, Mma. We shall see about that." And then to Mma Ramotswe she said, "As you were saying, Mma, after that man, Note . . ."

"I learned my lesson," Mma Ramotswe supplied. "I learned to tell the difference between a good man and a . . . not-so-good man. I met a man called Mr. J.L.B. Matekoni, a mechanic."

Calviniah brightened. "A mechanic, Mma? They make very fine husbands. They are famous for that. If a lady can find a mechanic, then she should not hesitate."

"I did not," said Mma Ramotswe. "But I must tell you, Mma, I had to wait some time before he asked me to marry him. I thought he'd never get around to it, but then eventually he did. And then, after we had become engaged, he took a long, long time to talk about a wedding."

Calviniah nodded at the familiar story. "We are going to have to change everything," she said. "In future, it is the women who are going to ask the men to marry them. It is the women who will decide the date and make all the arrangements. In that way, valuable time will not be lost."

They began their meal. The chips were perfectly cooked, as was the fish.

"And you?" asked Mma Ramotswe. "What about your husband, Mma?"

"He is a very good man," said Calviniah. "He is called Ernest. Sometimes people call him by the nickname Shiny, but I do not like that. He doesn't seem to mind, but I do."

"Why have a nickname when you have a perfectly good name already?" asked Mma Ramotswe.

"Those are my thoughts too," said Calviniah. "It is a male thing, I think. Men are always giving one another these names. Ernest has a friend who is called Trousers. I don't know why they use that name, but that is what they call him. His real name is Thomas, but they call him Trousers. None of them knows why."

"And family, Mma? Do you and Ernest have children?"

Calviniah nodded and then averted her eyes briefly. "I had heard about you, Mma. I heard that . . ."

"Yes," said Mma Ramotswe quietly. "My baby is late."

Reaching across the table, Calviniah placed a hand gently on Mma Ramotswe's arm. "I'm so sorry, Mma. I'm so sorry about that."

Mma Ramotswe inclined her head. "It was a long time ago now."

"I know. But your heart must still be broken, Mma."

Was it? Mma Ramotswe thought about her friend's words. There were so many things in this life that we had to regret that we sometimes forgot those things that belonged to the distant past. Or the pain was dulled, which was a different thing, of course.

"We have two foster children," she said. "We love them very much."

For a few moments Calviniah was silent, before continuing, "Yes, we love our children so much, don't we? And we expect them to love us back, but—" She broke off, as if she felt she had already said too much.

Mma Ramotswe waited.

"Then they go off," said Calviniah. "They go off and find their own friends. They start living their own lives and there is no place for you in those lives. That is what hurts."

"That has happened to you, Mma?"

Their eyes met, and Mma Ramotswe had her answer.

"My first-born is a girl," Calviniah said. "Nametso. She is twenty-four now. She has a job in Gaborone—a good job in the diamond-sorting office. You know that place out near the airport?"

Mma Ramotswe knew it. It was in that building that Botswana collected the diamonds from its open-pit diamond mines—a trickle of brilliance wrested from thousands of tons of raw rock. A job at the sorting tables was highly valued, and any parent would be proud of a daughter who worked there.

"We were very close," Calviniah continued. "And then . . ." She shrugged. "Suddenly she had no time for me."

Mma Ramotswe frowned. Teenagers did that—they gave their parents the cold shoulder, sometimes even pretended not to have anything to do with them, out of embarrassment—that could be comic, but it was also normal enough. Had this happened here, and was Calviniah simply over-reacting? "I think that sort of thing can happen, Mma," she said. "But they tend to grow out of it. Some people may just take a little longer than others." She remembered just such a case—a teenage boy, the son of neighbours, who had been at pains to reject his parents, studiously ignoring them or, at best, listening to them with a pained expression. That had gone on for years, and then, suddenly, at the age of nineteen his behaviour had changed, and he had become helpful and protective. "He suddenly realised that we might die," said his mother. "You don't think of that when you are fourteen, fifteen, and then it occurs to you and you change. That is what happened, Mma Ramotswe."

Mma Ramotswe told Calviniah about this boy, but her friend simply shook her head. "No, Mma Ramotswe, you don't understand. This didn't happen when she was a teenager. This happened just a few months ago. It was that recent."

Mma Ramotswe looked pained. "I'm sorry, Mma."

"I don't know what I've done to deserve it," sighed Calviniah. "I've tried to remember if it was something I said, but I can't think of anything." A look of anguish came over her face. "I would never have hurt her deliberately, Mma. She is my first-born, my own flesh and blood."

Mma Ramotswe lowered her voice. "Of course, Mma. Of course she is."

She asked Calviniah whether she had asked Nametso directly what was troubling her. She had always believed in asking direct questions, an approach which surprisingly often produced the answer one was looking for. If you wanted to know what people thought, ask them, and you might find out what you needed to know.

Calviniah assured her that she had done that. "I did ask her, Mma," she said. "I said, 'If there is something wrong, you should tell me.'"

"And?"

"She looked away. She didn't say anything. Then she told me that she was busy and I would have to go. Her own mother, Mma. She was too busy for her own mother."

For a few moments they were both silent. Then Calviniah made an effort to pull herself together. "But we have heard enough of my troubles, Mma. Let's talk about the old days. Let's talk about the people we both knew."

It was with some relief that Mma Ramotswe agreed to this suggestion. Her friend's account of her alienation from her daughter had saddened her, but she suspected that many of these family tiffs proved to be just that—splits that would heal themselves in the course of time. And anyway, she was not sure if she could do much to help in that respect—what she could do, though, was to encourage Calviniah to think of something more positive. And so she reminded her of one of their teachers at school who had been known as Mma Forget-the-Words because of her habit of starting a song and then getting tied up in knots of confusion over what came next.

"There are some people who are not destined to sing," said Calviniah, and they both laughed.

"Even if they know the words," Mma Ramotswe added. She thought of Mr. J.L.B. Matekoni, who liked music, but who did not have a good ear for it. "I have a mechanic's ear," he said. "I'm sorry about that, because I would like to be able to sing."

She had thought of a mechanic's ear, and had decided that it would have its advantages in at least some situations. "But you can hear what an engine is saying to you," she pointed out.

He had nodded. "Perhaps. Because they do talk to us, you know, Mma Ramotswe. Some engines have a lot to say."

They talked about one or two other people. Mma Ramotswe remembered Calviniah's cousin, who had gone to live in Maun, in the far north of the country, and had raised a brood of eight children. Then there was the woman who ran the small shop behind the hill at Mochudi, the woman whose husband had lost his sight and sat in a chair outside the store and felt the sun upon his face; he had smiled a great deal and had asked people who spoke to him whether they were happy—for he was, he said, and if he could be happy in his world of darkness, then they would have no excuse for not being happy themselves. "I don't think I knew then what he meant," said Calviniah, "but I think I do now."

"So do I," said Mma Ramotswe. "I hadn't thought of that man for a long time, Mma. Perhaps we should think about him a bit more often."

"He will be late now," said Calviniah. "So many of the people from those days are late."

"But still with us," said Mma Ramotswe, softly, thinking of her father, that great man, that fine judge of cattle. He was still with her, and no matter how many years passed, he would still be there.

"Yes," agreed Calviniah. "They are."

Neither said anything for a few moments. Their table was shaded by the spreading branches of a tree, a large umbrella thorn. In the foliage above them, a fluttering of wings gave away the presence of a pair of Cape doves, lovers of course, engaged in the flattery of courting birds, the puffed-up feathers, the soft cooing, the turning away of the female in the face of the male's wanted-but-unwanted advances. A feather drifted down, dancing through the air, and Mma Ramotswe smiled. "They're very happy up there," she said.

"They don't have our problems," said Calviniah. "They don't need to worry."

"Do we?" asked Mma Ramotswe.

They took their time to finish their lunch. There was still much to talk about, and much to laugh over too. The waitress returned, casting a disapproving eye over the empty plate on which Mma Ramotswe's chips had been.

Noticing the direction of the waitress's gaze, Mma Ramotswe said, "They were very good, Mma. Thank you."

Calviniah smiled. "I ate some of them," she said to the waitress. "I wouldn't want you to think that Mma Ramotswe ate them all herself."

The waitress looked pained. "It is not my business to tell people what to eat," she said. "If they wish to eat things that are not good for them, then that is their business, Mma, not mine."

She took the plates away. Calviniah looked at Mma Ramotswe. "There are many people around telling us what is good for us," she said. "Don't do this, don't do that. Who do they think they are, Mma? The government?"

"They mean well," said Mma Ramotswe.

Calviniah snorted. "But what about them? Who tells them what to do?"

Mma Ramotswe shrugged. "I don't know, Mma. But isn't it a good sign, don't you think? Isn't it a good sign that people worry about other people? That they want other people to be careful?"

Calviniah agreed, but only reluctantly. "We are not children, Mma. We don't like to be told: Don't do this thing, don't do that thing. Not all the time."

"Perhaps not."

"It would be better," Calviniah continued, "if they said to us: here is some advice, but it is your life and you must decide yourself. They could even not tell us directly, but leave the advice lying about on tables, perhaps, Mma. Booklets and so on. With *Good Advice for You from the Government* printed on the front—so that we know. That might be better, I think, Mma Ramotswe."

"Perhaps," said Mma Ramotswe.

Calviniah looked thoughtful. "Sometimes it's difficult to know what to do, isn't it? How can we tell what is right? That's the question, I think, Mma."

Mma Ramotswe looked up into the branches of the tree. *How could we tell? How could we?*

The sun filtered down through the canopy of acacia. Above its delicate, spreading branches was the sky, which went on forever, it seemed, into a thin, singing blue. Nothingness, just air. How could we tell what we had to do, because we were very small, really, and our feet were stuck on the ground, and we could not see very far? And then the answer came. It had been there all along, of course, and she had always known it: we knew what we had to do because there were all those people, our ancestors, who had faced exactly the same problems as confronted us, and who had worked out what was the right thing to do. We only had to listen. We only had to close our eyes and wait for their voices to come to us on the wind, perhaps, or in the stillness of the night. That was all we had to do.

"Oh," Calviniah said suddenly. "There's somebody else I've remembered."

Mma Ramotswe waited.

"Poppy," she said. "Remember her? She was in our class too. The one who went off to Francistown and became rich because she had that big store? Remember her?"

Mma Ramotswe did. She had forgotten about Poppy, but now she came back to her. They had all liked Poppy, and when they heard of her good fortune, people had been pleased rather than envious.

"Well," said Calviniah. "She has no money any more. Gone."

"Oh?" said Mma Ramotswe. "Where?"

"Who knows?" replied Calviniah. "I don't, I'm afraid." She shook her head sorrowfully. "Well, I have my suspicions. I don't think she will be very happy."

Mma Ramotswe lowered her eyes. She hated hearing about the unhappiness of others. There was so little time in life, so little, and yet there were so many who were obliged to spend those precious few years we had on this earth in unhappiness.

"Not that she *has* to be unhappy," Calviniah continued. "You can lose all your money and still be happy."

"And you might not have any in the first place," observed Mma

Ramotswe. "There are many people who do not have any money at all, Mma, and yet are happy with the world."

Calviniah agreed. "That's true enough, Mma Ramotswe."

Mma Ramotswe looked up. "You have your suspicions? You said you have your suspicions? Tell me about them, Mma."

CHAPTER FIVE

AT THE HAPPY CHICKEN CAF

THAT EVENING, Charlie met Queenie-Queenie at the Happy Chicken Caf. This was a small restaurant in a cluster of shops not far from the old Standard Bank; its sign had suffered the loss of a final *e*, and the accidentally shortened name had stuck. It had been a favourite haunt of Charlie's for some months, although its prices were, he thought, a bit on the steep side. In fact, Charlie was rarely in a position to buy a piece of chicken, restricting himself to the occasional free meal, given to him by Pearly, the restaurant's owner, a woman who was vaguely related to his mother. Pearly had a soft spot for Charlie, and recognised that according to the rules of the old Botswana morality, as an older relative she had at least some responsibility for him. That was how it was: nobody was left alone, unrelated, and uncared for—somewhere, in the vast tangle of human relationships, everybody could say to at least someone: *I am one of your people.*

Of course, the operation of this system of solidarity was not always simple. While there might be one person who recognised your claim, there might equally be another—sometimes in a position of authority—for whom the claim meant little or nothing. In this case, the doubter was Mr. Potso, the chef who fried the chicken, a thickset man with only one eye, who was Pearly's lover, and who resented Charlie's claims on her.

"This boy," Mr. Potso complained to Pearly. "This boy who hangs about sometimes: Who exactly is he?"

"He's my cousin's son. Not my close cousin, you know, but one of my mother's people from way back. I forget exactly where and when, but way, way back."

Mr. Potso was not impressed with the credentials of this kinship. "There are many people," he said. "There are so many people who were related a long time ago. We all go back to Adam, remember. We are all his cousins."

Pearly laughed. "That was a long time ago, Potso."

"That is what I'm saying," countered Mr. Potso. "I'm saying if you start looking for relatives, then there are relatives under every stone." He paused. You have to be careful, he thought; you have to be careful not to push women too far, because sometimes they can turn around and say, I've had enough of you. They could do that, and then they turn you out and where are you then? That was why you had to be careful, especially if you had only one eye. You could miss things if you had only one eye.

"All I'm saying," he continued, "is that once you start picking up relatives, then you can end up with a lot of them. That is all I'm saying."

"That is true enough, I suppose," said Pearly. It was not a matter that she had given much thought to, but she was often impressed with Potso's observations of the world. He might only have one eye, she had once said to a friend, but he sees a lot with that eye of his.

Mr. Potso was emboldened. "And then, if you're not careful, you end up with one hundred relatives on your doorstep—all of them hungry. All wanting something from you. And then along will come the baboons. They'll say, 'Don't forget about us! We are your cousins too—a long way back. What about us? What have you got for us to eat?'"

Pearly laughed. "I don't think so, Potso. If baboons come to your place, you chase them back into the bush. You say, 'Get back where you belong.' That's what you say, Potso."

Potso smiled. "They're clever creatures, Mma. Don't underestimate them."

"I don't. They understand a stick waved at them. I think they are clever enough to understand that."

Mr. Potso was a keen reader. He had borrowed a book from the library and was reading his way through it, slowly, because of his eyesight problem. "The baboons will say something to you, Mma," he began. "They'll say, 'Have you not heard of this fellow called Darwin?' That's what they will say, Mma. Those clever baboons—that's what they will say."

"Who is this Darwin, Rra?"

"He is the one who said that people and baboons are cousins, Mma. All people come from baboons in the old days, right at the beginning. They are our ancestors, way back, I think. That is what he said—I'm not saying that, Mma. Not me."

"Just as well," said Pearly, and laughed. "You're reading too much, Potso. There is limited space in our heads, you know. You can't put more and more stuff in there."

Charlie knew that Mr. Potso was resentful of him. Like so many young men, it did not readily occur to him that anybody could dislike him; a young man is like a puppy in that regard, assuming without any doubt the approbation of others. Puzzled by the cool disregard of Pearly's lover, he had tried to ingratiate himself, but without success.

He had even tried to win him over with humour, telling Mr. Potso a joke that he had heard and that he thought might appeal to the older man. He had expected laughter and male conspiracy, but had been greeted with a fixed stare.

"And then what happened?" Mr. Potso said eventually.

"Nothing more happened, Rra," explained Charlie. "That is the end of the story, you see." He paused. "It is a very amusing story, Rra, I think."

"So the man put the cattle-brand on the seat of the other man's trousers," said Mr. Potso. "What's so amusing about that?"

"Well, he hadn't been expecting it—that other man," said Charlie. "He was a bit surprised, you see."

"Of course he would be," said Mr. Potso. "And it must have been very painful for him. I do not think it funny. And he shouldn't have been seeing that man's wife, should he?"

Charlie did not try humour again. Nor did he succeed with compliments directed towards Mr. Potso's fried chicken. When Charlie praised him for the crispness of his chicken wings, Mr. Potso simply sighed and said that anybody could fry chicken and that there was no great art to getting crisp results. And when Charlie agreed with a view that Mr. Potso had expressed as to the competence of a local politician, Mr. Potso had pointed out that he was not at all serious in his earlier comments and that in reality he believed the opposite of what he said. "Sometimes people mean the opposite of what they say, Charlie," he had said. "You should be able to work that out by now."

After that, Charlie had given up, concluding that for some inexplicable reason Mr. Potso was determined to thwart him. From then on, although he remained polite to the chef, he warily kept his distance.

And now, as Charlie sat in the Happy Chicken Caf, waiting for Queenie-Queenie to arrive, he glanced surreptitiously at Mr. Potso through the open kitchen hatch. After a few minutes, the chef appeared from the kitchen, wiping his hands on a scrap of kitchen towel.

"Have you ordered?" Mr. Potso demanded.

Charlie shook his head. "I am waiting for company," he said.

"Company?"

"Yes, company, Rra."

The chef rolled his eyes. "And if everyone came in here and waited for company? What then? There would be the whole of Botswana sitting here, just in case any company dropped by. And all the people wanting to buy fried chicken, where would they be? Standing outside, I think."

Charlie bit his lip. "I will be ordering chicken when my girlfriend comes."

The chef rolled his eyes again, and Charlie's gaze was drawn to the mucus-white of the eyeballs. He did not like Mr. Potso, and, in particular, he did not like his eyes.

"So, you have a girlfriend. It seems that anybody can get a girl-friend these days."

Charlie said nothing.

"Even people you never thought would find a girlfriend," Mr. Potso continued. "Even those people seem to be able to find somebody." He shook his head in mock wonderment.

Pearly appeared from the kitchen. Mr. Potso looked in her direction and left Charlie.

"That is the number one useless man in the country," Charlie muttered to himself, and felt all the better for the observation, however private and unheard it may have been. He might have dwelt on his humiliation had it not been for the arrival a minute or so later of Queenie-Queenie.

"You've been waiting for hours," she said. "My fault. All my fault."

"I have not been waiting long," said Charlie. "Just ten minutes, maybe. Listening to that useless chef."

Queenie-Queenie glanced towards the kitchen door. "You do not need to listen to that man," she said. "My father says he's a rubbish man. No good. That's what my father says."

Charlie brightened. "I don't pay any attention to what he says. I never have."

Queenie-Queenie smiled. "He's jealous of you, I think. He's jealous because you are so handsome and clever. That is why he's rude to you, Charlie."

Charlie demurred. "I do not think that I—" He broke off. He could not believe what she had just said. She had said that he was handsome and clever. Nobody, let alone a girl, had said that to him before.

"Anyway," said Queenie-Queenie. "We have better things to do than think about that man."

"I know," said Charlie.

Queenie-Queenie sat down opposite him. "Are you going to have chicken?"

Charlie affected nonchalance. He could say that he had already eaten, and that he did not want anything more. That was not true, of course; he had not eaten, and the smell of the fried chicken wafting in from the kitchen was impossibly tempting. But the truth of the matter was that he could not afford two helpings of chicken—one for him and one for her.

"I'm not all that hungry," he said. "You have some chicken."

She looked at him with concern. "If you don't eat meat, then you'll get thin. You'll get knocked over. You should not be too thin."

"If you eat too much fried chicken," said Charlie, "then your arteries get clogged up with chicken fat. I have read all about that."

Queenie-Queenie was not impressed. "Then why are chickens

not all dead?" she demanded. "If chicken fat was so dangerous, then chickens would be dying all the time. But they are healthy, Charlie. You see them all over the place. They are very healthy."

"They are different," said Charlie. "We have these arteries, you see; chickens do not have arteries." He paused. "Or I don't think they do."

Queenie-Queenie made an insouciant gesture. "I don't think we should talk about all that. There are so many things they say we should not do. Don't eat this, don't eat that. Don't cross the road in case you get run down. Don't get out of bed in the morning in case you slip on the mat and break your ankle. We're warned about these things all the time."

"We could talk about other things," agreed Charlie. "There are many things to talk about."

"Such as marriage," said Queenie-Queenie. "That is one of the things that people can talk about."

Charlie had not expected this. Their relationship had been an on-off affair, and they had separated before this. He was hesitant. "Maybe," he said. "That is one thing, I think, but there are many others, of course."

"But none of them as important as marriage," persisted Queenie-Queenie.

"I never said it was not important," said Charlie.

Queenie-Queenie was studying him, and he found it slightly disconcerting. "It has been very hot," he said, in an attempt to change the subject. "The rain will have to come soon, I think."

Queenie-Queenie ignored this comment about rain. People were always talking about it—rain, rain, rain—and none of that talk, she felt, would make the rain come any sooner. If anything, it could tempt the rain to stay away, just to spite those rain-obsessed people. But no, she should not think that way: everything depended on rain, and if the weather spirits—not that they existed, of course—should ever know that she was thinking along these seditious lines, then it might make matters worse. So she put such thoughts out of her mind, and looked again at Charlie.

"Marriage is the number one thing," she said to Charlie. "If you can think of a more important question than that of who you spend your life with, then I'd like to know what that question is." She stared at him expectantly, and then added, "No? No suggestions?"

Charlie looked up at the ceiling. "Some people say that money is more important," he said, and added, hurriedly, "I am not saying that. That's not me. But there are people who say that. Money—everything is about money."

Queenie-Queenie wrinkled her nose. "Money is nothing, Charlie. Love is everything. That is the difference between the two: money, nothing; love, everything."

Charlie frowned. Queenie-Queenie came from a family that had money—money and trucks. If you had money and trucks behind you, then it was easy to say that money was nothing—and trucks, for that matter. It was only too easy. But if you came from where he came from, which was nowhere, really, and you had no money at all, you would never say that.

Queenie-Queenie expanded on her theme. "If I had a choice, Charlie, between money, here on this hand, and love, here on this hand . . ." She held her hands out towards him, and Charlie saw how soft the skin was, and the carefully tended nails. He swallowed hard. These were not hands that had been obliged to do the laundry or mix the mortar for the wall of the *lelapa,* the low mud-wall that bounded the traditional Botswana household. These were not even hands that had needed to do the kitchen work that most women had to do, and in the more progressive households, was even expected of men. These hands had done nothing.

"If I had to choose between the two of them," Queenie-Queenie continued, "what do you think I would choose, Charlie? You tell me. Think about it for a little while, and then you tell me what I would choose."

Charlie sat back in his seat. Mr. Potso poked his head out from the kitchen to stare at Queenie-Queenie. Then he transferred his gaze to Charlie, curling an eyebrow as if to say, *Her! What's she doing with somebody like you?*

Charlie echoed her question. "Which one would you choose?"

"Yes, which one?"

Charlie made a hopeless gesture. "Oh, I know that. I know that you would choose love. That is what you've already said. You said that money is not the big thing . . ."

Queenie-Queenie raised a finger. "No. Wrong. Money."

Charlie could not conceal his surprise. "But you said . . ."

"I didn't. I was talking about both. I never said that I would prefer love to money. I said that if I had money, then I would also like to have love. Love is more important than money—I did say that—but you can't live on love by itself. You need money. You have to eat. So what you do is you make sure that you have money in the first place, then love will come. You say, 'I am ready now for love, because I have money,' and love will come."

Charlie listened to this in silence. When she had finished speaking, he simply said, "Oh."

"So you agree with me?" asked Queenie-Queenie.

He did not answer immediately, and so she said, "I'm glad that we agree about this important thing."

He opened his mouth to speak, not knowing what he intended to say, but feeling that he should at least express a view. But before he could say anything, Queenie-Queenie continued, "That is why you do not need to ask me to marry you. I know that this is what you would like to do because we both think the same way about this thing."

He struggled to make sense of what she was saying. He did not need to ask her to marry him: What did that mean? That he should not ask? Or that he should? Or did it mean that they did not have to talk about the matter any longer?

He said, "Well, that is very interesting, Queenie. But are you going to order some fried chicken?"

She looked at him reproachfully. "This is no time for fried chicken."

Mr. Potso was staring at them again, this time more intently. "Potso thinks it is. Look at him. He is always thinking that we should order something. All the time."

She did not follow his gaze. Potso was nothing to her.

"No," she said. "You do not need to ask me to marry you, Charlie. These days, women can ask men to marry them. So if anybody asks us when you asked me, you can just say, 'It was not necessary—we decided to get married and that was it.' No need for formalities—not these days."

"Ha!" he said. "But we didn't decide, did we?"

This brought a flat rebuttal. "Yes, we did."

"When?"

"Just a few moments ago. I said that we agreed, and you said nothing. You didn't say, 'I do not agree.' You didn't say anything like that."

"I didn't know that we had agreed. How could I tell, Queenie?"

She brushed this aside. "That doesn't matter any longer. We don't need to go over the past—unlike some people. They are always saying 'You said this thing' or 'You said that thing' and disagreeing with one another all the time."

He looked away, summoning up the courage to tell her. He had no money. That was the issue. He could not pay what her family would be expecting. He could not even pay for two helpings of peri-peri chicken.

"I am very keen on you, Queenie," he said at last. "Every time you look at me, I think—here inside me, right here—I think, You are so lucky to have this lady. But then I think, How can I ever marry somebody like her when I have no money? How can I go to her relatives—to her father, to her uncles—and say all I have is a couple of hundred pula. They would laugh at me and say, 'Voetsek, you useless nothing man! Do not come around here unless you have at least thirty thousand pula, maybe forty.'"

Queenie-Queenie laughed. "But you don't just have a couple of hundred pula. You must have more than that."

Charlie shook his head. "That is the truth, Queenie. I have almost no money left."

"What have you spent it on?"

"Nothing."

"Then why do you say 'left'? If you have no money left, that means you have had some and it is gone now."

Charlie looked miserable. "It was never there. An apprentice detective does not get paid very much money."

"But you will not be an apprentice forever, Charlie."

He shook his head. "Sometimes I think I will. I was an apprentice mechanic for a long, long time. And I never became a fully qualified mechanic. Fanwell did, but I did not. And now I'm an apprentice detective but nobody can tell me how long that will last. Maybe forever, I think. I will be a very old man one day and still an apprentice. And then I will be dead and I will probably be an apprentice dead person too."

Charlie had not expected Queenie-Queenie to laugh, but that is how she responded. And once her laughter died away, she said, "But Charlie—you do not have to worry about that. My brother, Hector, is always making money on deals that he does. You've met him. You like him. He buys things cheaply and then sells them on. He is very clever that way. He will make you a partner in one of his deals and that way you will have the money very soon. I will tell my father that you are just getting the money together and will soon be talking to my uncles about the *bogadi*. No problem, Charlie. No problem. We can get married soon."

Charlie remained silent.

"You see?" said Queenie-Queenie after a few moments. "You see, Charlie? Simple."

CHAPTER SIX

MEN ARE WEAK, MMA

MMA RAMOTSWE always fed the children early on school nights. This was to give them time to do their homework in their rooms before lights out at eight-thirty. Of course, both Puso and Motholeli protested that their bedtime was far earlier than that of any of their friends—indeed, earlier than any known bedtime of any child in all of southern Africa, but Mma Ramotswe was not one to be persuaded by such pleading. She knew it was true that some children stayed up until midnight, or even beyond, but she knew from a teacher friend what the consequences of that were.

"We have children coming to school in the morning half asleep, Mma," said her friend. "Then they doze through their lessons and nothing goes into their heads."

"And their parents?" asked Mma Ramotswe. "What are the parents doing?"

The teacher laughed. "They are drinking beer or dancing, maybe. I don't know. One thing I do know is that they are not there making sure that their children go to bed at a reasonable time, as people did in the old days, Mma."

"Because many of us didn't have electricity," said Mma Ramotswe. "We had paraffin lamps when I was young. Then we had electricity later on."

"You went to bed when it got dark," said the teacher. She paused. A look came to her face that is the look that sometimes comes to those who think of the past. "You cannot uninvent things, Mma. Electricity is a good thing, I suppose. And water that comes in a tap."

"And pills for TB and other diseases."

The teacher nodded. "All of that, Mma. That is all progress, and nobody would want to stop progress, would they, Mma?"

She looked at Mma Ramotswe. There was a note of wistfulness in her voice, a note suggesting that there were, perhaps, times when one might want to do just that—to stop progress. Not that one could admit it publicly, of course; progress was one of those things that everybody was expected to believe in, and if you did not, then you might be mocked and accused of living in the past. And yet, were there not things about the old Botswana that were good and valuable, just as there were things like that in every country? The habit of not being rude to people; the habit of treating old people with respect because they had seen so many things and had worked hard for so many years; the habit of keeping some things private that deserved to be kept private, and not living one's life in a showy way, under the eyes of half the world; the habit of being charitable, and not laughing at others, or speaking ill of them. These were things that everybody respected in the old Botswana, in that time, still remembered by some, before people learned to be selfish.

The teacher sighed. Spilled milk was spilled milk. "But there is still a problem of children who are half asleep in the morning."

At least that would not be a problem for Puso and Motholeli, Mma Ramotswe thought. And despite all their protests, when it came to eight-thirty they tended to be so tired anyway that they fell fast asleep within a few minutes of their light being switched off. That meant that she could busy herself with making dinner for Mr. J.L.B. Matekoni, who sometimes did not arrive home from the garage until just before eight.

That evening she had prepared a stew for him, served with a generous helping of pumpkin. That was his favourite meal, and she made sure that she served it at least twice a week. You could not give a man too much meat, she believed, although Mma Makutsi had recently drawn her attention to an article in the press that seemed to contradict that traditional Botswana wisdom.

"They're saying that you should have red meat only once a week," Mma Makutsi warned. "I have read about this, Mma. They say that you shouldn't eat red meat more than once a week."

Mma Ramotswe had listened carefully, but this went against everything she, and a whole generation of Botswana women, had had instilled in them by their mothers. "I don't think they can be talking about Botswana," she said, once Mma Makutsi had finished. "I think that advice is for Americans. Over there I think they should not eat too much meat—it's different here, Mma. We have always liked meat."

"The Americans like meat too," said Mma Makutsi. "They are always eating hamburgers, Mma. All the time."

"Well, that must be the reason for those articles, Mma. It is because the Americans are eating too many hamburgers. They are being told not to eat so many. We do not eat hamburgers—we like steak. That is different, Mma. That is well known."

Mma Makutsi shook her head. "No, Mma, you are wrong there. This is advice from the United Nations. It is for all people, not just

Americans. They are saying: do not eat too much red meat. That is what they are saying."

Mma Ramotswe sighed. "But we cannot stop feeding men meat. They will be very angry if we do that. They will say, 'Where is our meat, then?'" She paused. "And there is another thing I can tell you, Mma Makutsi. If you stop giving your husband good Botswana beef, you know what happens? Men are weak, Mma. They will go to some other lady who will say, 'I will cook you lots of meat.' That is what will happen. Even a very mild man is capable of doing that, Mma."

The discussion with Mma Makutsi had not changed her view that if a man liked to eat meat, then you would have to be gentle in getting him to change his views. You should not say, "No more meat!" as some people argued you should do. Rather, you should work at it slowly, showing him that there were many other delicious meals he might enjoy. There were all sorts of pasta—the supermarket where she did her shopping was full of these things, and there were any number of sauces you could add. And then, when you served meat you might cut down on the size of the servings in such a way that the man might not notice—until it was too late. Then, when only a sliver of beef appeared on his plate, you might say, "Is it worth bothering with such a thin piece of meat?" and answer your own question firmly, saying, "No, it would be simpler if we had just the vegetables," and then change the subject quickly so that he would have no time to argue the point. And the next day would be a day for pasta, with no sign of beef in the sauce, but with plenty of tomatoes, which, being red, were of a colour that men tended to like.

That night, though, dinner was composed of beef and pumpkin, even if there was less beef than usual, and rather more pumpkin. As they sat down to the meal, Mma Ramotswe said grace, which she sometimes missed when the children were not at the table.

"We think of our brothers and sisters who have nothing," she said.

"We think of people who have lost what little they have. We think of those who go to bed hungry tonight. Let us not forget those brothers and sisters as we sit down to our meal."

She had been looking down at her plate as she spoke the grace, and now she looked up as Mr. J.L.B. Matekoni raised his eyes and muttered, "Amen." Then he said, "Those are good words, Mma. It is good to think of those who are not as fortunate as we are."

"It is, Rra," she said. "We need to remind ourselves from time to time of our good fortune."

"And think of the many men who do not get much meat," said Mr. J.L.B. Matekoni, looking down at his plate.

Mma Ramotswe was silent at first, but then she said, "This is very good pumpkin, Rra. It was the best they had in the supermarket. The biggest, I think. There was enough for three days."

"It's these agricultural scientists," said Mr. J.L.B. Matekoni. "They're developing new varieties of pumpkins all the time."

Normally, she might have replied to that. Pumpkins were a subject of some interest to her, but that evening her own words, the words of the grace she had uttered just a few moments ago, came back to her. *We think of our brothers and sisters . . .* She thought of Calviniah, and of their conversation over lunch, under that tree, with the doves in its branches. *Our brothers and sisters . . .* There were some people who laughed at religion, who said it was all about nothing, a nonsense dreamed up by the superstitious and the fearful, but that, really, was what it was about. It was about love and friendship rather than about selfishness and suffering. Calviniah, an old friend, was her sister; just as much as her half-sister down in Lobatse, or Mma Makutsi, or the woman who sold oranges on the roadside outside Tlokweng, or the woman who read the news on Botswana television, the woman who was far too thin by traditional

Botswana standards, but who had a very pretty face that made men get up close to the television to see more of it. All of these people, known and unknown, obscure and renowned, were her sisters. And their brothers were her brothers too: the man you saw outside the Princess Marina Hospital, who had pustules all over his skin, the man who stood guard in the supermarket to stop people from sampling the food as they pushed their trolleys down the aisles, the prisoner she had seen staring despondently out of the police truck as he was taken to the magistrates' court for sentencing—all of these were her brothers, with all that brotherhood entailed.

She sighed. It was hard sometimes, because some of the people who were meant to be your brothers and sisters were difficult people, dirty in some cases, selfish and calculating in others, even smelly, but they were still your brothers and had to be treated as such. There were no exceptions; you were not told, *You must love your neighbour—provided, of course, that he is presentable and not too noisy and does not drink or smell or wipe his nose on his sleeve* . . . You were told, *You must love your neighbour.* And then, just as you managed that, you were given the even more difficult instruction, *You must love your enemies.* That was a hurdle at which many people fell, because one thing was always abundantly clear: your enemies did not love *you*. But you had to grit your teeth and love them, even if your enemy was somebody like Violet Sephotho, with her husband-stealing and her nakedly self-centred ambitions. If she were to go to Trevor Mwamba himself, who had been the Bishop of Botswana, and say to him, "Do I really have to love Violet Sephotho?" he would incline his head and say, "I'm afraid you must, Precious." And she would do it for Bishop Mwamba, she would try to love even Violet, although she would not pretend it would be easy. At the same time, of course, that might be just too much of a request to make of Mma Makutsi. Mma Ramotswe would not like to have to say to her, "Violet Sephotho is your sister, Mma," because the reaction she should expect would not be a positive one.

Calviniah . . . Calviniah was her sister, and at lunch she had made a request of her. It was not uttered as a request—not in words that were normally used for asking—but the intention behind it was as clear as if it had been spelled out.

She looked at Mr. J.L.B. Matekoni. "Calviniah," she said. "The woman who was at the wedding."

"The one you thought was late?"

"Yes. That lady. I had lunch with her."

Mr. J.L.B. Matekoni nodded. "What did you have?" He looked at his plate again. "Meat?"

Mma Ramotswe did not answer the question. "She's unhappy."

Mr. J.L.B. Matekoni waited. If a woman was unhappy, in his experience this could mean that there was a badly behaved man in the background. That was not always the case, but it was often so.

"She has a daughter," Mma Ramotswe continued. "She works as a diamond sorter."

"She won't be unhappy about that," said Mr. J.L.B. Matekoni. "That's a very good job. Lots of people would give anything for that job."

"I know that," said Mma Ramotswe. "The daughter must be pleased. But I don't think it's anything to do with the job."

"Illness?" asked Mr. J.L.B. Matekoni. "Is she sick?"

"No, I don't think it's that. The daughter has become very unfriendly towards her. Calviniah cannot understand why."

Mr. J.L.B. Matekoni finished the last piece of meat on his plate. "Children can break your heart," he said. "I knew a man whose son did not speak to him for ten years. Then he came home and expected his father to give him money. After ten years of silence."

"Why?" asked Mma Ramotswe. "Why would you not speak to your father for ten years?"

"An argument over cattle," replied Mr. J.L.B. Matekoni. He smiled. "Cattle never argue over people, but people always argue over cattle."

"I think Calviniah was asking for help," she said. "I think she wants me to do something."

"You could speak to her, I suppose," said Mr. J.L.B. Matekoni.

"I could. But she might just tell me to mind my own business. People don't like outsiders to interfere in their private family business."

Mr. J.L.B. Matekoni said that he understood that.

"But I still have to do something," said Mma Ramotswe. "And there's another thing . . ." She mentioned Poppy, the woman who had lost all her money.

"Money lost is money lost," said Mr. J.L.B. Matekoni. Then he said, "Poppy?"

"Yes. She was at school with us in Mochudi. She went to Francistown."

Mr. J.L.B. Matekoni pushed his empty plate across the table. "I know about that woman."

Mma Ramotswe frowned. "There will be many Poppies. It is a popular name."

"No, it is the same one," said Mr. J.L.B. Matekoni. "She had a big store up in Francistown. There would not be two Poppies who had a store."

Mma Ramotswe asked him whether he knew how she had lost her money.

"She met a man," he said. "He was called Flat. That was his name; it was not a nickname. Flat Ponto. He used to work in the motor trade. He was quite a good mechanic, but he had a reputation for being lazy. You know how it is with some people—they're good at what they do, but they don't do enough of it."

Mma Ramotswe laughed. "I've known people like that, Rra. If people had batteries, then you might think that theirs needed charging. Not enough energy."

Mr. J.L.B. Matekoni looked down at his plate again. "Perhaps they're not getting enough meat, you know. Sometimes that's the explanation."

There was silence.

"Meat has lots of iron in it," Mr. J.L.B. Matekoni continued. "Iron makes your muscles strong. It gives you the energy you need to do things." He paused. "I'm not saying that's always the explanation, but I think that in some cases—some cases, Mma—that might be what's happening."

"Possibly," said Mma Ramotswe, looking straight ahead. "But this man she met . . . the mechanic, the iron-deficient one . . ."

"He became very religious," said Mr. J.L.B. Matekoni. "He joined one of those marching churches, but I think he found all that marching a bit too much."

"Perhaps it required too much energy," remarked Mma Ramotswe. "And this poor man, with his iron problem, couldn't keep up."

Mr. J.L.B. Matekoni nodded. "Something like that happened, I expect. Anyway, you know what he did? He started his own church. He called it the Church of Christ, Mechanic."

Mma Ramotswe's eyes opened wide with astonishment. "What a strange name, Rra. What did he mean?"

Mr. J.L.B. Matekoni shrugged. "He was not trying to be funny, Mma. He thought that it was a good name. He thought that Jesus would have been a mechanic if there had been cars. He was a carpenter, you see."

"I know that," said Mma Ramotswe. "And this church of his—did anybody join?"

"Oh, yes. There were many people who joined. Two hundred, I heard."

Mma Ramotswe thought for a few moments. "Well, there's nothing wrong with that, I suppose. I don't think that God really cares what church you belong to. I think it's much the same to him whether you are Christian or Jewish or Muslim. He listens to everybody, I think."

Mr. J.L.B. Matekoni thought that she was right. He was not a man with a very sophisticated theology, and there were times when he had his serious doubts. But when all was said and done he thought that there was something beyond us, something other than the human, and that if you closed your eyes and thought about this thing long enough you could hear its voice within you. That was enough for him.

"One of my customers goes to his church," he went on. "He is very pleased with it. He said that they have a big *braai* every Sunday lunch time, with lots of sausages. They go to the Notwane River in the rainy season, otherwise they have their picnic near the dam. And they sing hymns while they eat the sausages. He says it is very spiritual. That's the word he used, Mma—*spiritual*. They do the baptism in the river or the dam. They put them right under the water, still wearing their clothes."

She pictured the scene. She saw a river and the sinners being led into the water and being submerged, and all the time the people on the banks would be singing and eating sausages. She smiled.

"There are worse things to do on a Sunday," she said. "It is better to be doing those spiritual things than sitting idly at home or in some shebeen somewhere, drinking."

He agreed. "You're right, Mma. I was not criticising this man and his church. But I would say, though, that he seemed to do quite well out of it all."

Mma Ramotswe's antennae homed in on this. Africa was full of prophets who had done well out of their prophecy. Other places, too, had the same problem—not just Africa. She had discovered a wonderful English word for which there seemed to be no precise Setswana equivalent—*charlatan*. She savoured the sound of it— *charlatan*. It seemed to describe a certain sort of person very accurately, she thought. Was this man, this Flat, a charlatan?

"My customer told me that they were very happy in the church," Mr. J.L.B. Matekoni said. "He said that the Reverend Flat Ponto had converted a very rich woman to the church and that she had given him a car for use in his ministry."

Mma Ramotswe groaned. It was a familiar story. Rich women, it seemed, made the same mistake time and time again: whether they were ensnared by a natty dancer or a smart dresser or a minister who had invented his own church, the aim of the man was always the same—to part the rich woman from as large a proportion of her funds as possible before her family or friends were able to intervene. She had seen this happen on more than one occasion, and it never ended well. Oh, there were stories where the scheming man was exposed in time, but those were only stories. In real life it did not happen that way. The man got the money and the woman was left high and dry.

"And you're sure this lady was Poppy?" she asked.

He nodded. "That's what my customer said."

Mma Ramotswe groaned again. "And the car? Was it . . ." She hesitated. You should not be prejudiced against one sort of car, because cars are innocent—they know no better. But it was no use beating about the bush. "Was it a Mercedes-Benz?"

Mr. J.L.B. Matekoni did not need to respond; she saw the answer in his eyes.

"It was," he said. "A new one, too."

Mma Ramotswe rolled her eyes. "Oh, the foolishness of women," she muttered. "I mean, the foolishness of *some* women."

"And men," said Mr. J.L.B. Matekoni. "There are some very foolish men."

She said that he was right. Foolishness was something that afflicted men and women equally. Neither sex had the monopoly of wisdom, she said, although on balance she thought that women might perhaps have just a little bit more sense than men. But only a little bit, and it was not a point that she would care to make, normally, as Mma Ramotswe liked men, just as she liked women, and did not think it helpful to put a wedge between them. People were people first and foremost, she felt, and it was only after you had judged them as *people* that you should notice whether they were wearing a skirt or trousers, not that that was grounds for distinction these days.

She looked up. "Have you ever seen a man wearing a skirt, Mr. J.L.B. Matekoni?" she asked.

His face registered his puzzlement. "I have not seen that, Mma. And why would a man want to wear a skirt? What's the point of that?"

"I don't know," she said. "Men sometimes do strange things, of course." She was certain of that, at least; the strangeness of human behaviour was something of which anybody following her calling would be only too well aware. Anything, it seemed, was possible, such was human ingenuity in the pursuit of its goals. Mma Potokwane had once expressed views on this, saying that nothing would ever surprise her when it came to human nature. She remembered her friend's words. "People are very odd, Mma Ramotswe. They think odd thoughts and they do odd things. You can never be sure with people." Mma Potokwane was right, as she almost always was. She knew these things because she had been a matron for so long and had looked after children in whose lives, in the background, was almost every conceivable human disappointment and tragedy.

He shrugged. "If they want to wear ladies' clothes," he said, "then I suppose they should be allowed to do so." He shook his head. "Although I wouldn't recommend it if you're underneath a car fixing it. Overalls are the answer, Mma, for that sort of thing—for both men and women. Overalls."

Overalls, thought Mma Ramotswe. Was that the answer to all these issues that people were worrying away at—issues of who was a man and who was a woman? If we all were to wear overalls, would that argument simply go away? It would be nice to think that it would, as Mma Ramotswe wanted people to be happy in whatever way they needed to be happy, but somehow she doubted whether the provision of overalls for everybody was really the answer.

CHAPTER SEVEN

MONDAY, NOTHING; TUESDAY, NOTHING

THE DAYS THAT FOLLOWED this conversation with Mr. J.L.B. Matekoni were unusually quiet ones in the No. 1 Ladies' Detective Agency.

"Something will turn up," said Mma Makutsi, as she stared idly out of the office window. "It always does, I find."

Seated at her desk, Mma Ramotswe looked at the empty pages of her diary. *Monday, nothing; Tuesday, nothing;* and so on, stretching out to an indeterminate future. "People often say that business is either famine or feast," she said. "And I think that's right, Mma Makutsi."

"It definitely is," said Mma Makutsi. "Phuti says that it's the same in the furniture business. One moment everybody is desperate to buy beds and sofas and so forth. Then, the next day, nothing. No sales. It's as if everybody who could possibly want a bed or a sofa has got one. And you think, Is this the end of the business?"

Mma Ramotswe did not like to say that this was exactly the question that had occurred to her. The No. 1 Ladies' Detective Agency did not make a great deal of money. Indeed, at the end of most months, when the books were examined and outgoings subtracted from sums received, the resulting profit, if any, was minuscule. That did not matter too much, of course, as long as salaries were covered; they had no rent to pay, the office being attached to the premises of Tlokweng Road Speedy Motors, which was owned by Mr. J.L.B. Matekoni. If one had to have a landlord, then there was a very good case for having one's husband as one's landlord.

"Somebody will knock on the door," said Mma Ramotswe. "Somebody will come in and say that her husband is spending too much time in the office with his secretary, or the petty cash is disappearing in a mysterious way, or their daughter is seeing a suspicious boyfriend who won't give anybody his real name and insists on simply being called Joe."

Mma Makutsi laughed at that, remembering a case where that was exactly what had happened, and she and Mr. Polopetsi had discovered that Joe, as he called himself, was wanted by the police on several charges of handling stolen property. "I think you are right, Mma," she said. "Any moment now a new client will turn up."

But no new client arrived, and when they closed the office at five that evening, there had not been so much as a telephone enquiry. The only call, in fact, had been a wrong number. Mma Makutsi had answered that, and when it became apparent that the call was really intended for the office of a local refrigeration company, she had nonetheless tried to interest the caller in the agency's services. After all, one never knew what might be going on in the private life of an unexpected and misdialling stranger.

"You've come through to the No. 1 Ladies' Detective Agency," she announced. "I know that this is not the number you wanted, but since you're on the line, are you sure that you do not have a problem that we can help you with?"

This had not been well received by the woman at the other end, who took umbrage at the suggestion that she might be in need of a private detective. "I am not that sort of person," she said, slamming down the receiver in a way that suggested to Mma Makutsi that she was precisely the sort of person who might need the agency's help.

"People can be very rude," said Mma Makutsi. "If you dial the wrong number, the least you should do is listen politely to the person who answers."

That was a Tuesday, and the Wednesday seemed to be heading in much the same direction. By the time mid-morning tea was served, Mma Ramotswe had decided that if nothing came up within the next half an hour she would yield to the promptings of her conscience to do something for Calviniah. She would find Nametso and have a word with her about her mother's feelings. It was possible that she would get nowhere, but there was no harm in trying. It was possible that Nametso might simply not realise the hurt she was causing her mother and respond accordingly; alternatively, she might resent and rebuff any outside attempt to broach the subject. Either way, Mma Ramotswe felt that there was nothing to lose.

She mentioned her intention to Mma Makutsi, who agreed that helping an old friend in this way was the right thing to do. "If you go out, Mma," she said, "then I shall go out too and investigate this husband case—the one who appears to be so keen on studying mathematics."

Mma Ramotswe smiled. "By all means, Mma. It will be better than sitting in the office twiddling our thumbs." She paused. "Mind you, I think you're barking up the wrong tree, Mma, if I may say so."

"We shall see, Mma," said Mma Makutsi. "Sometimes, you know, it's a question of finding the right tree by barking up a whole lot of trees, some of which may be the wrong ones. You never know. The tree knows, of course, but you don't."

Mma Ramotswe looked at her assistant as she tried to make sense of this remark. She was not quite sure what Mma Makutsi meant, but then that was not all that unusual. There were many occasions on which Mma Makutsi made a pronouncement that seemed to be full of meaning and yet, on close examination, meant nothing at all. This might be one of those, she thought; or it might not be, which left her none the wiser about anything, and so she rose from her chair without further ado and proceeded, as Mma Makutsi might put it, to her tiny white van. She had a plan—not much of a plan, but then investigations had to start somewhere, and shaky grounds were better than no grounds at all. She would go to the diamond-sorting building and speak to the receptionist—if there was one. Receptionists usually knew more about what was going on than anybody else, including general managers, deputy general managers, and managers of any description. From the point of view of a private detective, indiscreet receptionists were gold mines of information, provided, of course, they could be persuaded to reveal what they knew. In general, Mma Ramotswe had found that people wanted to confide, and that all that was necessary was the provision of a sympathetic ear.

NOW SHE STOOD OUTSIDE the discreet building that was the headquarters of the Botswana Diamond Sorting Consortium. Into this building, with its modest four floors, were delivered the gems wrested from the great open-cast mines of the Kalahari, the end result of the reduction of millions of tons of ore into pellets, and the extraction from those pellets of the diamonds themselves. These arrived in sealed safe-boxes, packed by machine and unexposed to any human hand. Only once they were in the diamond-sorting building would they be opened and the stones within spread out on large sorting tables. At that point, the sorters began their work, expertly flicking stones into piles according to size and brilliance.

Mma Ramotswe had read about the process in an article in the *Botswana Daily News*. This had explained the training of the sorters, and the strict security measures surrounding the diamonds. Botswana's diamonds were clean, the paper pronounced, and elaborate steps were taken to keep them that way. Temptation, of course, was the enemy, and everything possible was done to remove the occasions for that. Mma Ramotswe had stared at the photograph in the paper of a pile of diamonds on a sorting table. A *pile* of diamonds—and to think that these were handled by ordinary people whose lives could be changed beyond recognition by just one of these glittering stones. Such a small thing, a diamond, and yet a thing of such power.

The sorters were allocated parcels of raw stones. These were weighed to the last fraction of an ounce, and signed for on the basis of weight. The slightest discrepancy, the smallest whisker of difference between weight signed for and weight later returned to a supervisor, would set in motion a process of rigorous searches and revealing X-rays. It was no use trying to swallow a diamond; an X-ray would show exactly where in the human body the stone was concealed. Nobody, it was said, had ever succeeded in smuggling so much as a single carat out of the high-security sorting area.

She parked her van in the parking place beside the building. There were no trees there, she noted—this was too grand a place, too modern for such things. She disapproved: some people thought that progress was synonymous with the cutting down of trees and the planting, instead, of concrete. They were wrong, she felt: concrete cut you off from the land and stopped the earth from breathing. Concrete was hardness and silence; it had no voice, as other building materials had. Wood brought a memory of trees, thatch of reed bed, mud of the place from which the earth had been taken. The people who commissioned and built large buildings thought nothing of that, but ordinary people, people who did not think always of money, had always turned to trees for shade, and she saw no reason for that to change. If that was progress, then she would have none of it. And yet, she thought, I am a modern lady and have no desire to go backwards rather than forwards. It all depended, she felt, on where you thought forwards was.

She sighed as she left her tiny white van out in the full glare of the sun. She knew that when she came back to it—even only a few minutes later—the burning rays would have heated the interior to the point of discomfort. She would have to open both doors and wait for the seats and the steering wheel to cool. If only they had kept a few trees . . .

A man was walking towards her—a man in a blue uniform with a badge on each shoulder. This badge, the same on each side, said *Security Consultant,* and now, reaching Mma Ramotswe, he looked at her over the rim of a pair of rectangle-framed glasses.

His greeting was polite, in spite of his stern expression. Following the old Botswana custom, he enquired about her health and whether she had slept well. On both of these matters, she gave a positive report.

"So, Mma, what are you doing with your van?"

He gestured to the van, which looked distinctly out of place among the opulent vehicles on either side of it.

"I am parking it, Rra," Mma Ramotswe replied. She hesitated. She did not want a confrontation with somebody described as a *security consultant,* but in her experience a firm response to officialdom could set a more positive tone for any subsequent encounter. This was a parking place—there was a notice that made that clear—and she had availed herself of it. There was nothing to say that only important people, or expensive modern cars, could use this space. This was a small square of Botswana, and she was a citizen of Botswana. Her van, although old and small, was a duly licensed Botswana car that had the same rights as any vehicle.

The security consultant continued to look at her over the top of his spectacles. "I can see that you have parked, Mma. I can see that."

Mma Ramotswe waited.

"Why have you parked here?" he asked.

"I have come to speak to somebody in the sorting office," she said, nodding in the direction of the building's front door.

He frowned. "Who is this person, Mma? And what is it about?"

"It is a personal matter," she replied, and knew immediately that this, although the truthful answer, was the wrong one to have given.

The guard's frown deepened. "It is not possible to talk to people here about personal matters," he said. "It is not allowed. You must go away."

Mma Ramotswe studied his uniform. The buttons, which were cast in brass, had the symbol of a diamond incised on them. The shirt, buttoned down at the collar, had been impeccably starched.

"I must say that your uniform is very smart, Captain."

The effect of this was instantaneous, just as she thought it would be. It was her practice, developed over years of experience of dealing with people who occupied junior rungs in any hierarchy, to promote the holder with a rank above that which they held or were ever likely to have held. Thus a sergeant of police, immediately and unambiguously distinguishable by the chevrons of his office, became a sub-inspector or even a full inspector, while an inspector became a superintendent. Even those at heady levels—those who were real superintendents—were susceptible to the tactic, and could be seen to swell visibly when addressed as Deputy Commissioner. Flattery, perhaps, but there was a wrong sort of flattery and a right sort, and this was the latter because it gave somebody a boost and it was always deployed for a good reason—not to curry favour, but to help a good cause. And the good cause in this case was clear enough: a mother wanted her daughter back from a puzzling and needless estrangement that had sprung up between them; what could be more defensible than that?

Captain! A smile played about the security guard's lips—a smile of pleasure rather than bemusement. Here was one who might be to the outside world a mere *security consultant,* but who, in his inner heart, was on the frontline of a worldwide battle against the forces of disorder and chaos. Those forces were ubiquitous and cunning; they took no hostages and struck in a way that was as underhand as they were ruthless. Ranged against them were men and women in a rainbow array of uniforms, each battling in his or her particular way a common enemy: people who challenged the accepted order in ways small and large. Here was one of them—a person who thought she could park in a dedicated parking place as casually as if she were by some roadside in a dusty village in the back of beyond, and who then explained that she wanted to talk to some employee about a purely personal matter. And what would that be?, he wondered. An arrangement for a wedding, perhaps, or for a church bazaar—something as petty and inconsequential as that. Really! That was the trouble with some people: they loved talking at great length about these small things, and all the while, elsewhere, people were working hard without any of these silly discussions. How could people complain if all the strides that were being taken in so many fields were being taken in places where wasting time like this was not permitted, where nobody parked where they shouldn't?

Those were the thoughts that crossed his mind, and yet this was a traditionally minded Botswana woman of well-kept appearance and respectful demeanour. And she had called him "Captain," which was the rank that he should really have held if the diamond authorities had given proper thought to the matter. She clearly understood how demanding his job was, and how vital. He could not be severe with her; firm, yes, but not severe. She was a sort of auntie, really, and he would treat her with the courtesy with which an auntie should be treated.

The instruction to go away was rescinded. "I'm sorry, Mma, I didn't mean that you should go away right now—I did not mean that."

Mma Ramotswe was gracious. "I could tell that you didn't, Rra. I could see that you were not the sort of officer to tell a lady to go away just like that when all she wanted to do was to speak to somebody."

Officer! He had served for four years in the Botswana Defence Force and knew that the term *officer* should not be used lightly. He had been promoted to corporal and had served honourably in that role in the days when that great man, General Khama, had been there, and the general had once singled him out for praise. He had said, "That NCO is doing good work," and the reference had been to him; there was no doubt about that because the general had been pointing at him as he spoke the words. His platoon commander had heard them, and nodded in his direction—a nod of encouragement and congratulation. That was not the sort of thing one easily forgets. *That NCO is doing good work.*

"No, Mma, I did not mean go away right now. I meant you cannot stay there, but you need not go immediately."

"Thank you, Rra. And can I speak to the person I want to speak to?"

That was another matter—not one in which discretion could be exercised. "That is more difficult, Mma. They . . ." He cast his eyes up towards the top floor of the building, where dwelt the senior management. "They don't allow that, Mma. This building, you see, is very secure. Even now they are watching us with their cameras. All the time, there are people watching, watching."

"They have to be careful," said Mma Ramotswe. "If nobody was watching, then what would happen? There would be people coming around all the time hoping to pick up a few diamonds."

He nodded his agreement. "Exactly, Mma. That is why we have these rules." He paused. "Could you tell me who this person is? Perhaps I could leave a note for him."

"It is a her," said Mma Ramotswe. "Her name is Nametso. She is one of the sorters. She is the daughter of an old friend of mine, Calviniah, from the old days in Mochudi."

The guard relaxed even more. "Mochudi," he said, savouring the word in his mouth, lingering over it, as one might a culinary treat. "I had an uncle who lived there. He was a porter in the hospital. He worked with Dr. Moffat back in those days."

Mma Ramotswe clapped her hands together. "Dr. Moffat, Rra! My father knew Dr. Moffat—and I did too. Mrs. Moffat—I used to visit her when she lived in the Village here in Gaborone."

The guard shook his head with pleasure at the memory, and at the connection this conversation had established.

"My uncle said that Dr. Moffat never lost his temper with anybody. Sometimes a doctor or a nurse could do that, you know. But he did not. He just said, 'Please don't do that,' or, 'That's not a good thing to do.' Something like that."

Mma Ramotswe nodded. "That is often the best way of dealing with such things," she said. "I have heard people say that you don't change others by shouting at them."

The security guard hesitated. In his days in the Botswana Defence Force he had done a great deal of shouting. Indeed, he had enjoyed a reputation of having one of the loudest voices in the entire army, but he was younger then, and you might change your views as you became older and more aware of the complexities of the world. And so he said, "That is very right, Mma. You do not change people in that way."

It was a pity, he thought. There were so many who were crying out to be changed and who would benefit from a few pieces of advice delivered at maximum volume. It was a pity.

"This Nametso," he said. "I think I know her. I know all the sorters because they are given permits to park in this car park. There is only one of them called Nametso."

Mma Ramotswe listened. "So you know her, Rra?"

"Yes." He turned around and gestured to a section of the car park immediately behind him. "That is where she used to park her car. Every day, she would park in the same place—right over there."

Mma Ramotswe followed his gaze. "Used to, Rra? Is she no longer working here?"

"Oh, yes, she is still working here. If you have a job as a diamond sorter, you don't give that up too readily, I can tell you."

"I don't suppose you do," said Mma Ramotswe. "But now she's parking somewhere else? Or is she coming into work by bus, maybe?"

He turned back to face her. "No, nothing like that. She's still driving in. You mentioned the Village earlier on. That is where she lives. You know those flats near the university?"

She did. "They aren't too far from my business." She bit her tongue. She had not intended to reveal what she did; it could only complicate matters.

It was too late. "Your business, Mma? What business is that?"

"I work in an office," Mma Ramotswe said vaguely. "Not a big office—just a couple of people. But tell me, Rra: Why is Nametso not parking here any longer?" She assumed that it was a shade issue, and felt that here at least was something on which she and Nametso would agree—too much concrete and too little respect for trees. Our natural umbrellas, she thought. That's what trees were: our natural umbrellas.

But this was not the reason. The security guard thought for a moment, and then, with what Mma Ramotswe thought was a rather condescending smile, gave his answer: "Envy, Mma. You know what envy is. It is our big problem here, although we don't like to talk about it. Envy."

Mma Ramotswe looked at him in surprise. "Envy, Rra?" She could not work out what he meant. Envy? Of what, and on whose part? Were there some people who did not have a parking place who would be envious of those who did? That was possible, she thought—just. But there did not seem to be a shortage of parking places attached to the building—in fact, judging from the many empty spaces, there seemed to be rather too many. And that's what happens, she thought grimly, if you cut down all your trees.

The security guard spoke patiently, as if explaining something elementary to a person who might not be expected to grasp a simple enough matter. This made Mma Ramotswe feel momentarily annoyed: there was a certain sort of man—usually an older man— who still harboured an old-fashioned attitude towards women. Women, they thought, had to have things explained to them by men. It was hard to believe that there were still men who took that view, even when women had fought back so successfully and exploded the nonsense behind it. Yet such men still existed, as Mma Makutsi had once said, because they were weak within themselves.

"If you know that you're not very good at something," she had said. "If, for example—and I am just giving an example here, Mma; I am not talking about any particular man—if you are a bit unintelligent in the head . . ." That was an expression that Mma Makutsi used from time to time; an odd expression, thought Mma Ramotswe, because where else could one be unintelligent but in the head? And yet it had a certain charm to it, and she had found herself using it once when hearing from Mma Potokwane of a man who had decided to clear a patch of land by fire and had succeeded in burning down his neighbour's house. "That man is a bit unintelligent in the head," she had said to Mma Potokwane, who had vigorously agreed. "And in other places too," the matron had said. "Unintelligent all over the place, Mma, but yes, certainly very unintelligent in the head."

"If you are unintelligent in the head," Mma Makutsi continued, "and you are a man—and I am not saying that *all* men are unintelligent in the head, Mma Ramotswe . . ."

"I know that, Mma Makutsi. I didn't think you were saying that."

"Because there are some women who talk like that, Mma. Some of them—you know, these ladies who are fed up with men and are saying to us that men are finished—those ladies who, incidentally, Mma, often do not have husbands, I might point out . . ."

Mma Ramotswe was not sure of the relevance of that. It was possible to have a husband, she thought, and at the same time be able to identify and criticise bad male attitudes and behaviour. "I do not think that is always true, Mma . . . ," she suggested mildly.

"Oh, it is, Mma Ramotswe. You and I are not unkind to men, are we?"

Mma Ramotswe agreed. "I would hope that we are not unkind to anybody," she said. "Why be unkind?"

Mma Makutsi did not address that more general question. "No, I'm telling you, Mma. Those ladies who are always saying men are rubbish, are saying that because they have not found a man for themselves, Mma—not even a rubbish man. So they say that all men are no good and it makes them feel a bit better." She drew a deep breath before continuing. Her large round spectacles caught a shaft of light and glinted. "If all men are no good, then who would want a man,

Mma? Nobody, I think. Then they feel better about not having a man. I'm telling you, Mma, that is how the human mind works. It is psychology, you see. Psychology lies underneath everything. Under every table."

It had been a long statement from Mma Makutsi. It was wrong, Mma Ramotswe felt, but it had some basic insights that were probably true. Mma Makutsi was right in saying that those who criticised something often did so because they wanted that very thing and did not have it. That was surely true. But she was not certain that one should look at all criticism in that light.

"If you are unintelligent in the head," Mma Makutsi continued, "then you are going to boost yourself, Mma Ramotswe. And how do you do that? You belittle other people—you say that *they* are unintelligent in the head. Do you see that?"

Mma Ramotswe did, and Mma Makutsi went on, "And so if you are a man and you are worried about how small your brain is—and some men, Mma, have *very* small brains. Big bodies, maybe, Mma. Lots of muscle and whatnot, but their brains?" She shook her head, and Mma Ramotswe for a moment pictured Mma Makutsi's brain inside it: the same brain that had guided her to that famous ninety-seven per cent in the final examinations of the Botswana Secretarial College. "Their brains, Mma Ramotswe, not much, I'm afraid. And so those men—it is those men I'm talking about, Mma—they are the ones who say that women are not very good at certain things and that men should be left to do them. They say that because they know that women are actually better than them at doing whatever it is they are talking about."

"Very possibly," said Mma Ramotswe. "In many cases I think that is probably what's going on, Mma."

Mma Makutsi lowered her voice. "And here's another thing,

Mma—just between you and me. There are men who are always talking about how good they are with ladies. You know, in paying attention to ladies in that way, Mma. In doing the sort of thing that men like to do with ladies. You know what I'm talking about, Mma?"

"I think I do, Mma," said Mma Ramotswe, looking away.

"Well, here's something, Mma," Mma Makutsi continued. "Those men who keep boasting about that, they are the ones who, I'm sorry to say, Mma, are unfortunate in that department, Mma, and who do not have many lady friends. You know what I mean?"

"I think I do, Mma. But look, we must get on with the letters—they are building up and we have answered none of them . . ."

That had been the end of that conversation, but the memory of it came back as she stood in the car park with the security guard who was looking at her in that way which might have been condescension; which might, just might, have stemmed from the fact that he felt that life had not brought him what he wanted, and so he needed to boost himself in the way identified by Mma Makutsi. Just possibly.

And he had referred to envy, which certainly was a factor in village life in Botswana. Everybody has some little failing, and Mma Ramotswe knew that a failing of her countrymen was an occasional tendency to be envious of the possessions of others.

"It's her car, you see, Mma," the security guard explained. "She is worried that others will be envious of her car."

Mma Ramotswe smiled. "Ah! I was wondering, Rra. So there are junior people in the building who have no car and would be envious. I can see how that might be so."

The security guard shook his head, with elaborate patience. "No, Mma. Not that. It is the sort of car that is the problem. She has a Mercedes-Benz, you see."

"A Mercedes-Benz!"

"And not just an ordinary one," the security guard continued. "It is a new one—very smart. Everything included. Special tyres and so on. All made by Germans."

"By Germans," Mma Ramotswe muttered. She was thinking . . . Where did Nametso get a Mercedes-Benz?

"A wealthy daddy," said the security guard. "She must have a wealthy daddy. That is how a young woman like her gets hold of a Mercedes-Benz." He paused. "Would you like me to take a note inside for her?" he asked.

Mma Ramotswe hesitated. "That's kind of you, Rra, but I think I need to go away and think about something."

"About what, Mma?"

"About things I need to think about, Rra. There are so many of them, I find."

"That's very true," he said. "Very true, Mma—make no mistake."

"But thank you anyway, Captain."

Captain! The word hung in the air like a shining, benevolent sun, imparting to those below a glow of warmth and pride. *Captain!* One word, one small word, could bring such pleasure, just as one word, one equally small word, might cause such distress. *Envy, Mercedes-Benz*—those words were, in the circumstances, thought Mma Ramotswe, deeply significant.

CHAPTER EIGHT

THE TRACK MARKED *PRIVATE LIFE*

WHILE MMA RAMOTSWE was engaged in conversation with her new friend, the informally promoted security consultant, Mma Makutsi was on her way to the home address of the teacher from whom Mr. Mogorosi, the husband until recently under suspicion, was receiving instruction in mathematics. This was a small house near the Mechanical Trades College, the sort of house which she might expect to be favoured by a government official on the cusp of promotion but unable yet to afford something in one of the more expensive suburbs. Such a person would be just outside the zone of comfort enjoyed by the next rung down on the social and economic ladder—a comfort that, paradoxically, came from not having to compete with those around you. Where everybody is poor, or on a tight budget, then there is little or no pressure to flaunt your possessions—everybody is in it together. Once you haul yourself up to the next level, though, life can become competitive. And one had to worry, too, about falling. The nearer the bottom, the less devastating is the prospect of a fall.

Mma Makutsi had driven to this house with Charlie, who had been briefed on the story that they would come up with if they found the teacher in.

"We are going to enquire about mathematics lessons," said Mma Makutsi. "I shall be your auntie. I shall be enquiring about lessons for my nephew—you."

Charlie giggled. "But I am not your nephew, Mma."

"Of course you aren't," said Mma Makutsi. "This is to get information, Charlie." She paused. "Haven't you heard of cover stories?"

"Oh, I know all about those," said Charlie. "You don't have to tell me about all that, Mma."

She glanced at him. Charlie had so much to learn, she thought; so much that it made it almost impossible to know where to start. That was the problem with ignorance: it tended to be so vast and so all-encompassing that tackling it became rather like struggling with a weed that had established itself in all parts of the garden. If you plucked the weed in one corner, then its offshoots might simply proliferate elsewhere behind your back.

"So," said Mma Makutsi, "you let me do the talking, Charlie. Understand? I'll do the talking."

Charlie nodded. "You're the boss, Mma."

She liked that. Young men like that could be difficult when it came to accepting female direction. They still thought—or some of them did—that being men gave them the right to give orders to women, even when the women were older and more qualified than they. They had to be disabused of that belief, even if some pockets of society continued to believe in this unwarranted male assumption.

They parked the car directly outside the gate. The house had an unusually large garden for a place of its size—it was, thought Mma Makutsi, a double plot. With the city continuing to grow, that would mean it was now worth a fair amount—one could sell it and move out to a much bigger place on the outskirts of the city, or in a neighbouring village, such as Tlokweng. That's what she would do, thought Mma Makutsi, if she lived in a place like that.

She opened the gate. "There's a car, Charlie," she said.

She pointed to the side of the house. Just visible behind a creeper-covered water butt was the rear section of a pick-up truck.

"Somebody's in," said Charlie as they began to walk up the path that led to the front door.

Mma Makutsi shook her head. "No, Charlie," she admonished, "you cannot draw that conclusion." She sighed. "Have you read that book we lent you?"

"The one by that man—"

She cut him short. "Not *that man,* Charlie. Mr.—"

Now he interrupted. "Clovis Andersen?"

"*Mr.* Andersen to you, Charlie," she admonished him. "Yes, that book—have you read it?"

Charlie was defensive. "I've looked at it," he said. "I've been very busy, Mma."

She sighed again; they were almost at the door. "If you bothered to read it, you would know what he says about not jumping to conclusions." She pointed to the side of the house. "All we know is that there is a car parked there. That does not mean the person who normally drives that car is inside the house. She—"

"Or he," muttered Charlie. "We don't know whether the car belongs to a man or a woman, Mma—do we?"

She did not reply. They were at the door now. She had noticed that the paint was scuffed and that a general air of neglect seemed to hang about the building. She glanced at Charlie and pointed to the unmaintained paintwork. "See that?" she whispered.

Charlie shrugged. "Paint costs money, Mma."

Mma Makutsi knocked on the door, calling out the greeting *Ko! Ko!* as she did so. She knocked again. Charlie looked at her expectantly. "Nobody here, Mma."

Mma Makutsi knocked a third time. "People sometimes take time to answer, Charlie. You never know."

Charlie reached forward and hammered loudly on the door. "They might be deaf, Mma Makutsi," he explained.

Mma Makutsi remonstrated with him. "You don't need to knock the door down."

It now seemed clear that nobody was in.

"We'll come back some other time," said Mma Makutsi.

Charlie frowned. "What about the back, Mma? Should I take a look round the back?"

She asked him why, and he replied, "There might be something suspicious."

Mma Makutsi laughed. "Something suspicious? Don't let your imagination run away with you, Charlie. You think you'll find a big clue?"

"There might be one," he said resentfully. "Sometimes you don't know what you're looking for until you find it. Your Clovis Andersen—"

"*Mr.* Andersen."

"Your Mr. Andersen probably says that in his book. It's the sort of thing you're always quoting to me. You and Mma Ramotswe—you'd think that was the only book in the world, the way you go on about it."

She gave him a discouraging look. "All right, go and take a quick look. I'll see you back at the car."

She made her way back down the path. At the gate she hesitated; somebody had taped a note to the gatepost—a small brown envelope.

She bent down to examine it. On the front of the envelope she could just make out the words SEE INSIDE. She stood up straight and looked about her. Had the envelope been there when they arrived? She did not think so, but she could not be sure. She looked down the road. There was no sign of anybody.

She saw Charlie emerge from behind the building. He spotted her and gave a cheerful wave.

"Anything?" she asked him when he reached the gate.

The young man shook his head. "I didn't think I'd find anything, but it always pays to be thorough."

Mma Makutsi inclined her head in agreement. "So, no clues, then?"

"I told you, Mma. Nothing."

She waited a moment and then pointed to the envelope. "Perhaps you were looking in the wrong place, Charlie," she said, a hint of satisfaction creeping into her voice. "What do you think this is?"

Charlie reached out, and before Mma Makutsi could stop him, he had detached the envelope from the gatepost.

"You shouldn't have touched it," hissed Mma Makutsi. "That could be evidence."

Charlie looked at the envelope. "Evidence of what, Mma? Has a crime been committed?"

"I did not say anything about crime, Charlie. It could be evidence of something else." She paused. "And that note is not addressed to us. We must always remember that our powers of investigation are limited. We are *private* detectives, Charlie; we are not the Botswana Police. We can't go round doing this, that, and the next thing."

Charlie looked again at the envelope. "It says SEE INSIDE, Mma. It is addressed to the general public; it is not addressed to anybody in particular."

"It is on that lady's gate," said Mma Makutsi, pointing to the house they had just visited. "It must be for that mathematics lady."

Charlie held the envelope up to the sun. "Then why did they put it on her gate, Mma? If it was for that lady, then why not put it on her door, or even under her door? That would be the normal thing to do, wouldn't it?"

She had to admit that he had a point. And yet, she was still reluctant to open a sealed envelope that had been intended for somebody else, even if the identity of that person remained unclear.

"I think I should open it, Mma," said Charlie.

She was about to say no, but she did not speak quickly enough. Charlie had now inserted a finger under the corner of the flap and torn it open. There was a folded piece of paper inside. He extracted this and began to read, silently.

"What does it say, Charlie?"

He looked up. "It is very odd, Mma," he said, handing the note to her.

She read out the message, which was written in capital letters, as with the invitation on the envelope. *I CAN ADD JUST AS WELL AS ANYBODY,* the message ran. *SO I KNOW THAT TWO PLUS TWO MAKES FOUR, YOU BAD RUBBISH WOMAN!*

Charlie waited for her response, but Mma Makutsi was examining the note again. "Well, Mma," he said after a few moments. "That looks like a clue to me."

She looked up from the note. "A clue to what, Charlie?"

He shrugged. "It tells us that she's a bad woman. That's what it says, doesn't it? A bad woman."

"And what does that mean?"

"It means that . . ." His voice trailed off. What did it mean? He was not sure.

It was for Mma Makutsi to provide the answer. "It means that this lady—whoever she is—has at least one enemy."

She folded the note and took the envelope from Charlie. "I'm going to take this away," she said.

"Why?" he asked. "Why not put it back where we found it?"

"Because it is a threat, Charlie. It is an anonymous letter, and I don't think it right that the lady who lives in this house should be threatened like that."

"Even if she is bad? Even if what the note says is true?"

"Even then," said Mma Makutsi.

She tucked the note into a pocket.

"We need to get back to the office," she said. "We can talk to Mma Ramotswe about it there."

Charlie shrugged again. "I'm just the assistant," he said. "Obviously nobody pays any attention to what I think . . ."

"That's right," said Mma Makutsi. "They don't."

Charlie kicked at the dust out of sheer frustration. "Why do you think I'm so stupid, Mma Makutsi?"

She felt a sudden pang of guilt. She did not think Charlie stupid. She did not dislike him. In fact, she found that she liked him more and more as time went by.

"I was only joking, Charlie. I listen to you, you know. It's just that sometimes . . ."

"Sometimes what, Mma?"

"Sometimes I forget that you still have a lot to learn and I judge you by standards that are too high. That is my fault—and I'm sorry about it. I shall try to avoid doing that in the future."

They began to walk the short distance to the car. As she walked, Mma Makutsi thought she heard a small voice from down below, down at the level of the rough ground and stones.

Change of tone there, Boss!, said the shoes.

She looked at her shoes. It was absurd. Even now, after years of interventions on the part of her shoes, she found that they surprised her. Nobody's shoes ever talked to them—they just didn't. But then Charlie said, "Did you say something, Mma?"

Mma Makutsi shook her head. "Sometimes one hears things when nobody's talking," she said. "But you shouldn't pay attention to such things, you know. It's just imagination." She tapped her forehead. "That's where these things come from, Charlie."

MMA RAMOTSWE LOOKED UP from her desk when Mma Makutsi and Charlie returned. She had picked up the mail on her way back to the office and had just finished sorting it. There were several items for the garage—bills, by the look of them—and two letters for the agency, one addressed to her personally, as Mma Ramotswe, and the other indirectly as *The Detective Woman on the Tlokweng Road (please place in relevant post-box, thank you)*. It was a tribute to the conscientious staff of the sorting office as much as to Mma Ramotswe's reputation in the wider community that the letter had been delivered appropriately. It was not the first time, though, that a vaguely addressed letter had found its way to its proper destination. On another occasion she had received a small parcel addressed to *The woman who drives a white van, comes from Mochudi, and is married to a mechanic of some sort, Gaborone (I think)*. That was a gift from a woman to whom she had given a lift on the road to Lobatse. The woman's car had broken down, and Mma Ramotswe had driven out of her way to deliver her safely to her home some twelve miles outside Lobatse. The woman had wanted to thank her but had not noted down her name and address. She had enough information, though, from their conversation to come up with that description and trust to the good will and knowledge of the Post Office to do the rest. They had had little difficulty in identifying Mma Ramotswe and had in due course placed the parcel in the agency's post-box. It was an embroidered handkerchief, lovingly worked with small representations of creatures of the bush: a dik-dik, that tiny, timid antelope; a long-snouted anteater; a guinea fowl with minute white spots. Mma Ramotswe had expected no thanks for what she had done. You helped other people—you just did. Had her van broken down, then she would have hoped that somebody would have done the same for her, and she thought that they would.

She had slit open the letter addressed to *The Detective Woman on the Tlokweng Road* a few minutes before the return of Mma Makutsi and Charlie, and had absorbed the contents.

Dear Detective Lady, the letter had begun. *I am sorry I do not know your name and do not have your post-box number. I believe, though, that you were recently engaged by my wife to investigate my behaviour. I have heard that you have now written to my wife and told her that I am not having an affair. I do not like to be rude, Mma, but may I ask you: How can you be so sure? You discovered that I was visiting a lady, and yet you tell my wife that I am an innocent man and that she should not divorce me. How do you know I'm innocent, Mma? Do you really think that I go to that lady to learn about mathematics? If you think that, Mma, then you are very foolish. Yours truly, L.D.M. Mogorosi, BA (University of Botswana).*

Mma Ramotswe had read through the letter twice, and then sighed, and it was while she was trying to work out its implications that Mma Makutsi returned. She picked up the letter and began to pass it to Mma Makutsi.

"Well, Mma Makutsi, everything is becoming more complicated. I have received a letter—"

She got no further. Breathlessly, Mma Makutsi brushed the letter aside. "Oh, there are always letters, Mma. Every day there are letters. We can deal with the mail later on. I have some very important information to tell you about."

"Very important," said Charlie. "We have found a very important piece of evidence."

"But this letter," Mma Ramotswe said. "This letter is—"

Once again she got no further. "I'm going to make some tea," said Mma Makutsi. "And while I'm making tea, I shall tell you what happened."

Mma Ramotswe made a gesture of resignation. When Mma Makutsi had the bit between her teeth, as she did now, there was no point in trying to deflect her to another agenda. "All right, Mma," she said. "I am listening."

"Well," began Mma Makutsi, "I went to the house of the mathematics teacher—"

Charlie corrected her. "*We* went, Mma. I was there too. It was a joint investigation."

"Very well, Charlie, *we* went to this house and we knocked on the door."

Mma Ramotswe waited politely. These preliminaries were not really necessary, but Mma Makutsi always insisted on them, quoting Clovis Andersen as the authority for the need to make a report as full as possible. *It's the small details,* he wrote. *At the time they may not seem important, but later on you may regret not writing them down. You never know what will be relevant at a later stage. Therefore, list everything—all steps taken, all people interviewed—even the weather may be worth saying something about.*

Remembering that now, Mma Makutsi added, "I knocked three times."

"And she was not in?" asked Mma Ramotswe.

"I knocked once as well," Charlie chipped in. "That made a total of four, Mma. Three knocks from Mma Makutsi, and one from me."

"Very interesting," said Mma Ramotswe. "And then?"

"Then I told Charlie to go and take a look round the back," said Mma Makutsi.

"You didn't tell me," said Charlie. "I said: I'll go around the back. I said that, Mma."

Mma Ramotswe suggested that it did not matter. The important thing was that Charlie went around the back. "And what did you find, Charlie?"

"Nothing," said Charlie.

Mma Ramotswe raised an eyebrow. She was unsure what the denouement of this account would be, but it was obviously something sufficiently dramatic to have produced Mma Makutsi's state of heightened excitement. "Then?" she prompted.

"Then I went to the gate," said Mma Makutsi. "I went to the gate and found a note, Mma. It was an envelope that said *SEE INSIDE*."

Charlie traced the words in the air with his index finger. "Those were the exact words, Mma Ramotswe: *SEE INSIDE*."

Mma Makutsi resumed the narrative. "I have the letter right here, Mma. It is a threat. It is a very serious threat to that lady from some unnamed party." She stressed the last two words to give them an almost melodramatic effect. Charlie was impressed; the phrase *unnamed party* would be noted down and would recur.

She had put the letter in the small bag in which she carried her spare glasses and keys. Now she took it out, unfolded it, and handed it to Mma Ramotswe. "Read that, Mma," she said. "Just read that."

"'I can add just as well as anybody,'" read Mma Ramotswe. "'So I know that two plus two makes four, you bad rubbish woman!'"

She looked up, and saw Mma Makutsi and Charlie watching her expectantly. Then Charlie said, "You will see that it is not signed, Mma. It is an anonymous letter."

Mma Ramotswe nodded. "That is not all that unusual. Most threats are anonymous."

"I have a very low opinion of people who write anonymous letters," said Mma Makutsi disapprovingly. "Only a coward threatens another person without coming into the open."

Mma Ramotswe said that she thought it wrong to threaten people in any circumstances. Threats were no more than the verbal expression of the violence that she had always disliked so much. As was swearing, which was another form of violence, even when it was directed against the world in general rather than an individual target. She did not like that, and yet it seemed to her that people now resorted to it so casually, as if it was nothing exceptional. What were they like *inside,* she asked herself, these people who used such language all the time; what were they like inside?

"You should talk to people rather than threaten them," she said.

"Talk first, then threaten," said Charlie.

Mma Ramotswe exchanged a glance with Mma Makutsi. "No, Charlie," she began, but then thought that this was not the time to correct Charlie once again. It sometimes seemed to her that if they kept a list of the occasions each day on which they upbraided Charlie for one thing or another, it would be a lengthy one. It was so easy to fall into a critical way of addressing somebody like Charlie, who appeared to require constant rebuke. Mr. J.L.B. Matekoni had noticed this when Charlie and Fanwell had been apprentices—"I am like a tape or a record stuck in one place," he said. "Don't do this, don't do that; use that wrench, not this one; don't tighten that too much, and so on and so on . . ."

The kettle had now boiled and Mma Makutsi made the tea.

"Red bush for you, Mma," she said, handing a mug to Mma Ramotswe.

"Not for me," said Charlie. "I don't drink that stuff."

"That stuff is very good for you, Charlie," said Mma Ramotswe, nursing the mug in her hands, blowing across the top to cool the steaming liquid. "You should pay more attention to what you put down your throat . . ." She stopped herself. There she went again: more advice, more criticism. The young man needed to be left alone.

But Mma Makutsi was not thinking along those lines. "Mma Ramotswe is right, Charlie," she scolded. "You eat such rubbish. All the time. I've seen you. Chips, chips, chips. What is in that stuff? Do you even know?"

"Potatoes," said Charlie. "Chips are potatoes and they are good for you. They make you strong."

He flexed the muscles of his arms. "See? Big, strong. Powerful." He paused. "Not weak and flabby like those people who eat lettuce all the time. A big storm comes up and what happens to them, Mma Makutsi? I'll tell you—they are blown away. Woosh! Goodbye, lettuce-people!"

Mma Makutsi bristled. "You are very stupid, Charlie. Your head is full of chips, maybe. You eat too much potato and your brain begins to look like a potato, you know."

Mma Ramotswe intervened. "Please! Please! We do not need to talk about lettuce and potatoes and such things. We need to talk about this letter you have found."

"Yes," said Mma Makutsi, giving Charlie a look that suggested it was his fault that these topics had been broached. "This letter, Mma—who does it come from? Who is this unnamed party, do you think?"

Mma Ramotswe took a sip of her red bush tea. "Somebody who doesn't like the teacher woman."

Charlie raised a finger. "*If* it was for that teacher woman," he said. "*If* . . . We don't know, do we? Clovis Andersen . . ." He paused, smiling with satisfaction at the reference. "Clovis Andersen would say: What do you know? Do you know anything?"

Mma Makutsi looked scornful. "You're quoting Clovis Andersen, Charlie? Have you actually read that book? You have not. So how do you know what he says?"

Charlie laughed. "He is always saying the same thing. Clovis Andersen says blah, blah, blah! I have heard it all—all the time, you go on about Clovis Andersen and what he says. It is always the same, Mma Makutsi—every time. Exactly the same. So now I know what that guy says without needing to read his book."

This was heresy, and for a few moments Mma Makutsi was almost too shocked to respond. Yes, it was heresy, and a gross slur against a trusted authority. It was almost as bad—almost—as if somebody were to question the reputation of the Botswana Secretarial College.

Mma Ramotswe sought to reduce the temperature of the conversation. "Let's not argue about Clovis Andersen," she said. "But I might just say that Mr. Andersen would always say—and he did, you know, although I forget on which page—that there is often a clue under your nose, right there. And I think there might be one here that settles the question as to whom this letter was addressed."

"A clue?" asked Charlie. "But there is no name. All I'm saying is that this note might have been for somebody else—who knows? Maybe the person dropped it . . ." He thought for a moment before continuing, "Yes, what if somebody had dropped it? Somebody walking along the street drops it, and then some other person—some other party—comes along and picks it up and thinks, Oh, some party has dropped a letter he was taking to another party, and then that party—the party who picks up the letter—thinks, I should put it somewhere

where that first party will find it. And so he sticks it to the nearest gatepost." He paused. "So that would mean that this unnamed party is somebody else altogether—somebody who has nothing at all to do with this teacher woman."

Mma Makutsi looked confused, but Mma Ramotswe simply sighed. "I don't think so, Charlie."

Charlie looked reproachfully at Mma Ramotswe. "Why not, Mma?"

"Because," she explained, "this note is clearly directed at a mathematics person. That is why it talks about being able to add. That is how you might speak to a person who knows all about mathematics. You would say, Yes, but I can add two and two—if you wanted to be rude, of course, which this person clearly wants to be."

The logic of this was irrefutable; Charlie looked deflated.

"But it is a good idea nonetheless, Charlie," Mma Ramotswe added hurriedly. "It is exactly what we should be doing in our job— exploring possibilities." She turned to Mma Makutsi. "Don't you agree, Mma?"

She did agree. Furthermore, she was now of the opinion that the letter confirmed her earlier view—that the client's suspicions about her husband were well founded. "This letter is clearly from a woman who has discovered that this lady is having an affair with her husband." She paused, watching, with some pride, her deduction sink in. "So that, Mma Ramotswe, amounts to corroboration. That is what Clovis Andersen calls it—corroboration. It is evidence that points in the same direction." She paused again. "Corroboration is very important, Mma."

Mma Ramotswe took a sip of her tea. "Possibly, Mma Makutsi. Possibly."

Mma Makutsi's spectacles caught a beam of sunlight and flashed it back across the room. "Not just possibly, Mma. Definitely."

Charlie nodded. This conclusion may have been reached by Mma Makutsi, but he had played a vital part in the discovery of the evidence, and he should by rights get at least some of the credit. "That is my view too," he said gravely. "That lady—that mathematics lady—is interested in other things than equations and stuff. Oh yes, I can tell you that! She is interested in men too, I'd say. Lots of men. Two men plus two men makes four men. That's what ladies like that think. The more men the better. A man for Monday and then another one for Tuesday. And when Wednesday comes along, well, there's a man for Wednesday . . ."

Mma Ramotswe held up a hand. "Excuse me," she said. "I don't like to throw cold water—except where some cold water is needed. So I must point out that the note could have been written by our client herself. Had you thought of that, Mma Makutsi? Charlie?"

For a while, the question hung in the air unanswered. But then Mma Makutsi shook her head. "No, Mma. I don't think that is likely. That lady—our client—knows that her husband is not having an affair. You told her that. You said that he was having mathematics lessons."

"That is true," Mma Ramotswe conceded. "But what if she didn't believe me? What if she thinks that the mathematics lessons are just cover for an affair?"

Charlie saw the force of this interpretation. "Yes, that's quite possible, I think. There are plenty of mathematics teachers who just pretend to give lessons, but are really carrying on with other women's husbands. It's happening all the time, I think."

Mma Makutsi gave him a withering glance. "That's complete nonsense, Charlie. Where are these mathematics teachers? Name one. No, you can't, can you? You think you can say things with no evidence to back them up, but you can't, you know."

"I don't think we should bicker," said Mma Ramotswe mildly. "It never helps to bicker."

Mma Makutsi shrugged. Mma Ramotswe might not require facts and figures for her assertions, but she was not going to fall into that trap. Mma Ramotswe, of course, was only too ready to attribute sayings to the late Seretse Khama, first President of Botswana, and a great man in so many respects. If there was a point she wanted to make, then she would say that Seretse Khama said something along those lines. But Mma Makutsi did not believe that Seretse Khama had said half the things that Mma Ramotswe insisted he had said. Why, one lifetime would hardly be enough to pronounce on as many subjects as that. You would have to get out of bed early every morning in order to start saying wise things before breakfast, and then you would spend much of the rest of the day making observations about the world and its workings, about human nature, even about the best way of taking mud off a pair of boots or cleaning a kitchen window. Much as she admired Seretse Khama, she did not think that he had given an opinion on everything.

"I still think—," Mma Makutsi began, only to be interrupted by Mma Ramotswe.

"Let's leave it where it should be—as an open question. This letter may be from some other lady, or it may be from our client. So the teacher may be innocent—as I thought she was—or, if the letter is from another person, then she may not be so innocent. I have had a letter myself this morning."

She picked up the letter that had been usurped by the note Mma Makutsi had found.

"Oh yes," said Mma Makutsi. "You said you'd received a letter." She was not particularly interested, as she was still thinking of the note and the possibilities it raised.

"It's from the husband," said Mma Ramotswe, passing the letter to Mma Makutsi.

"What husband?" asked Mma Makutsi.

"The husband of our client—Mma Mogorosi. She is the one we've been talking about. The husband of that lady."

Mma Makutsi glanced at the letter but did not bother to read it. "He'll be saying, 'Thank you for clearing me, Mma.' That's what he'll be saying—and what man wouldn't, Mma?"

Mma Ramotswe smiled. "Perhaps you should read the letter, Mma." She almost quoted Clovis Andersen, but refrained. She was sure he had said—in one of his chapters somewhere—that many people read into things the meaning they want to find; that was why it was so important to read everything twice, not just once, or not at all, as Mma Makutsi seemed to be doing.

Mma Makutsi adjusted her spectacles and began to read. Her expression changed as she went along, and ended in outrage. "He is a very shameless man," she said. "There is no end, Mma, to the shamelessness of men—no end at all."

Charlie asked if he might read the letter, and it was handed to him. His reaction was to laugh. As he handed the letter back to Mma Ramotswe, he said, "If you want to understand men, ladies, then you *need to think like a man.* Yes, you have to put yourself in a man's shoes."

Mma Ramotswe accepted the challenge. "All right, Charlie. That is a very good point. So I am now thinking like a man. I have heard that a private detective lady has said I am not having an affair. Why should I tell her she's wrong?"

Mma Makutsi joined in. "Because you want her to divorce you. You want to get rid of her, but you do not think that people will approve of your divorcing her. So she must do it."

"Why?" asked Charlie.

"Social pressure, Charlie," said Mma Makutsi. "Many people have odd ideas about this sort of thing. They think it's all right for a man to have affairs as long as he continues to support his wife and family. They do not like him to throw a woman out."

Mma Ramotswe agreed. But there was something in the tone of the letter that puzzled her. She turned to Charlie and encouraged him to continue.

"I do not think this has anything to do with a divorce," he declared. "It is quite different—if you think like a man." He paused. They were rapt. He was pleased that they were taking him seriously. "I'll tell you what he is thinking, Mma Ramotswe. He is thinking: this woman thinks I am no good with women. This woman is thinking that I am unable to get any girlfriends—that I am just a useless husband-type who has nobody thinking lustful thoughts about him. How dare she? She doesn't know that I am a big Romeo-type with lots of women hanging about me all the time. She doesn't know that, and so I had better tell her."

It was not what they had expected, and it took a few moments for either of them to react. Then Mma Ramotswe said, "Vanity?"

Charlie nodded. "Yes, Mma. Vanity. Every man thinks he is the best thing ever when it comes to women. Every man thinks that. I can tell you that—one hundred per cent for sure."

Mma Makutsi hesitated. "Maybe, Charlie. Maybe a bit. But you are also a bit wrong. There are many men who think that about themselves—I have met many, many. But you cannot say all men think that way."

"But they do," Charlie insisted. "That is how men think, Mma. I can tell you because I am one—I mean I am a man. I know."

"You are out of date, Charlie," Mma Makutsi said. "There are plenty of men these days who do not think about women like that. Or, rather, they do not think of themselves as being the best thing with women. Champions, if you see what I mean. Number one in the attractive-to-ladies department. First prize. Not every man."

Charlie stood his ground. "You are wrong, Mma. I told you: I know. I am a man myself. I know how men think. It's all here." He tapped his forehead—the seat, he imagined, of knowledge of the world and, in particular, of the ways of men.

Mma Makutsi made her point with a certain air of triumph. "What about men who like other men, Charlie? What about them? They will not think the way you're thinking."

There is a certain reticence in Botswana society that discourages direct reference to private matters. Now it came out, while they skirted this delicate subject.

"Mma Makutsi has a good point, Charlie," said Mma Ramotswe. "There are some men who prefer the company of other men."

Charlie stared at them. "There are not many men like that," he said quietly. "I was not talking about those men."

"But you can't ignore them," said Mma Makutsi. "Phuti has a man working in the furniture store who is wearing lipstick. He said he saw him putting it on."

Charlie frowned. "How could he tell it was lipstick, Mma? There are those things for sore lips—you know that balm stuff. It is for sore lips. Maybe it was that."

"It was lipstick," said Mma Makutsi. "Phuti knows the difference between lipstick and that stuff. He saw it with his own eyes."

"That does not make him a man who likes other men," said Charlie. "Why should men not wear something if they want to?"

"Anyway," said Mma Ramotswe, "it doesn't matter who you like. If you are kind and good to people, then you should be left in peace. Nobody should care—it's not their business."

Mma Makutsi agreed. "These days it is not important. And there are many men who like other men just a little bit, you know. Look at a group of men together—they are smiling and laughing and drinking beer and so on. All the time. They must like those other men. They must want to hug them from time to time."

Charlie shook his head vehemently. "No, Mma. They do not. They do not like to hug other men."

"Then that's very sad," said Mma Makutsi. "Perhaps they really do want to hug other men but have been told that they cannot, because it is not allowed." She remembered something. "I have read somewhere that all men feel a bit like that at some point in their lives. Just now and then. I have read that ninety-seven per cent do. Something like that."

She was taunting Charlie, who was unaware of it. "No, Mma," he said. "No, that is not right."

"Perhaps you should stop worrying about these things, Charlie. Perhaps you worry too much."

Mma Ramotswe decided that it was time to abandon this discussion, interesting though it was. "We shall have to think a bit more about this case," she said. "But perhaps not right now. I would like to tell you about what I found out this morning."

MMA RAMOTSWE TOLD THEM about her attempt to visit Nametso in the diamond-sorting office. She described the security consultant—"He was a security guard, really, but you know how everybody has become a consultant these days"—and she told them what he had revealed about Nametso. "He said that she now has a Mercedes-Benz, but she parks it elsewhere, not in the parking place she used to have."

"It's best to put a car like that in a safe place," said Charlie. "If you put it in a public parking place, then bang, some lady comes and reverses into you."

Mma Makutsi glared at him. "Some *lady,* Charlie? Why do you say some *lady*? Is it because you think we women can't drive safely? Is that what you think?"

Charlie made a conciliatory gesture. "I only said 'some lady' because I do not want to use sexist language, Mma Makutsi. If I said 'some man,' then you would come and say to me, 'Why are you always talking about men, what about ladies?' And so I say 'some lady' and you jump up and down and say, 'Why are you picking on ladies?'"

"You're not fooling me, Charlie," snorted Mma Makutsi. "You said 'some lady' because you think it is always ladies who are bumping into other cars in car parks. That is what you think."

Mma Ramotswe was staring at the ceiling. Over the last twelve months, she had bumped her van into two other cars, both of them in parking places. She had done no real damage, and the owners of the two cars in question had been understanding. One of them was a woman, and she had said to Mma Ramotswe, "Don't you worry, Mma. I'm always bumping into other cars myself." It was best, perhaps, not to mention that now, she thought.

And Mma Makutsi was thinking of how Phuti had come back from the Double Comfort Furniture Store one day recently and told her that his secretary had come into the office in tears because she had bumped into a furniture van in the off-loading bay at the back of the building. "He should not have been there, Rra," she said. "He normally comes at eleven in the morning. This was at nine. What was he doing there? It's his fault, Rra."

And yet Mma Ramotswe had read that women were safer drivers than men, and these stories were both unfair and inaccurate. It was young men who caused many of the accidents—young men like Charlie, who only wanted to go fast and show off to people in the back seat. They were the bad drivers, not women. That was well known. Indeed, it was probably the sort of thing that Seretse Khama himself might have said.

"It doesn't really make much difference," said Mma Ramotswe. "It seems to me that it is a reasonable explanation to say that she does not want her Mercedes-Benz to be damaged. But—and it's a big but, I think—the real question is this: Where does a young woman like that get a Mercedes-Benz?"

Mma Makutsi looked thoughtful. "Diamonds, Mma."

Nobody spoke for a good minute or so. Illicit activities in relation to diamonds was a sensitive subject in Botswana: the authorities took precious-stone offences extremely seriously.

At last, Mma Ramotswe spoke. "Are you suggesting she's been stealing from her employer?" she asked. "That's a very serious matter, Mma Makutsi."

Mma Makutsi defended herself. "I am not accusing anybody of stealing anything," she said. "All that I am saying, Mma, is this: If you work each day with very valuable things—small things—and then you start driving a Mercedes-Benz, what are people to think?"

"They would think that you're removing some of the diamonds," said Charlie. "They would think that you are selling these diamonds and have saved up to buy a Mercedes-Benz."

Mma Makutsi nodded. Further possibilities were occurring to her. "And if you have a Mercedes-Benz, would you want the people you work with to see you arriving for work in it? I do not think you would."

"No!" exclaimed Charlie. "No, you would not, Mma Makutsi. You are one hundred per cent right—not ninety-seven per cent, ha ha, but one hundred per cent right. You would not want people in the office to think you had been stealing diamonds and buying a Mercedes-Benz." He waited for his moment. He watched. He could come up with deductions every bit as significant as any of theirs. They thought he was just a man, and that men were hopeless at these things—far too clumsy in their way of looking at the world, thinking only of cars, girls, soccer; things like that. Mind you, he said to himself, I am one of those men who think about cars, girls, and soccer; but not *all* the time; there were times when he thought of other things. And now, unbidden, into his mind there came the image—and the smell—of a good Botswana steak, a T-bone that gave you something to gnaw on when you had eaten all the rest. He thought about food rather a lot, he had to confess. But so did women. Listen to the way they went on about clothes—and babies too. Women loved babies. They also loved shoes, he had noticed; especially Mma Makutsi, who had many pairs now, green, blue, red—all those colours, inside and outside; and bows and pieces of coloured glass, heart-shaped and stuck on the toe. Why would you have a piece of coloured glass on the toe of your shoe? What was the point of that? No man would do something like that, because men had better things to do, Charlie thought, than stick pieces of glass on their shoes.

Oh, there was so much unfairness in the way women thought about men. It was true, he conceded, that men had treated women unfairly in the past, but now things were stacked the other way and women were exacting their revenge. This is what you get for making us stay at home and stopping us from doing the things you thought it was your right to do; this is what you get. Well, yes; well, yes, but what will happen to all those young boys who grow up and find there's nothing for them to do? Charlie had sometimes wondered about that.

Women said that men were a big problem for them. Charlie had heard them saying just that. Now he thought: You are a big problem for us, because maybe you are a bit smarter than we are. Maybe that is true. But men could still do some things; men were still of some use. Women thought they were the only ones who could work out what was what; well, he would show them.

"So what does this person do, Mma Ramotswe? Mma Makutsi? Any ideas? Let me tell you: She says to herself, I will park round the corner so that nobody thinks I have stolen any diamonds. They will think I have walked to work because I do not have that much money." He drew breath. "That's what she would have said to herself, I think."

The end of Charlie's explanation was greeted by silence. Charlie thought: They do not like a man who can think for himself; that is what they think. They would prefer it if a woman came up with a good conclusion like mine. They would say, "Exactly, Mma," and "How right you are," just because she was a woman and all women will agree with everything that other women say. That is the way they work. That is the way they unite against us.

Injustice heaped upon injustice—in Charlie's view at least—and now just this silence.

Then Mma Ramotswe nodded and said, "Exactly, Charlie."

Mma Makutsi pursed her lips. Then she said, "How right you are." But then added, "Well done, Charlie. Sometimes you can get things right—if you're pointed in the right direction."

Mma Ramotswe thought about this. The thought of diamond theft had occurred to her, but she wondered whether it was feasible or likely. The security surrounding the handling of diamonds was legendary for its strictness. It could safely be assumed that nobody would get away with any attempt to circumvent it. And if that was the case, then Nametso must have bought the Mercedes-Benz with the proceeds of some other activity.

She raised this possibility with Mma Makutsi and Charlie. They listened attentively.

"We need to follow her," said Charlie when Mma Ramotswe had finished. "Follow somebody, and you find out the truth."

Even Mma Makutsi was impressed with this observation. "That is very good, Charlie," she said. "You are becoming rather a good *assistant* detective. Follow somebody down the track and at the end of the track you will find the truth."

"What track?" asked Charlie.

"Mma Makutsi is thinking of no particular track," said Mma Ramotswe.

"Actually, I am thinking of the track marked *private life*," said Mma Makutsi, examining her fingernails. "That is the track to follow, I think."

CHAPTER NINE

GOOD DRINKS, PLENTY FOOD

CHARLIE MET QUEENIE-QUEENIE that night at The Gaborone Dance Studio, a bar that prided itself on its dance floor. *The best music south of the Zambezi,* the club claimed on the lurid hoarding above its entrance. Below that boast, in somewhat less florid lettering, was the more practical advertisement: *Good drinks, plenty food.* No geographical distinction was asserted for these; certainly not that they were better than anything else obtainable south of any river. The place was popular, though, particularly among younger, more affluent government officials—it was not far from the headquarters of several ministries—and among aspiring socialites.

Charlie was wary of meeting there, on the grounds of expense, but had been assured by Queenie-Queenie that since the purpose of their tryst was a meeting with her brother, Hector, who had suggested it, he would pay for the drinks. "He has an account there," she said. "He always goes there to speak to his business associates."

Charlie had enquired as to what Hector's business was, and who the associates were. Queenie-Queenie had not answered directly, but had waved a hand airily. "He does business deals," she said. "With this person, then with that person. Then with somebody down in Mozambique, even. He sometimes goes there, Maputo. He says they have great seafood there. Big prawns. You like prawns, Charlie?"

Charlie had never tasted seafood of any description. He shook his head. "I do not eat prawns," he said.

"When we're married, Charlie, I'll cook you prawns. They have frozen prawns in the supermarket—you don't have to go to Mozambique, although we could go if we liked."

Charlie had never been anywhere, not even to Johannesburg. Would it ever be possible to go to Mozambique—with somebody like Queenie-Queenie? Dancing? Eating prawns? Staying in a *hotel*?

"And peri-peri chicken," Queenie-Queenie went on. "You must like peri-peri chicken, Charlie? Everybody likes peri-peri chicken—even vegetarians. They have a vegetarian version of it."

Yes, he liked peri-peri chicken.

"That comes from those Portuguese," said Queenie-Queenie. "When they were in Mozambique, they liked to eat peri-peri chicken. They said to people: 'You will eat peri-peri chicken.' And you did not argue with the Portuguese."

"No," said Charlie. "They were not very nice."

"There were some nice Portuguese," said Queenie-Queenie. "But they have all gone home now. That is African history, you see. People come and take what they want, and then they go home."

Charlie shook his head. "That was very bad. But it is finished now."

"I don't know," said Queenie-Queenie. "There are others. They are always looking for their chance."

Now Charlie sat in a booth at The Gaborone Dance Studio, nursing his drink—a small soft drink, mostly ice, served to him by a disdainful waitress who had looked at his trousers with what seemed close to contempt. And there was indeed an old oil stain that he had tried, and failed, to remove; how that had happened, he had no idea, as his work trousers were kept rigorously separate from his social trousers, but there it was—Queenie-Queenie had never said anything about his clothes, and he thought she probably did not notice. Women, thought Charlie, are keen for you to notice what *they* are wearing but are often not particularly interested in what *you* are wearing, which was just as well, he thought, because his clothes had a thin, scrappy look to them, like the skin of an undernourished cow, perhaps, or the cheap upholstery of an old car seat. It will be different, he told himself; it will be different in the future when I am somebody to reckon with: a leading private investigator, with offices in Gaborone and Lobatse, and possibly Francistown; with a secretary—no, two secretaries—and a switchboard to put calls in from one line to the other, and a room of his own, not one shared with two younger cousins, one of whom currently had a dry, rasping cough. You could not be angry with a cough, nor with the indignities visited on the other poor little boy, but you could yearn for freedom from such things, for escape from need, from the limitations of a world made small by poverty.

And he was looking down at his trousers when Queenie-Queenie came in with Hector, her brother, whose hobby was body-building and whose clothes clung to his body, tight and shining, safe from the condescension of any waitress.

Queenie-Queenie did not kiss him, but reached out briefly and touched his hand before she sat down beside him, all the while watching her brother, Charlie noticed, as if she were anxious that he should approve of her demeanour.

"Hector drove me here," she said. "He has been very busy, but he is happy that he can be here."

Hector had greeted Charlie formally. Now, still standing, he said, "Come with me to the bar, Charlie. I need a drink."

"The waitress will come," said Charlie. "They have a waitress here."

"That woman is no good," said Hector. "She knows nothing."

Queenie-Queenie nudged Charlie. "You should go with Hector," she whispered. "Then come back and we can talk."

Charlie rose obediently, and walked across the dance floor to the bar with the other young man. There was no band yet—just a tired recording from somewhere behind the bar, marred by a faulty lead to the speaker.

"This place needs a kick in the pants," said Hector. "They are no good, but this is where everyone comes. Have you been here before, Charlie?"

Charlie shook his head.

"You should come," said Hector. "As I said, everyone comes here. This is where all the big deals are done. Right here. This is where people see who's who, you know."

Charlie nodded. He had no idea who was who. I am really just a mechanic, he said to himself. I am not even a proper detective. I am not a big man who can walk about The Gaborone Dance Studio as if he owns it. This is not my place.

They reached the bar, where Hector offered him a beer while ordering himself a vodka and lime.

"Vodka goes with anything," he said. "You can have it with soda, with Coke if you like, with orange juice. Anything. You should try it some time. One vodka and you think: Problems? No problems any more. No problems."

"That must be very good," said Charlie. "Who hasn't got problems?"

Hector raised his glass. "Who hasn't got problems? Too true,

Charlie. Too true." He reached out and poked Charlie gently in the chest. "You've got problems, I'd say. Big problems too."

Charlie said nothing. Hector was right: he had problems.

Hector took a sip of his vodka and lime. "Queenie says you've asked her to marry you? Is that true?"

Charlie thought that it was not strictly true. He could not remember actually proposing to her; it seemed to him that she had simply assumed that he was about to do so, and had saved him the effort. But he would not say that now.

"That's true. We are hoping to get married."

Hector nodded. "Then that's where your problem lies," he said.

Charlie looked down at the floor. Money. Everything was reduced to money. At the end of the day, that was how the important decisions were made. Money.

Hector continued, "Because I think you have no money at all—correct?"

Charlie looked up briefly and nodded. "I have no money. I am very poor."

Hector made a noise with his tongue that was hard to interpret. It was not an encouraging sound. "You see, Charlie, you're basically nothing, aren't you? Mr. Nothing—big-time."

Charlie was about to nod again, but stopped himself. He was beginning, though, to feel angry. That was not the way things were meant to be—not here in Botswana, where every person had a right to have their dignity acknowledged and respected. The government said that all the time. And when the government spoke, it spoke with all the authority of the ancestors, way back, all the way back.

He summoned up his courage. "I am not Mr. Nothing," he said.

Hector's tone was mocking. "No? Then who are you?"

"Same as you," said Charlie. "Same as anybody else."

This momentarily deflected Hector. But he soon returned. "Okay," he said. "So you're not nothing in the sense of . . . of not being here at all, but . . . but don't you see a big problem here? You go to my uncles, my father even, and you say, 'I want to marry Queenie-Queenie,' and they say, 'You want to marry Queenie-Queenie?' And then they start to think about the money, Charlie, the money. And they say, 'We were thinking of fifty cattle, maybe one hundred, who knows?' And then they ask you how many cattle you have, and I don't know the answer to that, Charlie, but I think I can guess. I think you are Mr. Zero Cattle. Is that correct?"

"I have no cattle. It is true."

"You see," said Hector. "When I said you were Mr. Nothing, that's what I meant. And so you can't marry Queenie unless there's a big change in your life, Charlie."

Charlie looked away. The waitress was staring at him from the end of the counter. She seemed puzzled as to why Charlie was with Hector. Noticing this, Charlie felt some satisfaction; she had written him off, and now here he was, talking to this well-dressed and impressive body-builder—Mr. Something to his Mr. Nothing.

Hector leaned forward. He lowered his voice. "I can help you, Charlie."

Charlie drew in his breath. "Yes?"

"Yes. I can see my sister thinks a lot of you." He paused. "I can't see why. No offence, Charlie, but you know what I mean. Women are funny that way, aren't they? They go for useless men sometimes."

Charlie lowered his gaze. *I am not useless. I am an assistant detective. I have almost solved a big case today. The ladies congratulated me.* There was so much he could say to this person—if only he had the courage.

"So they insist on marrying some guy who's never going to get anywhere," Hector continued. "You ask them why, and they say—love. Would you believe it? That's what they say."

"Maybe that's what they want."

Hector ignored this. "And then, after a few years, they wake up one day and they have three children, maybe four, and they can't see why they married him and they say, 'Oh dear, look at me now, with all these children and this useless man—what can I do?' And the answer, of course, is nothing, because they're stuck with him." He shook his head. "It's very sad."

"Perhaps—"

"Let me tell you, Charlie. I have some business interests and I need people to help me. And I think I might have just the job for you."

Charlie pointed out that he already had a job. "I am an assistant detective."

Hector brushed this aside. "Of course, of course. You work for that fat lady. But this would not be a full-time job—it would be an evening job, for after work. You go to work and do your investigations or whatever, then you come to my place and you do some things for me."

Charlie asked what things these were.

"I am a partner in a money-lending firm," said Hector. "I used money that the old man gave me—he has this big transport company, you know. Anyway, he advanced me some money and I invested with this guy called Freddy, who has a money-lending company. We make small loans to people who've spent all their money and need something to keep them going until payday." He looked at Charlie. "You'll know what it's like to be short of money, won't you?" He rubbed two fingers together while looking pained.

Charlie nodded. "It's not easy."

"Yes," said Hector. "We make small loans, and then they pay us back when they get their pay. That's the theory."

"It doesn't work?"

"It works most of the time, but not always. Out of one hundred loans, you get paid back no problem in eighty of them. Then there are ten that are late, and then there are ten who don't pay back at all. Those are the ones you have to go and see—to remind them."

Charlie waited.

"And that's where you come in, Charlie," said Hector. "We need a new reminder. The last one . . . well, he had an accident. We need people who will go to visit these people and persuade them to pay us back."

"How?" asked Charlie.

Hector laughed. "Lots of people have cars these days. And if their car is grounded for a while, it's very inconvenient for them—very. That's where you come in. You are a mechanic, aren't you?"

Charlie nodded.

"Then it'll be simple," said Hector. "You go and take something out of the car—some important piece. You immobilise them. That's why I'm giving you this great opportunity, Charlie. I know you're a mechanic, and so you can do this sort of thing."

Charlie's eyes widened.

"You remove the distributor or something," Hector continued. "Maybe one or two of its wheels. Or you make sure the car won't start. And then they realise that we mean business, and you won't see them for dust—running around to make sure they pay us back and get their cars going again. Simple. Everybody's happy—or, at least, we're happy; they may not be."

Charlie stared at Hector open-mouthed. "You want me to sabotage their cars?" he asked. "Is that what you want?"

"You could put it that way, Charlie," said Hector. "But remember: You're the one who needs the money. You're the one who wants to get married to my sister. All that I'm doing is making it possible for you.

You work for me, and I'll give you the money to give to the old man."
He smiled. "Simple, you see. You should say, 'Thank you, Hector.'
That's what you should say, Charlie, my friend!"

Charlie mumbled something. It was possibly *thank you*, possibly not.

_____

CHAPTER TEN

AND WHAT WAS THERE TO REGRET?

I T WAS HIGH TIME, thought Mma Ramotswe, to visit her old friend, Mma Potokwane, matron, stalwart defender of orphans and other poor children, and maker of fruit cake—from a famous and unfathomable recipe. It was not that fruit cake was topmost in Mma Ramotswe's mind when she made the decision to travel out to Tlokweng—any friendship based on considerations of appetite would be a shallow friendship indeed—but one could not ignore the role that mutual enjoyment of food played in the enjoyment of human company. Mma Ramotswe was a stout defender of the idea that a family should eat together, and insisted on this in her own home, even if she and Mr. J.L.B. Matekoni often had to have dinner later than the two foster children because he was late back from the garage. On such occasions, she would feed Motholeli and Puso first, yet would always sit down with them at the table, even if she would be having her own dinner a bit later. And if she treated herself to a small helping of what was being served to them, then that was done out of respect for her own rule about eating together. And there was another rule at play here—the rule that stated that food prepared for children was almost always tastier than the food cooked for oneself. It simply was. How many parents, then, found themselves hovering over their children's plates, ready to swoop on any surplus or rejected morsel or, worse still, ready to sneak something off the plate while the child was looking in the other direction, or arguing with a brother or sister, or possibly having a tantrum. The closing of eyes that went with a tantrum could be especially useful in this respect; when the child came to his or her senses, the quantity on the plate may have been significantly reduced, thus providing the child who noticed it with a sharp lesson in the consequences of bad behaviour. Make a fuss, and your food will be eaten by somebody else: a sound proposition that Mma Ramotswe believed could be applied with equal force to many other situations.

She had not seen Mma Potokwane for some time, and as she drove along the corrugated dirt road that led to the Orphan Farm, a cloud of dust thrown up behind her white van like the vapour trail of a high-flying aircraft, she thought of the last occasion on which she and her friend had sat down together and had one of their wide-ranging conversations. They had talked about so much that a great deal of it was now forgotten, although a few topics remained in her mind.

There had been a discussion about Mma Makutsi and her latest doings. Mma Potokwane and Mma Makutsi had not always had the easiest of relationships in the past, both being women of strong personality and confirmed views. That had changed for the better, and now they enjoyed civil relations, even if they did not always see eye to eye in quite the same way as did Mma Ramotswe and Mma Potokwane.

"Mma Makutsi has many merits," said Mma Potokwane. "But nobody is perfect, is she, Mma?"

It was impossible to refute that. There were no perfect people, said Mma Ramotswe, even if there were one or two who were almost perfect. Mr. J.L.B. Matekoni, for instance, was almost without fault, but not quite. He was the kindest man in Botswana, Mma Ramotswe asserted, and one of the gentlest too, but he suffered from indecisiveness that he would undoubtedly be better off without. That had led to their long engagement and to her difficulty in pinning him down to a wedding date, an impasse eventually satisfactorily resolved by Mma Ramotswe's taking the matter in hand. Many men needed that firm treatment, she thought: they meant well; they had plans that sounded plausible in theory, but when it came to actually doing something, then women were far more effective. One should not be too hard on the weaker brethren, though, Mma Ramotswe told herself, because they also served—in their way.

"Mma Makutsi," she said, in response to Mma Potokwane, "is an unusual lady. She is very good at her job, and of course she did very well at the Botswana Secretarial College . . ."

"Oh that," said Mma Potokwane. "We have all heard about her ninety-seven per cent. I am not one to decry that, Mma, but nonetheless there must come a point at which you forget about your marks in exams all those years ago. I do not talk about my prize for being most improved girl in Standard Three. You have never heard me mention that, have you, Mma?"

"You were most improved girl, Mma? I should not be surprised by that. You must have had many prizes in your career, Mma."

Mma Potokwane shook her head. "Only one, Mma. That one. Since then there have been no prizes."

"Oh well . . ."

"I am not criticising Mma Makutsi," Mma Potokwane went on. "But sometimes I wonder about her shoes."

Mma Ramotswe had heard Mma Potokwane express such reservations before. "Shoes are very important to her, Mma. She gets great pleasure from having those fashionable shoes of hers. She loves them."

"I say that shoes are for walking in," said Mma Potokwane. "That is what I say, Mma. Or standing about in. They should be comfortable."

Mma Ramotswe glanced down at her friend's feet. They were on the large side, and they reminded her at that moment of the bottom sections of the concrete pillars of that new bridge on the outskirts of town; but she did not say anything about that, of course, as it is rude to make civil engineering comparisons when talking about a friend's personal features. "I have always thought your shoes looked very comfortable. They seem to have a lot of room in them. And they have very low heels too, which must help. And that wide shape too, Mma. We traditionally built ladies need to have wide feet for stability, Mma. That is very important, I think."

"My feet are a bit big," said Mma Potokwane. "My husband has small feet, but mine are generously proportioned. His shoes are too small for me."

And so the conversation had wandered on, touching briefly on politics—but leaving that subject quickly enough, to the relief of both of them—and then moving to the difficult issue of stopping children from eating too many sweet things. That last topic had been aired at the same time as second slices of fruit cake were embarked upon, and Mma Ramotswe had been briefly aware of that irony, but had reminded herself that they were talking about children, not adults, and that was clearly very different.

That afternoon, she parked her van in its accustomed position, under the tree that she liked to think somebody had planted many years ago with her in mind, as if that person knew—although of course he could not have known—that she, Mma Ramotswe, would in the fullness of time arrive and find it the ideal place for her. The world was not like that, she knew; we had to fit in with the world rather than the world fit in with us, but every so often it was nice to imagine that it was the other way round. And there was no doubt, she thought, that Botswana fitted her to perfection. It was the right size; it was the right shape on the map; the people who lived in it and the cattle they kept were just as she would want them to be; it was so perfect that she imagined that God himself had thought: I shall invent a country that is just right for Mma Ramotswe when she comes along, and I shall call it Botswana, and it will be a good place.

And as she stepped out of the van and closed its door behind her, she looked up and drank in the air and the blue and the emptiness that was the sky; a draught more satisfying than the sweetest water; and filled, at that moment, with the song of some bird that she did not know the name of, but that she had heard oh so many times, as a girl, as a young woman, as the person she now was. That bird continued to sing that same song, learned from its mother and father, to be passed on to the next generation of birds, small creatures even now sheltering in a hidden nest somewhere, ready for their moment of launch and the beginning of the dance about the skies of Botswana that would be their brief life. And she thought: Oh, I am so fortunate to be here in this land, to be standing under this sky, ready to see my old friend Mma Potokwane, and to drink tea with her and to talk about the things that we always talk about.

Unknown to Mma Ramotswe, that same old friend was looking out of her window, having heard the sound of the approaching van. She had watched Mma Ramotswe's manoeuvres under the habitual tree, and she had remembered how that morning she had told the farm manager, who looked after the vegetable patches and the fields, to move the tractor that he had parked under the shade of that particular acacia. She had explained that Mma Ramotswe would be arriving before too long and that it was important that her parking place be kept free, because she would expect it. The farm manager had readily agreed; the tractor would be moved. "The tractor can go anywhere; it is only a tractor," he had said. "Mma Ramotswe is a very good woman, and she is also the cousin of my brother's wife's sister."

Mma Potokwane watched as Mma Ramotswe made her way towards her office. Why had she suddenly stopped, as if she had forgotten something and had now remembered it? Why was she standing there, looking up at the sky? Of course, she did just that, she remembered; Mma Ramotswe would often stop and look at the sky; and this just went to show how wise she was, because looking at the sky was something that we all should do more often. Or so Mma Potokwane had read somewhere. People who looked at the sky, she had learned, are less likely to die than those who do not look at the sky. That was interesting and must have something to do with inner calmness and the way in which that calmness protects you from things that afflict those who are not calm—nervous conditions of one sort or another, and other illnesses too. Nerves were involved with everything, Mma Potokwane believed.

The water for the tea was already boiling when she welcomed her visitor into her office.

"It is still hot outside," said Mma Potokwane, as Mma Ramotswe sank into the chair in which she always sat.

"The heat will bring the rain," said Mma Ramotswe. "That is what I am hoping, Mma Potokwane."

"We are all hoping that, Mma."

Tea was served and the cake was wordlessly taken from its tin, given admiring looks by Mma Ramotswe, and served on Mma Potokwane's best plates, used only on occasions such as this—the visit of particular friends or members of the Orphan Farm Board of Management; or of Mr. J.L.B. Matekoni, for that matter, when he called in after performing some helpful task of machinery management, coax-

ing life out of a water pump that had lost the will to go on, or servic-
ing one of the farm vehicles or the ancient minibus—too ancient, he
said—that was used to transport the children. Mr. J.L.B. Matekoni's
ultimate reward for such acts of kindness, Mma Potokwane wryly
observed, might be in heaven, but on this earth, in the here and
now, it would take the form of an excessively generous slice of fruit
cake. He would eat it with relish, and would demur, but only briefly,
when a second slice was pressed upon him, and even a third. "My
wife would not approve," he would say, through a mouthful of cake.
"She says I must have only one slice if my trousers are still to fit. You
know how it is, Mma Potokwane."

And Mma Potokwane would laugh, and reassure him that eating
fruit cake was one of the things that a husband was entitled to keep
from his wife when the fruit cake in question was *deserved,* as this
undoubtedly was. "Deserved calories do not count, Rra," she said.
"You can count up all the calories you have had and then take away
the ones that were deserved. That is the total that you must look at."

He had laughed too, and said, "That is good to know, Mma Potokwane, because they are taking the fun out of everything these days,
and there is nothing left for many of us, I think. The government says
we must not do any of the things we like to do."

Now, Mma Potokwane blew across the top of her tea to cool
it down while Mma Ramotswe began to tell her about her latest
investigations. This was all done under an understanding of confi-
dentiality: Mma Ramotswe understood the need for confidence in
her work—that lay at the heart of the relationship with the client,
as Clovis Andersen stressed at so many points in *The Principles of
Private Detection*—but you had to be able to talk to *somebody* if your
work was not to get you down. It was also true that discussing a case
with another person served to illuminate certain aspects of it that
might otherwise not be spotted. How many times had Mma Poto-

kwane asked a question or made an observation that changed Mma Ramotswe's view of a situation; that suggested an explanation that had been eluding her simply because she had been looking at things from the wrong angle?

So she told her first about Nametso and her inexplicable coolness towards her mother. That behaviour was not uncommon, said Mma Potokwane, and it usually arose when a son or daughter was wanting to cut the apron-strings of an over-possessive mother. "People need to be able to breathe," said Mma Potokwane. "And parents sometimes stand in the way of that."

That was possible, said Mma Ramotswe. But what about the Mercedes-Benz?

"That," said Mma Potokwane, "sounds like shame. That is not an honest Mercedes-Benz."

"No," agreed Mma Ramotswe, "I do not think it is."

They moved on to Poppy, and to the loss of her money. Mma Potokwane rolled her eyes at the mention of the Reverend Flat Ponto. "I have heard of that man," she said. "One of the housemothers went to a meeting he held and she came back all fired up. She was gabbling away about this man and how he could change sinners into saints. She was so excited she was hardly making any sense."

"So what did you do?" asked Mma Ramotswe.

Mma Potokwane answered in a matter-of-fact way. "I pushed her."

Mma Ramotswe's eyes widened. "But you can't push people, Mma—not these days."

Mma Potokwane shrugged. "So people tell me. But how else do you get somebody who is hysterical to see sense? I don't see any other way. So I pushed her and then I persuaded her to stand under a cold shower for ten minutes, maybe a bit longer. And at the end I said to her, 'Mma, what is all this nonsense?' and she looked very embarrassed and admitted that she had been a bit excited. So I told her that if she saw that reverend again she would lose her job." She waited for a moment, aware that Mma Ramotswe was taken aback. "He is not a real reverend, you see. Those people who invent their own churches are not proper reverends at all. That one is a mechanic, I think."

But still Mma Ramotswe expressed surprise. People could not be fired on arbitrary grounds, she reminded Mma Potokwane. But Mma Potokwane was having none of that: "If you are a housemother, you have to be responsible and keep your head all the time. There are many little children relying on you, and we cannot have a house-mother who goes off and becomes hysterical because she has been listening to some windbag of a preacher—bogus preacher, should I say—can we, Mma?"

Mma Ramotswe did not argue the point. There was perhaps something to be said for Mma Potokwane's approach, she felt, even if she herself would find it hard to be so high-handed. "I suppose it was for her own good," she conceded.

"Yes," said Mma Potokwane. "It was." She paused. "And this poor woman who has had all her money taken away from her—what can you do for her? Will you be able to get it back?"

"I don't think so," said Mma Ramotswe. "She is an adult. She controls her own money and where it goes. I do not have any author-ity to act, you see."

Mma Potokwane looked thoughtful. Eventually she said, "Mma Ramotswe, do you think I could do something here? I know I have never interfered in these things that you do, but I think I might be able to help this poor lady."

"You would do that, Mma?"

"Yes. Why not?"

Mma Ramotswe bit her lip. "I don't like to be rude, Mma, but I must ask this: Would you respect the limits of what you can do? And by that, I mean: You wouldn't do anything illegal?"

Mma Potokwane was the picture of innocence. "Certainly not, Mma."

"It isn't really a fully fledged case," said Mma Ramotswe. "I am not acting for anybody. Nobody has come to me and asked me to help that woman."

"No, of course not," said Mma Potokwane hurriedly. "I can see that you're acting out of the goodness of your heart."

"In that case, Mma, it's up to you," Mma Ramotswe said. "You may wish to help her."

"Good," announced Mma Potokwane. "We'll sort out that reverend double quick. Bang. Like that. Bang."

Mma Ramotswe sipped at her tea. What did *bang* mean? It was the sort of thing that Charlie would say, but this was not Charlie—this was a respectable matron, a pillar (not in the civil engineering sense, of course) of the community. Mma Potokwane was a force to be reckoned with, and the Reverend Flat Ponto might be in for an unpleasant surprise. But if he preyed on vulnerable women, then he could hardly complain. Although he probably would—and vociferously too. The more that people are in the wrong, she thought, the louder their protestations on being brought to book. Clovis Andersen said something about that—possibly—but she could not remember chapter and verse.

THEY FINISHED THEIR TEA and the second slice of fruit cake. Then Mma Potokwane rose to her feet and suggested that Mma Ramotswe might care to visit one of the housemothers, Mma Tsepole, who had been asking after her. "She has been down in Lobatse visiting a sick relative, and I think she might like to be cheered up," she said.

They walked past the meeting hall and the children's *kgotla*. The older children had not yet returned from school, but there were groups of younger ones playing at various games. A small cluster of girls was drawing a hopscotch grid in the sand, watched by a couple of boys who had not been asked to join in but were awaiting an invitation. They stopped what they were doing when they saw Mma Potokwane, and waited for her to encourage them to continue.

"They'll spend hours on that," said Mma Potokwane. "Do you remember, Mma? Do you remember doing that yourself?"

Mma Ramotswe did. And there were songs, too, that went with skipping, but she could remember only a few snatches of them, a smattering of words: something about counting goats. It was so long ago, in the playground of the school on the hill at Mochudi, that place where she had started.

Mma Tsepole presided over one of the self-contained houses that lay at the heart of the Orphan Farm's structure. Each housemother looked after up to ten children, who would form the "family" of that house. She cooked for them, looked after their clothes, and allocated small domestic tasks to each child. If a child had no family in the out-side world, then this was the substitute, the housemother being the main anchor in what was in most cases a grossly disrupted young life.

She greeted Mma Ramotswe warmly. "I am glad you have come to see me, Mma," she said. "And you too, Mma Potokwane."

"I am not really here," said Mma Potokwane with a smile. "It is Mma Ramotswe you want to see."

The housemother invited them in, dusting her hands on her skirt as she led them into the kitchen. This was dominated by a large table, its surface scrubbed bare and laid with a row of white enamel plates. Against the wall on one side was a large range cooker, on the top of which two blackened and capacious cooking-pots sat. A thin layer of white ash from the wood used as fuel coated the floor at the bottom of the cooker; in the air there hung the smell of a bubbling stew and a faint trace of wood-smoke. For Mma Ramotswe it was a richly evocative combination, taking her back to the kitchen of her father's house in Mochudi, all those years ago, where there had been a wood-burning stove of much the same vintage. There, of course, was where the women who looked after her after her mother died, that succession of cousins on her father's side, would cook stews from which wafted an invitation as delicious and tempting as the one that Mma Tsepole was conjuring up for the children in her charge. Mma Ramotswe sniffed at the air and smiled. The children who lived in this place had no mother of their own, but they had what was undoubtedly the next best thing—somebody who watched over them and would make the stews that a loving hand produces for those who are loved.

There was more tea. This time it was not the red bush tea that she usually drank, but ordinary tea, which Mma Ramotswe would drink out of politeness, but with no great enthusiasm for the caffeine that she found made her feel a bit too enthusiastic, almost impulsive. But no harm would come from sharing one cup with Mma Tsepole, as they chatted about the housemother's relative in Lobatse—the one who had been ill—and about how she feared that this relative might not see out the year.

"There is nothing wrong with her," said Mma Tsepole, "other than the fact that she is very old, Mma, and her heart is saying, 'I am very tired with all this beating.' That is what happens, you know, Mma Ramotswe: your heart eventually says, 'Oh, my goodness, do I have to go on and on like this?'"

Mma Ramotswe nodded in agreement. "That is what happens, Mma. And I think that when it does, you should just say, 'It is time to go now,' and then you should become late without making too much fuss about it."

"Oh, that is very true, Mma Ramotswe," said Mma Tsepole. "That is what I always say. And that is what my auntie—the one down in Lobatse—says as well. She is ready to go, but there is a cousin down there who is always taking her to the doctor. And the doctor says, 'You are very old now, Auntie,' and my auntie says, 'Yes, I am very old and I do not want to trouble you.' And then the cousin says, 'But what about some more pills, please? Auntie needs pills.' And so it goes on."

"That is very sad," said Mma Ramotswe, taking a sip of the strong brown tea Mma Tsepole had given her.

"I will miss her," said Mma Tsepole. "She has seen so many things in her life, and all those old things, the things that happened a long time ago, she remembers. Every detail is there, Mma. She remembers Protectorate days, when we were still Bechuanaland. She remembers the old steam trains that came down from Bulawayo, and how the police band used to play at the railway station when the train came in. A band, Mma, playing for a train coming in. Can you imagine that?"

The question was rhetorical, but Mma Ramotswe could remember it. Life had been like that in those days, when there was not very much going on and the arrival of a train was something of an event. We had lost that sense of excitement, she felt, because now there was so much happening all the time and nobody paid attention to anything because they had seen it all before. In the days that Mma Tsepole was talking about, people waved to one another on the road. You did not need to know the other person, you just waved, because that was what people did. Now, of course, people just ignored strangers; they took no interest in the story of the other person because they had no time for such things.

Mma Tsepole enquired about various people known to Mma Ramotswe, and Mma Ramotswe assured her that as far as she knew, they were well. Then there was a lengthy discussion about the merits of macaroni cheese. Was this, in Mma Ramotswe's opinion, a good food to serve to children twice a week, say, or should it be kept as a special treat? Some people said one thing, Mma Tsepole complained, and others said the opposite. Whom was one to believe, especially nowadays, when everybody considered themselves experts on everything? Mma Ramotswe had no idea, and nor did Mma Potokwane. "Perhaps we should believe nobody any longer," said the housemother, somewhat sadly, and then added, by way of a tactful afterthought, "Except Mma Potokwane, of course." And Mma Potokwane had laughed and said, "Do not believe me, Mma, except some of the time, perhaps."

Mma Ramotswe became aware that a child had entered the kitchen. She and Mma Potokwane had seated themselves at the table, their mugs of tea before them, and suddenly she was just there; quiet and unannounced, a little girl still unsteady on her legs, but with that rootedness to the ground that comes with a low centre of gravity. She was barely three, Mma Ramotswe thought, although it was sometimes difficult with children who had been undernourished: a five-year-old might have the frame of a three-year-old if there had not been enough food. That was relatively rare in Botswana, but it still happened; there were still many poor people whose eked-out living was too small to give their children the start they needed. Poverty in Africa lurked on the edges of plenty, waiting for its chance to nip at the heels of those who did not get their fair share, and these children, every one of them, had fallen through the net of the traditional family and village systems of support. They were the children who had no grandmother to look after them on the death of their mother, or whose grandmother had simply too many children around her skirts to manage. The most burdened shoulders in Africa might also be the oldest.

The little girl stood just inside the doorway, a tattered soft toy in her hand, an ancient threadbare dog or cat—it was hard to tell, so loved and cuddled had it been. She was watching them with that intense, unremitting gaze of the young child, and her eyes now fixed on Mma Ramotswe.

Mma Ramotswe turned to Mma Tsepole. She raised an enquiring eyebrow, and Mma Tsepole nodded.

"That is little Daisy. She has a Setswana name, but the older children decided to call her Daisy. I think they had seen the name in a school book."

Mma Potokwane smiled encouragingly at the child. "Daisy," she said. "You say hello to these aunties."

But the child, for all the boldness of her stare, was too shy to speak.

"She is learning words," said Mma Tsepole. "I think I was telling you about that the other day, Mma Potokwane. Her words are coming at last."

Mma Potokwane nodded. "Sometimes children are too traumatised to speak when they get here," she explained. "Sometimes it takes months and months before there is anything. Then suddenly you hear the first *dumela*, the first hello, and it is like the coming of the dawn. You know, that moment when the sun first comes up over the trees and makes everything gold. Like that."

"She is talking to the other children now," said Mma Tsepole. "Just single words—you know how it is. *Water. Sun. Hot.* Words like that, but you can hear them." She paused. "And *Mama* too. You hear her say that."

Mma Ramotswe caught her breath; that the child should say that which she did not have: the missing bit of her world.

Mma Tsepole lowered her voice; this was her habit when talking about her charges, even if they were too young to understand.

"Her mother was ill," she said. Her voice lowered further. Now it was a whisper. "With that illness."

Mma Ramotswe knew what she was talking about. It had cut like a scythe through the land, and now, although there were pills that could keep it at bay, there were still those who were beyond the reach of medicines, or who were visited with other complications, and fell.

"Yes," continued Mma Tsepole. "The mother was ill, although it was not the illness that killed her. And the father . . ."

Mma Potokwane took over. "The father was no good. He drank, and he ended up in prison for a while. Then they lost sight of him. The village headman's wife tried to find somebody to take the little girl, but nobody could. That happens more and more. Too busy. Gone away. Too many children on their hands already—I'm not blaming them, but it's hard. It's hard for everybody."

"But this child's mother," said Mma Tsepole. "Now that is very sad. They lived up north, near Maun. You know how it is up there, Mma Ramotswe. There are elephants—too many elephants, many people say. And they walk past the villages sometimes and destroy their crops."

Mma Ramotswe nodded. She knew about this—Mr. J.L.B. Matekoni had been discussing it the other day. "It is not the elephants' fault," he said. "Where are they to go? If they go up north they will be shot. They feel Botswana is their place too." Now she said, "Yes, it is hard for everybody—people and elephants."

Mma Tsepole continued, "The mother of this child—she was working in the fields, although she was ill. She was still working. And the child was with her, playing, when the elephant came. There was another woman there, on the other side of the field, and she saw the elephant coming and she shouted to warn this child's mother. But she did not hear, and the elephant was angry because it had that condition that elephants get, where their eyes water. And the people up there know to keep well away from an elephant when it is like that."

Mma Ramotswe was silent. She saw the scene: the field, the sun, the struggling crops, the woman tending them. And the elephant, a grey shape that came out of nowhere, as elephants can do, and that could move with such swiftness and agility, like a great dancer, when angered or afraid.

"The elephant killed the mother," said Mma Potokwane. "The other woman saw it all happen—and so did the little girl. The elephant picked the mother up and threw her, as those creatures do, and then trampled her. The child saw it happen."

Mma Ramotswe closed her eyes. "The poor child." It was not much to say, she knew. The poor child.

"They shouted at the elephant and banged an old tin bath they had at the fields," said Mma Tsepole. "That made it turn away. Sometimes they lose interest, you see. It turned and went away before it could kill the child too."

Mma Potokwane shrugged her shoulders. "She will not remember it in the future. I think she remembers now—maybe that is why she says *Mama* sometimes—but she will forget. Children forget. They forget the most terrible things, Mma, if they are young enough."

"But later, when they are older, Mma," said Mma Tsepole. "I think it is different then."

Mma Potokwane nodded gravely. "Yes, it can be very different."

Daisy had moved. Now, a few hesitant steps later, she was beside Mma Ramotswe's chair, looking up at her. Mma Potokwane smiled. "See, Mma, she has come to you."

Mma Ramotswe turned in her chair and gazed down at the little girl. "She is very pretty," she said.

"Yes," said Mma Tsepole. "I think she is, Mma. She has those eyes—you know the eyes that some of them have. She has those."

Daisy now reached out and took hold of Mma Ramotswe's hand that had been half proffered to her. The tiny hand fastened onto a finger and gripped tight.

"She's holding your hand," whispered Mma Potokwane. "Look, Mma. She is holding on to you."

Mma Ramotswe moved her hand slightly, but the child did not relinquish her grip. She leaned over and picked her up, taking her to her bosom. The child held on. She buried her head in Mma Ramotswe. She clung to her.

The two other women were silent. There was nothing that they could say.

"Yes," Mma Ramotswe whispered. "Yes, my little one."

And then she kissed the child gently, on her head, and put her free hand on her back and hugged her closer.

"Yes, my little one. Now you have met Mma Ramotswe. That's who I am. I am Mma Ramotswe."

She thought of those moments, so infinitely painful to the memory, and therefore not thought about very often, when she had held her baby who died. How small the infant had been—a scrap of humanity—but how vast the chasm of sorrow it had opened in her. She struggled with the memory, and after a short while she put it out of her mind and was back in this room, with her two friends, and this strange little girl who seemed to have taken to her so quickly.

"I must put you down, little one," she whispered, and began to detach herself from the child. But Daisy was not to be put down, and held on all the tighter, struggling to remain exactly where she was, in the arms of Mma Ramotswe, nestling at her chest.

Mma Potokwane leaned over towards her friend. "They can cling very tight, Mma," she said. "After they have lost the mother, they can cling very tight."

Mma Ramotswe nodded. She understood, and she stopped trying to put Daisy down. Instead she rose to her feet, still holding the child, and walked over to the other side of the kitchen, to the door that gave out onto the back yard.

"Look," she said. "Look out there. Can you see the trees? And look, there's a bird there, on that branch. Can you see it?"

The child looked, but soon turned her head back to Mma Ramotswe and the comfort of her bosom.

"And look—look up there. That's the sky, you see. It goes for a long way. And out there, not far away, is the Kalahari. And at night there are many stars there, you know. High, high—many, many stars."

The child uttered a sound that she did not hear very well. It could have been anything, but it was probably nothing, she thought.

"Maybe you're hungry," she said. "Maybe that is what it is."

Mma Ramotswe looked at Mma Tsepole, who reached for a battered tin box and took out a plain rusk. "They love these," she said to Mma Ramotswe. "Milk rusks. I make them for the children." She handed the rusk to Mma Ramotswe, who offered it to Daisy. A small hand reached for it but did not put it in her mouth. She held the rusk, which shed crumbs on Mma Ramotswe.

"She's not hungry," said Mma Potokwane. "And we should wait a little, I think, so that she can have food with her pill."

Mma Ramotswe frowned. "Her pill, Mma?"

Mma Potokwane sighed. "The mother was ill, Mma, as we told you."

It took Mma Ramotswe no more than a few seconds to grasp the significance of this. She gave an involuntary gasp. "Oh, Mma Potokwane . . ."

"Yes," said Mma Potokwane. "That is how it is, Mma. It is hard, I know. It is very hard."

Mma Ramotswe kissed Daisy again, and held her more tightly.

She rocked her gently, as if in an effort to calm her—although the child was not upset.

Mma Tsepole turned away. She could not bear it; she could not bear it. And yet she had to, because this was her job and you could not allow your emotions to get the better of you. Others would have to do the weeping, because a housemother in tears was no help to the other children. A housemother had to be brave.

Mma Potokwane lifted her mug and took a sip of tea. "These children have very special needs, Mma. It would be good if we could give little Daisy more attention, but there are so many children. Mma Tsepole has to look after . . . How many is it, Mma?"

"Eight now," said Mma Tsepole. "And there are two more coming, you said."

"Possibly," said Mma Potokwane. Then, to Mma Ramotswe, "We have a helper for this child, thanks to one of the firms that support us. They have paid for a young woman to look after her. But we have no accommodation for her—the young woman, that is. She has to travel over from the far side of the village every day, and then go back at night." She paused, and addressed Mma Tsepole again. "Where is that girl, Mma?"

"She has gone to the stores," said Mma Tsepole. "She'll be back in an hour, maybe. I am covering in the meantime."

Mma Potokwane nodded. "You see, Mma Ramotswe, it is a bit hard for us. We have to balance all these needs. This child needs this thing, that child needs that thing, and a third child needs something else altogether. It isn't easy."

"No," said Mma Ramotswe, kissing the top of Daisy's head again. "It cannot be."

Mma Potokwane hesitated. She glanced at Mma Tsepole, who intercepted her glance, but said nothing. Then she continued, "Of course, it would be ideal if somebody were to offer to take this child—and the young woman. It would only be for a month or two, because we have found a home for this child. There are some good people who are going to take her, but their new house is still being built and it is not yet ready. In the meantime, it is very hard for the helper to get in here every day at the right time. And she cannot travel back in the dark, so she has to leave early and there is nobody to look after the child."

Mma Ramotswe understood. "It must be hard—with all these children. I can see that, Mma Potokwane."

Mma Potokwane brushed a fly away. "If there were somebody," she continued, "who had unoccupied servants' quarters, for example, at the back of their yard, where the young woman could live. That would be very good." She paused. "It wouldn't cost them anything, of course, because we get money for the young woman from that firm, and the government also gives us some money to support the child. So there would be no cost at all."

There was a silence. Another fly buzzed against the fly screen on the kitchen window, looking for freedom in that quarter but unaware of the open door behind it.

"It would be a great help, that," agreed Mma Tsepole. Then, "You foster two children already, don't you, Mma?"

"I do," said Mma Ramotswe. "They are with us forever now."

"That's very good," said Mma Tsepole. "Children like security. They like to have one person who is just theirs, you see."

"I understand," muttered Mma Ramotswe.

Mma Potokwane put down her cup. "You don't by any chance have unoccupied quarters at the back of your yard, do you, Mma?"

LATER, AS SHE LAY IN BED and contemplated what she had done, Mma Ramotswe thought: it was the tea that did it. It was the tea that had made her say what she said. It was the tea.

But she had never once regretted what she had done under the influence of tea, and would not start doing so now. And what was there to regret? Motholeli had been so pleased to discover Daisy, and Puso, although usually indifferent to younger children, had listened carefully as she told him how Daisy had lost her mother. "That's very sad," he said at the end. "I shall try to make her happy."

"We all shall," said Mma Ramotswe, dispelling there and then the last of her doubts as to her admittedly impetuous decision. If you could not help in a case like this, when you had been given so much, and when your friend, Mma Potokwane, spent every minute of her working day trying to make life better for these poor children, then what could you do? Of course you had to do it. Of course you had to say to Mma Potokwane, "Well, as it happens, Mma, we have the room and the young woman will be able to look after her during the day when I am at the office, and yes, Mma, there is always enough love for some of it to be given to a little girl who has had these things happen to her." And Mma Potokwane, for her part, had to say, "Well, Mma Ramotswe, it's good that you should say that because I thought this might just be the right thing for this child, and we can sort out the paperwork later on—not that I am a great believer in paperwork. Why wait, when she so obviously wants you to look after her; see how she still holds on to you? See that? That is a sign, I think."

Mr. J.L.B. Matekoni had been uncertain what to say. He wondered whether he should ask Mma Ramotswe why she had not consulted him, but decided against it. If husbands started to question their wives' decisions, then where would it end, and what purpose would it serve? You could not undo what your wife had done. Some men tried it, he knew, but they almost always failed, because women so often did the right thing, and the right thing may be beyond undoing. It was far better to accept what had happened and make the best of it. It was also the case, he reflected, that Mma Ramotswe usually got her way. She was so nice about it, so disinclined to be insistent or pushy, but she usually got him to do what she wanted—and he was happy enough about that when all was said and done.

And in that spirit he had crept into the room at the back of the house to be shown where Daisy was asleep in a cot borrowed from a Zebra Drive neighbour. And there, seeing the sleeping child's head upon the pillow, he had unexpectedly found himself in tears. A handkerchief was pressed into his hand by Mma Ramotswe, who said, "There, Rra, there." And then they had closed the door quietly and made their way back to the kitchen and their waiting dinner. It was always the strongest men who were the first to cry, thought Mma Ramotswe. Some people said it was the other way round, but they were wrong, she told herself; they were simply wrong.

CHAPTER ELEVEN

ROUTINE ARM-WORK (FOR LEGS)

AT MORNING TEA TIME the next day, Mma Ramotswe outlined to Mma Makutsi and Charlie what she had in mind to do about Nametso. Charlie, she suggested, should take up position in the van, discreetly parked, ready to follow Nametso when she left work that evening.

"People leave that sort of office at five on the dot," she said. "They are always ready to pack up and go the moment the clock says the working day is over."

"Unlike us," said Mma Makutsi. "We self-employed people are always working odd hours. If the work is there, we do it."

Mma Ramotswe agreed, refraining from pointing out that both Mma Makutsi and Charlie had always had a very keen sense of when it was five o'clock.

"I shall come too," offered Mma Makutsi. "I think this is a sensitive matter, Mma, and . . ." She looked at Charlie. "I think there is a need for a senior operative."

Charlie looked to Mma Ramotswe for support. "That's very kind, Mma Makutsi," he said. "But I am sure I shall manage."

"No," said Mma Makutsi. "You do not need to thank me, Charlie. It is for the best."

Mma Ramotswe made her decision. There was something about this case—if one could call it a case—that made her uncomfortable, and she wanted to watch over it carefully. Diamonds were involved, and you did not tread lightly with diamonds—not in a country that prided itself on the careful regulation of the industry. Diamonds were sensitive, and Charlie and Mma Makutsi might easily wander into something that would have to be handed over to the authorities. "I shall come too," Mma Ramotswe announced. "That way there will be many eyes watching her."

"Six," said Charlie. "Six eyes, Mma."

"That's correct, Charlie," she said. "Six eyes. Three pairs."

At four-fifteen, in time to beat the traffic that built up after five, the three of them left the agency in the tiny white van, with Charlie at the wheel, Mma Makutsi in the middle of the ancient bench seat that Mr. J.L.B. Matekoni had installed in the cab, and, up against the passenger door, its uncomfortable broken handle pressing into her side, Mma Ramotswe. They were so squashed that in unspoken agreement their breathing fell into a sequence, with Charlie breathing in first, while Mma Makutsi breathed out, and this gave room for Mma Ramotswe to fall into synchronicity with Charlie. In this way they drove slowly along the street that approached the diamond-sorting office and found, more or less exactly where they had expected it, a gleaming silver Mercedes-Benz parked in between a pick-up truck and a modest, somewhat battered car bearing a large *Be Careful* sticker.

"There," said Mma Ramotswe, wanting to point, but unable to disentangle her elbow from Mma Makutsi's rib cage.

"That's the car," said Charlie, swerving in his excitement. "That'll be her car, Mma."

"Don't park too close, Charlie," said Mma Makutsi. "You don't want her to see us."

Mma Ramotswe thought: And how could they possibly avoid being seen? Two women and a young man shoehorned into a cab meant for two, if not one, in a van listing markedly to the left and emitting, she now noticed, a small cloud of steam from its front. That was worrying, she thought, and made a mental note to draw Mr. J.L.B. Matekoni's attention to it, although she was loath to do so. He was looking for an excuse, she suspected, once again to urge her to retire the van and replace it with something more modern. She would have to resist that, because one did not lightly retire an old friend, which is what it would seem like to her.

As luck would have it, Charlie found a spot not far away that was in the process of being vacated by another driver, and the van fitted neatly into that. This afforded them a view of the Mercedes-Benz, but from such a distance that would allow them to slip out without it being too obvious, they hoped, that they were following the driver. Once the van was parked, Mma Ramotswe opened her door, not completely, but sufficiently to allow for a release of the pressure.

Charlie was gazing across the street, in the direction of the parked silver car. "Why does that sticker say *Be Careful?*" he asked. "You see it? It says *Be Careful*. That's all: *Be Careful*."

"That is good advice," said Mma Makutsi. "You have to be careful."

"About what?" asked Charlie.

Mma Makutsi was patient. "About everything, Charlie. You have to watch out these days." She half turned to Mma Ramotswe. It was still a bit difficult to move, even with the passenger door partly open. "That's good advice, don't you think, Mma? The sort of advice Charlie should listen to, wouldn't you say?"

"I am always careful," protested Charlie. "Always. Crossing the road. Coming to work. Going home. Careful, careful, careful."

"I'm sure you are, Charlie," Mma Ramotswe said. She stopped. They had parked facing a dry-cleaning depot. This had a door in the front and a large shop window through which they could see the counter and several large machines beyond it. A young woman had emerged from this door, holding a large folded plastic bag in which a dress was stored. As she came out into the light, the young woman blinked, shading her eyes from the low-angled rays of the sun. At that moment, her gaze met Mma Ramotswe's, and Mma Ramotswe knew that this was Nametso. She had never met her, and had no idea of her appearance, but she knew, almost instinctively, that this was the woman she was there to observe.

Nametso looked puzzled, evidently wondering about the odd combination in the van: the two women, one of them tradition-ally built, the other with large round spectacles—far too big for her face—and hints of a troublesome skin; and the young man with the rather loud shirt, staring at her as if he recognised her.

Mma Ramotswe looked away, whispering to the others, "Don't stare, don't stare. Just look somewhere else."

"She was staring at me, Mma," Charlie whispered. "She is the one who was staring."

"Now she has seen us," muttered Mma Makutsi. "How can we follow somebody who has seen us? We are finished, Mma Ramotswe."

But Mma Ramotswe was not one to give up so readily. She pointed out that there was no reason to suspect them of taking an undue interest in her. From her point of view, she said, they were just a van full of people who had probably come into town from some-where out in the bush and were gaping at everything they saw. They could be people who had perhaps never seen a dry-cleaner's place before and were marvelling at the machinery. Sometimes you saw that in town: people, particularly elderly people from outlying areas, would come into the city and be astonished by what they saw. You noticed them standing on street corners simply staring and wondering how all these people could be living in one place and going about their business like this. And where were the cattle? What was there for the cattle to eat here where the only grass seemed to be that grown in front of houses—which would have been heaven for cattle, if only they were allowed to eat it.

Nametso crossed the road and, as they expected, unlocked the silver Mercedes-Benz.

"You see," said Charlie. "I told you." He craned his neck. "I know that model. It is very expensive. One hundred and sixty-three horsepower. That's max. Automatic gearbox, one, two, three—"

"Yes, yes, Charlie," said Mma Makutsi. "But just concentrate. We have to get ready to follow."

Mma Ramotswe squeezed herself back into her share of the seat and, breathing in, just managed to get the door shut. On the other side of the road, the reversing lights of the silver Mercedes-Benz flicked on.

"See those lights," said Charlie. "They come on automatically, of course. And there's an extra one you can switch on if you really need to see what's behind you in the dark. There's a camera in the car too, you know, and—"

Mma Makutsi cut him short once more. "We do not need to hear all this, Charlie."

The Mercedes-Benz reversed out of its parking place. For a few moments it seemed as if the driver was hesitating, uncertain as to which way to go. Then the decision was made, and the car sped off down the road, heading away from the centre of town.

"Quick," urged Mma Makutsi. "We must not lose her, Charlie."

Charlie struggled with the gears, pushing Mma Makutsi's legs away from the lever. "It is very hard, Mma, if you are sitting like that."

Somehow Charlie managed to get the van under way. The other car, though, had almost disappeared, and Charlie had to coax the van's badly struggling engine to the limits of its capacity to keep up.

"Do you think she's noticed us?" asked Mma Makutsi.

Mma Ramotswe looked at the back of the Mercedes-Benz. "If she's looked in the mirror, perhaps. But people often don't."

By the traffic circle near the university gate, Nametso slowed down. It seemed for a few moments as if she was about to turn off to the left, but she did not, and continued to the far end of the road that skirted the university grounds. There were several large blocks of flats there, and it was through the gates of one of these buildings that the Mercedes now swung, braked sharply, and then came to a halt. Charlie slowed the van down to a snail's pace, keeping to the road outside. From there, they watched as Nametso got out of her car, retrieved her dry-cleaning, and walked the short distance into one of the flats.

"Now?" asked Charlie.

Mma Ramotswe told Charlie to park further down the road.

"This is not where she lives," said Mma Ramotswe. "Her mother told me she lived with some other people over near the railway station."

"So what is she doing here?" asked Charlie.

Mma Makutsi tapped the window. "I've been thinking," she said. "Some people have places where they live part of the time. They live there, but they don't live there all the time."

Mma Ramotswe waited.

"So I think this woman lives here," Mma Makutsi continued.

"She is leading a double life. She doesn't want anybody to know about her car. She doesn't want anybody to know about this flat."

Charlie whistled. "She is a big thief, then. She is definitely stealing diamonds. You can only have two lives if you're stealing something."

"Possibly," said Mma Ramotswe. She paused. "Of course, people who are leading two lives are usually very secretive. One of those lives will be led in the shadows, you know."

"So how are we going to find out?" asked Charlie.

Mma Ramotswe smiled. There were times when it was appropriate to quote Clovis Andersen, but there were also times when it seemed right to quote herself. Not that she would do that, of course, but she had always maintained that the best way of finding out about something was simply to ask somebody. There was always somebody who would have the information you needed, and, in just about every case, such a person would be happy to give it to you. It was just a question of finding out whom one should ask and then asking. It was no more complicated than that.

She smiled at Charlie. "We ask."

"Who do we ask, Mma?"

The answer to that was simple. "Who are the people who see everything that goes on, Charlie? Neighbours. They are the ones. Neighbours know everything, Charlie. And they are also usually the ones who are keenest to talk."

Mma Makutsi gestured towards the block of flats. "Over there, Mma?"

"Yes," said Mma Ramotswe. "There are plenty of neighbours over there, and I think that they will be keen to talk to us." She paused. Windows were open. A smell of distant cooking drifted over from the nearest of the flats. People were home, and of course they would talk—especially about a young woman who appeared to own a silver Mercedes-Benz and who had something to do with diamonds.

Mma Ramotswe opened her door and began to manoeuvre herself out of the van. Mr. J.L.B. Matekoni was right about at least one thing: a more modern van would not only be more reliable, but would have more room. "People have been becoming more traditionally built over recent years," he had pointed out. "And the people who make cars know that. They have made the seats much bigger, Mma. You would find that out if you let me buy you a new van."

He was right, but there was more to life than just having more room to spread out in. Having more room did not in itself make you happier; having something you loved did that, and she still loved her van, just as one might love a comfortable pair of shoes, or a scarf somebody gave you—somebody you had in turn loved very much—or a teacup from which you had drunk your tea for years and years. Such love did not go away when something new and shiny came along.

"We shall all go," she said. "I'll go and speak to the people in the flat on the left. Mma Makutsi, you take the neighbours in the flat upstairs, and Charlie . . ."

"But what do I say?" asked Charlie. "I can't just go up to their door and say, 'Tell me all about your neighbour, please.' They could say, 'What business is it of yours?' and tell me to go away."

Mma Ramotswe smiled. "You have a story, Charlie. You say you're looking for somebody and ask them if that person lives next door."

"Yes," said Mma Makutsi. "Then they'll say, 'Oh no, that person doesn't live there. That is a young woman called Nametso.'"

"And then?" asked Charlie.

Mma Makutsi took off her spectacles and gave them a cursory wipe. "Then you say, 'Oh, I think I know her. Is she the one from Molepolole?'"

Mma Ramotswe joined in. "Mma Makutsi is right," she reassured Charlie. "It is what Clovis Andersen calls routine arm-work."

Mma Makutsi corrected her: "Leg-work, Mma. He calls it leg-work."

"It is all the same," said Mma Ramotswe. "Arm-work, leg-work— it is all the same thing. It is what we do, Charlie, and I think you are getting better and better at it."

He beamed with pleasure. It was so easy to make Charlie happy, thought Mma Ramotswe. Indeed, it was so easy to make anybody happy. All that was required was a kind word or two—a kind word that cost nothing, and yet could have such a profound effect.

"Yes," she said. "You are doing very well, Charlie."

His smile broadened. "You are like my mother, Mma Ramotswe," he said. And then, becoming aware of Mma Makutsi's gaze upon him, he added, "And you, Mma Makutsi, you are like my auntie."

"Thank you, Charlie," said Mma Makutsi—a bit primly, thought Mma Ramotswe, but then he had described her as his aunt, and aunts, of all people, could be allowed to be prim.

But Mma Ramotswe thought: this young man is not yet there. She was not quite sure where *there* was, but it was the place that he wanted to get to, a place where he would not be poor, where he would be able to feel proud of himself, a place where he would be some-thing. He might get there, but it would be something of a miracle if he did, given the odds stacked against him.

CHAPTER TWELVE

MMA BOKO DISAPPROVES

MMA BOKO LOOKED at Mma Ramotswe over a pair of tortoise-shell half-moon glasses.

"I like your glasses, Mma," said Mma Ramotswe.

Mma Boko removed them self-consciously. She giggled. "They are just for reading, Mma. You know how it is? They are printing everything much smaller these days. All the time they are making it smaller."

Mma Ramotswe smiled. "Or our eyes are changing, Mma. They are becoming tired and they think, This is much smaller now."

Mma Boko replaced her glasses. "There are many things I am happy *not* to see," she said. "When I look around town these days, I see many things that I think should not be there—many things that I do not like."

Mma Ramotswe knew what she meant. "Oh, you are right, Mma—you are very right. There are things that you would never have seen in the past." And there were things that you would have seen in the past that you would never see today—and thank heavens for that. There had been cruelties and injustices that would never be tolerated today.

But that was not what interested Mma Boko; disapproval is less effort than approval, and, for those who disapprove, twice as satisfying.

"I'll give you an example, Mma," said Mma Boko. "I'll give you an example of something that will shock you."

Mma Ramotswe said nothing. She wanted to tell Mma Boko that nothing would shock her, as in her profession she had seen just about everything. But then she realised that she had not; the bad behaviour with which the No. 1 Ladies' Detective Agency was concerned was not really all that bad. They saw selfishness and greed; they saw infidelity and other forms of disloyalty; they saw vanity, and its cousin, insecurity. They did not see the major cruelties, nor the great frauds and dishonesties.

"Tell me, Mma," she said.

Mma Boko drew in her breath. "You know that place?" she began.

Mma Ramotswe frowned. "What place, Mma? There are many places."

Mma Boko waved her hand vaguely in the direction of the Tlokweng Road. "That place they call River-something. That place where there are shops."

Mma Ramotswe nodded. "I know the shops. I go there for groceries. That supermarket—"

Mma Boko raised a finger. "That supermarket, Mma—yes, right there. I was there with my friend Mma Magadi—you'll know her, I think."

Again, Mma Ramotswe frowned. Mma Magadi? Somewhere in the back of her memory, the name chimed with something. But that was the problem: so many names chimed with something, and yet it was impossible to establish what that something was. "I'm not sure,

Mma," she replied. "The name is a bit familiar, but . . . but, I'm not sure."

HER HESITATION was in part occasioned by a concern that denying knowledge of somebody might give offence. Mma Ramotswe was reasonably well known in Gaborone—not because she had courted prominence in any way, but because people drove past her business sign on the Tlokweng Road (one could hardly miss it) and they were naturally curious as to who these No. 1 detective ladies might be. And then there had been the occasional article in the paper, including one entitled THE ONE HUNDRED AND FIFTY MOST INFLUENTIAL WOMEN IN BOTSWANA (PART ONE). When Mma Makutsi had spotted that one morning as they were drinking tea in the office, she had let out a whoop of delight. "Look, Mma!" she exclaimed. "Look! We are in the list of . . ." She consulted the article. "The one hundred and fifty most influential women in the world."

Mma Ramotswe had peered over Mma Makutsi's shoulder. "In Botswana, Mma," she had corrected her.

"Yes, that's what I said, Mma. The one hundred and fifty most influential women in Botswana."

Mma Ramotswe had not pressed the point, but as her eye ran down the columns in the double-page spread, she realised that there were several reasons why Mma Makutsi's delight might soon turn sour.

Mma Makutsi pointed to a line in the article. "There it is, Mma. Number ninety-seven. The No. 1 Ladies' Detective Agency . . ." She trailed off.

"They always get these things wrong, Mma," Mma Ramotswe said hurriedly. "I'm sure that they meant to mention you too."

"Ninety-seven," muttered Mma Makutsi.

Mma Ramotswe swallowed hard. That was doubly unfortunate. If anybody had the right to the number ninety-seven, then it was Mma Makutsi, with her unassailable claim to have climbed to the heights of ninety-seven in the final examinations of the Botswana Secretarial College. And yet here it was on the printed page: *Number Ninety-Seven, The No. 1 Ladies' Detective Agency is the creation of Precious Ramotswe, Mochudi-born private investigator and solver of those oh-so-difficult mysteries! Move over, Mr. Sherlock Holmes, and let the lady from the Tlokweng Road get to the bottom of things!*

Mma Ramotswe was immediately apologetic. "These journalists," she expostulated. "They are always getting things wrong! Making things up! Writing such nonsense about things they know nothing about." She paused, dismayed at the only-too-apparent failure of her words to pour the necessary oil on these troubled waters. "And here they are—forgetting to write about you, when they must have meant to include you."

No, Mma Makutsi was not to be that easily pacified. "There is no mention of me," she said. "I am clearly a person with no influence."

"Oh, you mustn't say that, Mma. This is a ridiculous piece of nonsense. They make these things up to fill the pages when there is no news—when the politicians have all gone back to their villages and nobody is saying anything for the newspapers to write about." She watched Mma Makutsi, who remained unconvinced.

"Look," Mma Ramotswe continued. "This list is no use at all, Mma. Who is one of the most influential ladies we know? It is Mma Potokwane, without any doubt at all. But is she in this list? Do we see her name here? No, we do not."

Mma Makutsi snatched the paper from Mma Ramotswe, peering at the list of names. Suddenly she pointed indignantly at the now-crumpled sheet. "Oh yes, Mma? Oh yes? What is this here, then? Number eighty-one: Mma Silvia Potokwane. See? And just in case they are talking about another Mma Potokwane altogether, what does it say? It says, *Mma Silvia Potokwane is the well-known matron who has looked after hundreds of children over the years. She does not live in a shoe, this lady, and she certainly knows what to do!*"

Mma Makutsi lowered the paper and fixed Mma Ramotswe with an accusing stare. "I think that is definitely our Mma Potokwane, Mma. I think there is no mistake about that."

Mma Ramotswe was silent. The situation was irretrievable, she decided. But there was more to come, and this was heralded by a sharp intake of breath from Mma Makutsi as she glanced once more at the newspaper. For a moment she appeared to struggle, and then, wordlessly, she thrust the paper at Mma Ramotswe, her finger jabbing at a place on the list where, with utter shamelessness, was to be seen the name of Violet Sephotho, at number fourteen—*fourteen!*—with the following encomium: *A lady whose fingers are in every pie, Violet Sephotho B.A. is the mover and shaker who puts Gaborone on the map! Onward and upward goes this lady of the future.*

Mma Ramotswe's jaw sagged. Mma Makutsi had every right to feel outraged. This was an abomination.

"B.A.?" shouted Mma Makutsi. "Since when is Violet a B.A.? What did she get in the final examinations of the Botswana Secretarial College? I can tell you, Mma. Barely fifty per cent. And now she calls herself a B.A."

"Mover and shaker," groaned Mma Ramotswe. "I have never liked that expression, Mma. Now I like it even less."

"This country is finished," Mma Makutsi wailed. "If this sort of thing can appear in the papers, then this country is finished, Mma. Over. Finished."

BUT NOW, here was Mma Boko starting some story about a Mma Magadi and the supermarket.

"No, perhaps you don't know her," said Mma Boko. "But you might recognise her, because she is, like you, a large lady, Mma. She is larger, perhaps, and her children are all quite large too. Not tall, you understand, but large this way—out to the side and to the front. And at the back too. She has five of them, and I was in the supermarket when she came in with them. All five."

"That cannot be easy," said Mma Ramotswe. "Feeding five children will be a full-time job, I think."

Mma Boko agreed. She had had three children, she said, and although they were all grown up and away from home now, she still felt exhausted. Just think about the effort that had been required to get meals on the table, day in, day out, year after year. "People don't always know what it's like," she said. "They forget how hard it is to be a mother."

"And a wife," said Mma Ramotswe.

"Yes, and a wife, because a husband is just like a child in many cases, Mma. Not all the time, of course, but often. People forget that."

Mma Ramotswe waited for the conversation to continue. Sympathy had been expressed for this mother of five, but was that the point of her having been mentioned? Had she been the victim of some outrage that Mma Boko was now to report, or was there another reason for her appearance in this discussion?

It now became clear. "Having five children is no excuse," said Mma Boko. She spoke firmly. "No, Mma, even if you have five children, you are not entitled to take them into the supermarket and feed them there."

Mma Ramotswe sighed. "Ah, Mma. I have seen that sort of

thing happen. I have seen people sneaking a bite of something in the supermarket—and then not buying it." She paused. "Of course, sometimes it is very tempting. They put this food in front of you, and sometimes temptation is very strong."

Mma Boko was staring at her, and Mma Ramotswe quickly qualified her remark. "Not that you should give in to it, of course. I would never say that you should give in to temptation."

And yet, and yet . . . There were occasions on which she gave in to temptation, in spite of every resolution she might make not to yield. Doughnuts were such an occasion—and fat cakes too. And Mma Potokwane's fruit cake, come to think of it. And those chocolate bars with coconut in the middle. There were many, many temptations in one's way on the road through life, and one would not be human if one *never* succumbed.

"You are right, Mma," said Mma Boko. "When I am faced with temptation, I am happy to say that I do not yield. Not one inch, Mma."

Mma Ramotswe sighed again. "You are fortunate, Mma. You must be very strong. Sometimes I think that I am one of the weaker sisters. In fact, I know I am. Fat cakes, you see . . ."

"Then you must get the Lord to help you," said Mma Boko. "He is well aware of fat cakes."

There had been the feeding of the five thousand, Mma Ramotswe remembered. Had fat cakes been involved in that? She stopped herself. That was disrespectful. She glanced at Mma Boko. She suspected that she was as weak as the next person, in spite of all this talk of being above temptation.

"There is a very good reverend," Mma Boko said. "He is the one who helps people overcome temptation. I am lucky that I have met him."

Something chimed, but Mma Ramotswe was not sure what it

was. *A very good reverend . . .* But she wanted to get on with her conversation with Mma Boko, and it seemed that they would have to dispose of Mma Magadi first. "So this lady allowed her children to eat in the supermarket," she said. "That is not right. It is stealing."

"Not only that," Mma Boko continued. "That was shocking enough, Mma, to see this mother telling her children to eat things while she kept a look-out for the supermarket staff. That's a very bad example to a child. But there was something else. I had to go and inform the cashier, Mma. I went and told her that there were five children all eating things."

Mma Ramotswe nodded. "That was the right thing to do, Mma."

Mma Boko shook her head. "You would think they would be pleased. You would think that she would have said, 'Thank you for this information—we shall attend to it immediately.' You would think she would have said that, and instead, what did she say? She said, 'Mind your own business.' That is what she said—her exact words. *Mind your own business.*"

"But that is terrible, Mma. She should have done something."

"Exactly," said Mma Boko. "But that is what we are coming to these days, Mma. People don't care."

Mma Ramotswe allowed a few moments to pass, and then she said, "Next door, Mma. When I knocked on your door a little while ago and told you that I am a private detective wanting to find out about something, that was about next door actually."

Mma Boko said that this did not surprise her. "When you said you were a private detective, I assumed that. I thought you would be acting for that man's wife. And that is why I have been happy to speak to you."

"What man, Mma?"

"That man next door. He has a wife, you see, and he also has that young woman—that shameless young woman."

Mma Ramotswe coaxed out the facts slowly and skilfully. The flat was rented, Mma Boko told her, by a wealthy businessman— "He has many shops, Mma, and they say that he even owns a small mine somewhere up north." The businessman was married, and had three children, she believed. "Three innocent children, Mma, and the wife is innocent too—all innocent. But this businessman—I have never actually seen him, Mma, but I have been told all these things about him—this businessman likes young women. Men, you know, Mma, they are all like that. He has set this young woman up in this flat, and he lets her use that silver car too. A young woman—driving around in a car like that, Mma. That is very bad."

At the end, Mma Ramotswe thanked her for her frankness. Once again, her theory had been proved: if you wanted to get information about something, you had only to ask. Of course, you might get a lot of additional material, as she had just done: information about bad behaviour in supermarkets, for instance, and techniques for resisting temptation. She thought about that again. Something had been said about a reverend, she remembered, and that made her wonder.

BACK IN THE VAN, squashed up against one another once more, each revealed their results.

"Now, Charlie," Mma Ramotswe began. "You go first. You tell us what you found out."

"Nothing," said Charlie. "There was just an old man in the flat. He said that he never saw what was going on outside, as he had lost his glasses six months ago and had not bought a new pair yet. He said that he probably wouldn't bother, because there was nothing worth looking at any more."

Mma Makutsi laughed. "Some people lack curiosity, don't they?"

"He told me that he used to be a train driver," Charlie went on.

"As long as he had his glasses then," said Mma Ramotswe. "You wouldn't want to lose your glasses when you were driving a train. And you, Mma Makutsi—did you find out anything?"

Mma Makutsi had the air of one who harboured private information that she was only too eager to impart. "I found out something very interesting," she said.

"That's good," said Mma Ramotswe, with the air of one who already knew a secret about to be revealed.

"The flat I went to is occupied by a divorced woman," she said. "She is very lonely, I think, because she was keen to speak to me. I told her I was a detective and she said that she had thought of being a detective herself, but had never done anything about it."

"Ha!" Charlie interjected. "There are many people who think they can be detectives. I find that when I tell them what I do."

"Apprentice detective," Mma Makutsi said.

Charlie ignored this. "I tell them that I am a detective and they say, 'I could be that too. I'm very good at solving mysteries. I know what's what.' That sort of thing."

"This woman," said Mma Ramotswe. "What did she tell you, Mma?"

"She told me her life story," answered Mma Makutsi. "She came from Palapye originally. She went to a commercial college up in Francistown—those are not very high-level places, you know; they do book-keeping and things like that. No shorthand." She paused and gave a disapproving look, as might any graduate, *magna cum laude,* of the Botswana Secretarial College. "Anyway, she went to this college place and then came down to Gaborone. Then she met a pilot with an air charter company. You know those planes that go up to Maun and into the Kalahari?"

"A bush pilot," said Charlie. "They like landing on those little airstrips out in the bush. You have to watch out for those guys."

Mma Ramotswe looked puzzled. "Why is that, Charlie?"

"They think they're the tops," Charlie replied. "They think all the girls are there just for them."

Mma Ramotswe smiled. The uncharitable might say the same thing about young mechanics, but she would not.

"She met this pilot," Mma Makutsi continued. "They got married and she was very happy. Then she found out that he had women in all sorts of places. One up in Maun, one in Francistown, even one over the border in Angola. Wherever he landed, there would be a woman waiting for him. Can you imagine that? Can you just imagine it?"

Charlie closed his eyes. Mma Ramotswe thought he looked a bit dreamy, but she said nothing.

"This poor lady has been single since then," Mma Makutsi went on. "She has a job with one of the banks. She is a book-keeper, and she likes the job, but her boss is a woman who does not like other women to succeed. She will not recommend her for promotion."

Mma Ramotswe disapproved of that. Removing the ladder by which you had climbed up was a common enough practice—and a particularly nasty one, she felt. "That is very bad," she said. "Everybody is entitled to a chance. Everybody."

Charlie was listening. Yes, he thought. Yes.

"She gave me the full story," Mma Makutsi said. "It was only after she had finished this long tale that I was able to ask her about downstairs. And then, oh my goodness, did I get it all then! She does not like Nametso, Mma Ramotswe. She does not like her."

"Why?" asked Mma Ramotswe.

"Maybe it's the Mercedes-Benz," ventured Charlie. "I have found that many people do not like people with Mercedes-Benzes because they would like one themselves and do not have one."

Mma Makutsi nodded her agreement. "You're right there, Charlie. She went on and on about that. She said it was wrong for a young woman like that to have a silver Mercedes-Benz when there are many people much older than she is who have no car at all. She was very cross about that. So I asked her whether she had a car, and she said that her car had broken down and it was going to cost a lot to get it repaired. She said it needed a new gearbox."

Charlie winced. "That's not good news. A new gearbox is always expensive. If the gearbox went in this van, Mma Ramotswe . . ."

Mma Ramotswe made such a gesture as might forfend disaster. "I hope that doesn't happen, Charlie."

"I'm not saying it will, Mma," Charlie replied. "But in a vehicle as old as this, it's always a possibility."

Mma Ramotswe steered the conversation back to the woman in the flat. "She does not like Nametso. Maybe it was the Mercedes-Benz—"

"Not only that," Mma Makutsi interjected. "And I really can't blame her, Mma—and you won't either, once you hear what I have to tell you."

Mma Ramotswe waited.

"Nametso is seeing two men. The divorced lady says she hasn't seen much of them, but she is certain that there are two different men."

Mma Ramotswe frowned. This complicated matters. "And that was all she said about her?"

Mma Makutsi shrugged. "Yes. She did not know who they were." She turned to Mma Ramotswe. "What did you find out?" she asked.

Mma Ramotswe hesitated. Then she replied, "Same as you, Mma. I found out she has a male friend—a sugar daddy, it seems."

Charlie let out a whistle. It was a whistle of admiration, Mma Ramotswe thought, under the disguise of a whistle of surprise. "She's a naughty girl, this Nametso," he said. "Wow! Bad, bad!"

Mma Makutsi looked at him indignantly. "And what about the

men?" she asked. "What about the men, Charlie? Aren't they naughty too?"

"It's different for men," muttered Charlie.

Mma Makutsi rounded on him. "Did you say 'It's different for men,' Charlie? Did my ears deceive me?" She quivered with rage. "Is that how you think, after all this . . ." She floundered, but only briefly. "After all this *progress* we have made? After all the lessons that men have been telling us they have learned—nodding their heads and saying, 'Yes, yes, we understand and we shall try to behave better in the future'—after all that, and secretly they are thinking, We can still have a good time, though, and women will always be there to cook for us and make us feel better."

Charlie pursed his lips.

"Did you hear that, Mma Ramotswe?" asked Mma Makutsi. "Charlie said it's different for men. It seems that men can run around with all sorts of ladies and nobody will criticise them for it. One girlfriend, two girlfriends, even three—it's all the same. It's the way men are."

Mma Ramotswe looked reproachfully at Charlie. "I'm sure you didn't mean that, Charlie," she said gently.

Charlie looked abashed. "No, maybe not, Mma. It's just sometimes words slip out. Many men have that problem, Mma—words slip out when men forget what they're not meant to say."

"Well, let's not argue about it," said Mma Ramotswe. "The important thing is this: we have learned something about Nametso. The question now is, does this explain why she has suddenly dropped her mother? That's the question, I think."

"What do you think, Mma Ramotswe?" Charlie asked.

"I think it is guilt," said Mma Ramotswe. "I think she is ashamed of herself and does not want to see her mother because of that. She doesn't want her mother to find out where she is living—how the flat is being paid for by a married man. She does not want her mother to see her driving around in her silver Mercedes-Benz because the mother will then ask, 'Where did you get that car from?' That is what mothers think when they see their children in Mercedes-Benzes. It is only natural."

"What do we do, then?" asked Mma Makutsi.

Mma Ramotswe did not answer immediately. A minute or two later, though, she said, "I have no idea, Mma. No idea at all. Do you?"

"No," said Mma Makutsi.

"Charlie?" asked Mma Ramotswe.

"I think we tell the mother the truth," he answered. "We tell her and then she will know why her daughter is behaving as she is."

Mma Makutsi was worried. "I don't feel that will help that poor lady," she said. "Perhaps we should think about things before we do anything."

"That won't change anything, Mma," said Charlie.

"Perhaps not," Mma Ramotswe said. "But then there is never any harm in thinking, Charlie. You never know what will come from thinking."

CHAPTER THIRTEEN

A BIG THING OR A SMALL THING

MR. J.L.B. MATEKONI was late home that evening. Mr. Lefa Matabane, a regular client, had kept him in the garage, complaining that the engine of his car, a dispirited blue saloon that Mr. J.L.B. Matekoni had nursed for more than five years, was making strange sounds when it went above a certain speed.

"This car has its sneaky side," said Mr. Matabane. "You know that sort of car, Rra? A good car at heart, but with what these days they call issues."

Mr. J.L.B. Matekoni smiled. "Many cars have issues, Rra. That is why I am in business here. If cars didn't have issues, then there would be no Tlokweng Road Speedy Motors."

"And you would be doing something else, J.L.B.?"

He did not like the abbreviation. There were one or two people who called him J.L.B.—uninvited—and it grated. He was tempted to say, "I have issues with being called J.L.B.," but was too mild to do so. Instead he said, "I have never thought of doing anything else. I think I could only work with cars."

Mr. Matabane nodded. "That is what a true artist says. My dentist says that too. He says he would be very unhappy if there were no teeth. Teeth are everything to him. It is always teeth, teeth, teeth."

Mr. J.L.B. Matekoni looked at his watch. "Your car, Rra? This noise?"

"It is a sort of groan, I think. Everything is going normally, and then there is this groan when we get up to eighty kilometres. Groan. All the time, as if it has a sore stomach. Just like that. And it stays until the speed drops right back."

Mr. J.L.B. Matekoni stared at the car. There came a time with vehicles, and a mechanic usually knew when that time was. The problem, though, was that the owner of the vehicle often did not. There had been that old people carrier that Mma Potokwane had used to transport children—that had reached its time well before it was eventually scrapped; closer to home, indeed *at* home, there was Mma Ramotswe's tiny white van; and now there was Mr. Lefa Matabane's blue saloon with its bald tyres, its cracked upholstery, and its flaking paint that he had jokingly referred to as car dandruff—a comment that had not gone down well with Mr. Lefa Matabane, who had sighed and looked at him reproachfully.

All of these cars, he thought, had simply reached their time and should be allowed to go. We did that with people. A person who was very old and very tired, who did not want to linger too long, would be allowed to sit outside the house in the morning sun and dream about the past and would not be made to run about and do things that nobody of that age would want to do. Why would people not do the same with cars?

"I think your car may be tired," he said to Mr. Matabane. "Cars reach a point, Rra—"

He was not allowed to finish. "But it still goes, J.L.B.," came the retort. "If a car goes, why get rid of it? This car has been going for a long time, right from the beginning. It was over in Swaziland, you know. Before it came to Botswana. It gave good service there to a man in Manzini. It was a well-known car there, I believe."

And so there had been no alternative but to set out with Mr. Lefa Matabane for a test drive, which was inconclusive, because the evening traffic, with everybody wanting to get home, had prevented them from reaching the speed at which the groan would appear. The car had been left at the garage, with a promise that it would be looked at again the following day. Mr. J.L.B. Matekoni had been required to drive Mr. Lefa Matabane back home, and had been cajoled there to come inside and meet his brother-in-law, who was on a visit from Mahalapye, and who had gone on at some length about a car he had almost bought that had turned out to be stolen. It was a long story, and in spite of frequent glances at his watch, Mr. J.L.B. Matekoni had been unable to extricate himself for over half an hour.

Mma Ramotswe understood, of course. And it was not inconvenient for her, because there was rather more to do in the evenings now that there was a young child in the house. The helper, whose name was Pretty, had settled into the room in the back yard and had proved to be easy company and helpful in the kitchen. She was liked, too, by Puso and Motholeli, and they had all cooked their own dinner that evening, leaving Mma Ramotswe free to repair some of the clothing Daisy had brought with her.

By the time that Mr. J.L.B. Matekoni returned, the children were already in bed. Pretty had settled Daisy, who was tired and dropped off to sleep almost immediately, before she herself had taken a plate of food back to her own room. She had been shy about eating in the kitchen—"It is your place, Mma"—but Mma Ramotswe hoped that this would pass. "If you are with us, Pretty, then this is your place too." But Pretty had demurred—"You have a husband, Mma. You will want to be with your husband."

"She's very easy, that Pretty," Mma Ramotswe said to Mr. J.L.B. Matekoni as they sat down together on the verandah before dinner. This was their time together, and Mma Ramotswe had always cherished it—a time when the day's events could be talked about and put in perspective. It was a time, too, for silences—not long ones, or heavy ones, but silences during which they could think about what had just been said, or sometimes about what might have been said, but, for some reason, had not been.

"Daisy," said Mr. J.L.B. Matekoni. And then he sighed.

"Yes," said Mma Ramotswe.

"I'm not sure . . ."

Mma Ramotswe said nothing, and after a short silence, Mr. J.L.B. Matekoni continued, "You see . . ."

"Yes, Rra?"

"It's just that . . ."

And then silence, and he asked himself, How could I? How could I close my heart to that child? The answer was unspoken, but was as clear and unambiguous as if it had been announced at the top of his voice, or written in clouds across the sky: You cannot. You simply cannot, because life was full of tears and suffering, and if it was given to you to do something—anything, really—a big thing or a small thing, to make that suffering easier, then how could you refuse to do it? How could you dodge that moment? So he said, "I hope she is happy."

Mma Ramotswe's heart went out to him. This was the man she loved above all other men—apart from her father, of course, the late Obed Ramotswe. Not that there was any rivalry between them, nor conflict in their claims. Her father had never got to know Mr. J.L.B. Matekoni, but she knew that he would have approved of him because they both stood for all that was best in Botswana. If only he could come back—even for the shortest time, even a day—so that she could show him the man she had married and tell him how good he had been to her. Perhaps he knew, of course; perhaps he could see what was happening from that other Botswana where the late people were—that place of light and happiness and unfailing, gentle rain.

Rain . . . There were people, she knew, who did not like rain, who called rain bad or a nuisance; people for whom rainy weather was a curse to be endured. It was hard to believe that anybody could think that way, but she had been led to believe that in those far-off places, this is how people thought.

"I have been thinking of rain," she said now, because there was nothing more to be said about Daisy.

"Ah, rain," said Mr. J.L.B. Matekoni. "Well, we need rain, Mma. We would be blessed if there were rain soon." He shook his head. He had been out at the dam from which the town drew its water and had seen that it was reduced to a few disheartened puddles, and all about there was dry, caked mud, cracked by the sun.

"We are very fortunate that they decided to build that pipeline," Mr. J.L.B. Matekoni continued.

"Even if it turned out to be a bit leaky."

"Even so, Mma. It has saved us."

It had, she thought. The pipeline that brought water down from the far north of the country had allowed so much of their precious water to leak out, but it had still saved them from disaster.

"But still we need rain," she said. And then she changed the subject again and began to tell him about the day's uncomfortable discovery.

"You remember Calviniah's daughter, Rra? We talked about her."

"The one who works in the diamond office? The one who is ignoring her mother?"

She nodded. "She is treating her very cruelly. But now I think I have found the reason."

He looked interested. "It is unusual for a daughter to be like that. Sometimes a son won't care about family, but daughters usually do. So what lies behind it, Mma?"

Mma Ramotswe told him of their discoveries. He shook his head disapprovingly as she related her conversation with the neighbour, but when the second man was mentioned, his disapproval prompted him to groan. "That's very shocking, Mma. Two boyfriends. I have never heard of such a thing. Never!"

Mma Ramotswe expressed her surprise. "But, Rra, that is what they call two-timing. It is very common—surely you have heard of it."

"No, Mma, I have not come across it personally. I have heard of married men who have had a girlfriend—and I believe there is a lot of that going on—but this—"

Mma Ramotswe interrupted him. "Hold on, Mr. J.L.B. Matekoni," she said. "This is exactly the same thing."

"No, it's different, Mma. This is a woman with two boyfriends."

Mma Ramotswe was patient. Mr. J.L.B. Matekoni was an old-fashioned man, and she should not be surprised if he were to express old-fashioned views, but she could not let such double standards go unrebuked—at least gently. Mma Ramotswe did not approve of the strident hectoring of others that some people now engaged in, but she did believe that you could tactfully let people know that the world had moved on.

"No, Rra," she began. "We must expect the same standards from both men and women. Men cannot say there is one rule for them and another rule for women. We are all bound by the same rules these days."

"But you do not expect a woman to have two boyfriends," protested Mr. J.L.B. Matekoni.

"Then you must not expect a man to have two girlfriends," Mma Ramotswe countered. "We must treat men and women equally."

"Are you saying there is no difference between men and women?" asked Mr. J.L.B. Matekoni.

"I am not saying that, Rra."

He was smiling. It was a serious discussion, but he was nonetheless amused by it. Women were always insisting that no distinction should be made, but who did they turn to if there was some hard piece of physical work to be done? To men, he told himself. And if there was noise outside at night that needed investigating, then who was sent out to look into it? Who had to take the risk of coming face-to-face with a leopard, or even a lion? Men. That is what he thought. Men were still expected to do things that women were reluctant to do.

"I know that women do not think very highly of men these days," Mr. J.L.B. Matekoni continued. "I know that they think men are useless, Mma."

Mma Ramotswe denied this vigorously. "I do *not* think that," she said. "I am not one of those women who run down men."

Mr. J.L.B. Matekoni knew that this was true. Mma Ramotswe liked men, and was kind to them, just as she was kind to everyone. But there were women, he was sure of it, who seemed to enjoy belittling men. And it seemed to him that these women were allowed to say disparaging things about men, whereas men were definitely not permitted to say such things about women. Only the other day a member of the legislative assembly—a man—had found himself in terrible trouble for having said a political rival—a junior government minister—should go back to cooking in her kitchen. He had been heavily criticised for this—and rightly so, thought Mr. J.L.B. Matekoni—but there had been no criticism of a female politician who had recently expressed the view that girls were doing better at high school than boys because they were more intelligent. "Boys can be very stupid," she had said. "They are good at mak-

ing noise and disturbing the class—they are not so good at learning things and writing examinations." That was a double standard,
thought Mr. J.L.B. Matekoni, and he was fed up with people saying
unpleasant things about men and not being pulled up on it.

It was a complex issue—and a fraught one. But on one thing,
at least, Mma Ramotswe and Mr. J.L.B. Matekoni agreed: they did
not want the country torn apart by a war of accusation and counter-
accusation between men and women—an argument that seemed to
have made so many other countries unhappy with themselves. How
can you have a peaceful country where one half of the population
thinks that the other is wrong, or hostile, or determined to do them
down? What better recipe for unhappiness was there than that?

They skirted round the question of double standards. "The important question," Mma Ramotswe said, "is this: Is this the reason why
Nametso is avoiding her mother?"

Mr. J.L.B. Matekoni was not long in answering. "I think so," he
said. "If you do something that you know your mother will not like,
what do you do? You keep her away from the thing that will disturb
her. And you say to yourself: I am going to lead my life without her
poking her nose into my affairs. That is what you do, Mma."

"And that is what has happened here, Rra? Is that what you
think?"

"It is exactly what has happened," he said, adding, "I think."

She asked him what she should do. Should she tell Calviniah
that her daughter was seeing two men? How did one put that tactfully? Did you say, "Your daughter is being very wise, Mma. If you
want to avoid being left with one boyfriend, make sure that you have
a spare one all the time"? That was one way of conveying the information, but she was not sure that it would make much difference to
the recipient. No parent likes to hear that sort of news about their
offspring.

Mr. J.L.B. Matekoni thought for a while before he gave his answer. When he spoke, his opinion was firm. "You do not tell her anything about this, Mma Ramotswe. That is my advice to you. Stay quiet. Forget that you ever found this out about this Nametso lady. Say nothing, Mma."

She asked him why.

"Because it will not help for her to know this about her daughter. It will only make it worse if the mother comes along and chides her for carrying on with men."

"Why, Rra? Why will it make it worse?"

"Because the young woman will be angry with her mother. She will tell her to mind her own business."

As she considered this answer, Mma Ramotswe suddenly had a moment of epiphany. Yes, that would explain it. It was obvious, once one came to think of it.

"I think I know what to do," she said. "I think it is clear now."

He waited for her to explain.

"When a child behaves badly," Mma Ramotswe said, "it is often because it wants attention. That is so, don't you think, Rra?"

He shrugged. "I am not a great expert in these things, Mma. Usually it is women who know why children do the things they do."

"Well, I think that is true," Mma Ramotswe said. "Children behave badly because their parents are not giving them the attention they want. So the child thinks: If I do something bad, then at least my mother or my father will *have* to look at me."

Mr. J.L.B. Matekoni looked out at the darkening garden. The last rays of sun had gone now, and there was only a faint glow left in the sky. "But if she wanted her mother to see what she was doing, she would have told her about it. How can she expect to get her mother's attention if the mother has no idea what she's doing?"

"That is a very difficult question, Rra."

He nodded. "Well, what's the answer?"

Mma Ramotswe had a cup of red bush tea on the table beside her. She reached for this, but she had let it become cold, and so she put it down without taking a sip.

"What if the mother does know?" she asked.

"But you said that she's avoiding her mother. That is why I thought that Calviniah wouldn't know."

Mma Ramotswe nodded. "Perhaps, Rra. Perhaps. But what if she *does* know and doesn't want me to know that she knows? What if it is the mother who is ashamed of the daughter? What if Calviniah wants me to do something, but cannot bring herself to tell me what her daughter is up to?"

Mr. J.L.B. Matekoni sighed. This was becoming too complicated for him. He was on firm ground when it came to mechanical issues and the like, but he felt that the sort of complexities with which Mma Ramotswe had to concern herself in her work were sometimes beyond him. "Who can tell, Mma?" he said at last.

They lapsed into silence. A bird flew past the house, a late returner to the safety of its branch. Mma Ramotswe smiled to herself, a memory triggered. As a child, she had walked one evening with her father in the bush on the edge of Mochudi, a place of thorn trees and scrub grass, criss-crossed by meandering paths. Cattle walked that way, and somewhere in the distance there was the sound of cattle bells. The sun had set, but there were a few precious minutes of light left—a time when the sky was still pale with the day's last moments. And a pair of guinea fowl had suddenly clattered up in front of them, fussing and anxious, and had flown up into the branches of a nearby tree. Her father had said—and she remembered his words—"Night is not always a friend, my darling." It was a strange thing for him to say, and it was equally strange that she should remember his words with such clarity after all these years. But she nurtured any memory of that great man, her father, tended it as one might tend a delicate plant; always, forever.

She wondered what Mr. J.L.B. Matekoni was thinking about. She had reflected in the past on how two lives might be led as one, but only on the outside; on the inside very different thoughts might be in the minds of husband and wife. Was he thinking right now, for instance, of something somebody had said to him at the garage? Or of some mechanical problem that had not been resolved that day and would have to be dealt with the following morning? Or was he thinking of something altogether different? Money? Cattle? Or rain, perhaps, because everybody was thinking of rain now, so great was their longing.

"I don't want to disturb you," she said quietly. "You may be thinking of something important."

He laughed. "I am not thinking of anything very much, Mma. Just my dinner."

"Is that what men think about?" she asked playfully. "Mma Potokwane says it is. She says that men think of meat all the time. Steak. That is what she says."

"Some of the time, maybe," said Mr. J.L.B. Matekoni. "But I was wondering when we would be having dinner tonight." He glanced at his watch and then, becoming aware that she had noticed, he looked apologetic. "Although I am still happy to talk about this lady with her two boyfriends—and to tell you what I think you should do."

She was pleased. She wanted his view on what was to her an uncomfortable choice.

"I would do nothing," he said. "Calviniah is not a proper paying client, Mma. She is a lady who is unhappy because her daughter is being unkind to her."

She nodded. Calviniah was not a client—that was true enough—and yet she was a friend, even if one with whom she had lost touch.

"Because," Mr. J.L.B. Matekoni continued, drawing out the word as if to give himself time to think of what was to follow, "because, Mma, there is so much unhappiness in the world, and can the No. 1 Ladies' Detective Agency deal with all of it? I do not think so, Mma Ramotswe." He shook his head sadly. Mma Ramotswe, for all her talent, for all her generosity of spirit, could not deal with all that unhappiness—just as he could not rectify all the mechanical problems that beset the world. Everywhere, all the time, there were cars making peculiar noises, cars begging for a change of oil, cars listing to one side or another because of faulty suspension—oh, it hurt the head just to think of all those unattended mechanical faults—and yet Tlokweng Road Speedy Motors could not, on its own, bring an end to all of that.

"No," he concluded. "No, Mma. You cannot. You should think of other things now, and leave that young woman to lead her life in the way in which she wants to. Ladies who have two boyfriends will eventually trip up over one of them and learn their lesson. She will eventually call one of them by the other's name, or do something like that, and then there will be trouble." He paused. "And the poor mother will be there, I suppose, when the daughter comes back to her and says, 'Oh, Mummy, I have been a foolish, foolish girl.' And the mother will take her back, because that is what mothers always do, Mma. And that will be that."

She looked at him. Mr. J.L.B. Matekoni did not go in for long speeches, but this one, lengthy though it was, was firm and decisive.

"So you think I should forget about the whole thing, Rra?"

"Yes," he said. "And are you not hungry now, Mma? It is getting late and most people—not all, of course, but most people—will have had their dinner."

She sighed. "You're probably right. I should forget about it. And we should have our dinner."

He reached out to touch her lightly on the forearm. Mr. J.L.B. Matekoni was not physically demonstrative, but this gesture spoke volubly to all the love he felt for this woman, and for so much else in the world: for the kindness of women, for the touching concern a woman could have for the unhappiness of another, for the willingness of women to make dinner, day after day, for their husbands. There were men who cooked, Mr. J.L.B. Matekoni reminded himself, and perhaps he should do that himself—just to show her that he valued her so much and, incidentally, that he was not one of those old-fashioned men who would never change.

On impulse, he said, "Mma Ramotswe—would you teach me how to cook?"

She was unprepared for this, but touched. "I will do that, Rra. Yes, I will do that. When would you like to start?"

He had not thought about that. There were immediate projects, and there were more general projects. There was a difference. "Next month?" he said.

She smiled. "That will be a good time to start, Rra. When the rains come."

"Yes," he said. "When the rains come."

CHAPTER FOURTEEN

YOU SHOULD SEE HIS TEETH

WHILE MMA RAMOTSWE and Mr. J.L.B. Matekoni were having their conversation about Calviniah—and cooking—Charlie was standing anxiously at the front door of Queenie-Queenie's parental home listening to the loud barking of a dog. Queenie-Queenie had told him that her parents had a dog, and that in her opinion it was too dangerous to be kept in the house.

"That dog has big-time psychological problems," she said. "One of these days he is going to eat somebody—I mean, really eat them, Charlie. No, I'm not exaggerating: you should see his teeth."

Charlie made a face. "They should tie him up," he suggested. "They should tie him up in the back yard, where he cannot easily bite people who come to the house."

"They tried that," Queenie-Queenie retorted. "But he ate the rope. And he likes to sleep on the sofa. He is unhappy if he cannot sleep on the sofa. He growls and growls. He is a very bad dog, Charlie."

"I do not like dogs like that," Charlie muttered.

"Just ignore him," Queenie-Queenie advised. "If you look into the eyes of that dog, he will bite you. Just look up at the ceiling or out of the window; then he will forget to bite you. That's the best way of dealing with him."

Charlie did not enjoy that conversation. He was already intimidated by the thought of Queenie-Queenie's domestic circumstances—by the disparity between her social position and his—and to add the threat of an unfriendly dog hardly helped. He had also been worrying about Hector's offer of a job. He was not at all sure that he wanted to work for somebody who was prepared to sabotage the cars of his debtors, but he had not been sure how to refuse. If he said no, then Queenie-Queenie's father might well be offended—Hector, after all, was his only son, and he must approve of what he did. Yet, in spite of this uncertainty, he had made up his mind. He would refuse to do Hector's bidding—he would not work for him.

And now, on the evening of his first invitation to have dinner with her father—her mother was away—that dreadful dog was starting up. He drew in his breath and made sure that his shirt was tucked properly into his trousers. He had polished his shoes and bought a new pair of laces. He had paid his cousin five pula to wash and iron his second pair of trousers—his church trousers, as his mother used to call them—and they, at least, looked smart enough, although one leg was fraying at the bottom. Nobody would notice that, though, especially if he crossed his legs in such a way that the good leg obscured the bad one.

Queenie-Queenie answered the door. He noticed how she smiled when she saw him, and his heart gave a leap. She would not smile like that, he thought, if she did not love him. She loves me . . . The words, uttered but not sounded, brought on a feeling that Charlie had rarely, if ever, experienced before—a feeling of pride, of gratitude, almost of relief. Nobody had been proud of him before, or at least nobody had expressed it; and he was not sure if he had been loved, even by his parents. His mother had been too busy, with too many mouths to feed and with her work as a domestic servant for an ungrateful employer; she had not had the time to love her children, because all her energy was spent in simply keeping them alive. And his father had been a drinker who spent all his time in the shebeen, and sometimes did not even recognise his children when he came home. It was no surprise, then, that there had not been much family life and that everyone had gone their separate ways as soon as an opportunity presented itself. And now there was somebody for whom he was special: me, he thought, me! Charlie! Special!

Queenie-Queenie whispered, "You aren't nervous, are you?"

He looked down at his shoes, at his new laces, tied too tightly, perhaps. "Me?" He affected a laugh. "Why should I be nervous?"

But then he thought: I should be honest, because you must be honest with somebody who loves you. And so he said, "Yes, I am very nervous, Queenie. I am shaking inside my shoes."

She looked down at his shoes. "You have new laces, I see. They are very smart."

He smiled. "You like them?"

"Yes, I like laces like that."

She glanced over her shoulder, into the room that opened up from the entrance hall behind her. Charlie followed her gaze. There was bulky, expensive furniture of the sort he had seen in Phuti Radiphuti's furniture store: heavy chairs and a sofa covered in shiny grey leather. Those sofas cost more than he earned in a year, he reflected; more than his entire year's wage as an apprentice detective. He could buy one sofa, at the most, and then have no money for anything else for twelve months; no money for food, even, or for bus fares or new laces, let alone new shoes. He would just have a sofa to sit on and not even anywhere to put it, because there would be no money for rent. He would have to put his sofa under a tree somewhere, at the edge of town, and live on it, eating lizards and birds' eggs and even the remains of old sandwiches, crusts, thrown out of bus windows by passengers. He would sit on his sofa and eat such things and wait for something to happen.

Queenie-Queenie reached out and patted his shoulder. Even that had an electric effect on him, sending a shiver of pleasure down into his chest—into his heart, he felt; right into his heart.

"You don't need to be nervous, Charlie," she said. "The daddy is looking forward to meeting you."

Charlie swallowed. "You have told him?"

She shook her head. "Not in so many words. But I did say: 'Daddy, there is a really nice boy I want you to meet.' That is what I said, Charlie, and he said, 'I am always happy to meet nice boys, Queenie, if that is what you want me to do.'"

Charlie took some comfort from this, but not much. "What if he doesn't like me?"

Queenie-Queenie brushed this aside. "Of course he'll like you, Charlie."

"And if I tell him that we want to get married? What will he say then? Will he say, 'And how many cattle do you have?'"

"If he says that, then you should say to him, 'There will be plenty of cattle in the future.'"

That, thought Charlie, was not the way it worked, but he did not have the chance to express these doubts, as Queenie-Queenie had begun to usher him through the hall and into the room beyond. As he walked beside her, Charlie was aware of the fact that his shoes were squeaking. He had not noticed it before, and perhaps it was caused by the expensive wooden floor underfoot, but they were definitely squeaking. He tried not to put too much weight on his step, which helped, but led to his using a strange, rather exaggerated gait, as if he were walking on hot coals.

"You shouldn't walk like that," whispered Queenie-Queenie. "My father won't like a boy who walks like that."

Charlie bit his lip. He was not sure that it was a good idea to have accepted Queenie-Queenie's invitation. He did not belong here, in this house of expensive furniture, with its noisy floor and its . . . He looked up at the light fittings. He had never seen anything like this. Ten bulbs? Twenty? He had a single bulb in his room—a single, dim bulb that ran on electricity that he knew his uncle stole by attaching an illegal wire to a nearby cable. To live by stolen light, in a room shared with young cousins, one of whom still wet the bed, and another whose feet had an unpleasant odour, and now to be here, under the glare of a costly light fitting probably brought all the way from Johannesburg by some fancy electrician; that was to invite exposure. Queenie-Queenie's father would see through him immediately. He would say, "This is not what you are used to, is it, young man?" And he would have to hang his head and say nothing because there was nothing he could say.

Queenie-Queenie's father was sitting on one of the large leather sofas. On the wall behind him was a large picture of a giraffe, painted on dark velvet. Beside the sofa, on a glass-topped table, a table lamp in the shape of an eagle was surmounted by an elaborate tasselled shade in a silvery material.

"Ha!" said the father. "So here you are, Mr. Charlie."

Charlie had expected a traditional greeting, and was taken aback. He muttered a few indistinct words.

Queenie-Queenie's father said, "What?"

"I said I am very happy to meet you, Rra."

Queenie-Queenie's father acknowledged the sentiment with a

nod of his head. Then he introduced himself. "I am called Isaiah. That is my name. Isaiah."

Charlie bit his lip again. "I am Charlie," he said.

"I know that," said Isaiah.

"Charlie is a detective," said Queenie-Queenie. "I've told you that already, I think, Daddy. A private detective."

Isaiah raised an eyebrow. "Yes, I knew that too. You work for those ladies, don't you? That Mma Ramotswe."

"I do," said Charlie. "She is my boss."

Isaiah gestured for Charlie to sit down. The leather upholstery of the chair on which he sat squeaked in protest.

"Sometimes I think these chairs are still alive," said Isaiah. "I think they are saying to us: Do not sit on us too heavily, please."

Queenie-Queenie laughed, and Charlie followed her example. "You would not want a chair to walk away on its legs," he said.

This amused Isaiah. "That is very funny—a chair walking away on its legs. That is very funny."

This was followed by silence. Queenie-Queenie had now taken a seat on the sofa, beside her father. She glanced at Charlie before turning to address Isaiah.

"Charlie and I are going out together," she said.

Her father looked at Charlie. "So, you are going out. Where are you going?"

Charlie was not sure how to respond. Was this a joke, or was it an enquiry?

"Out," said Queenie-Queenie. "We go out together, Daddy."

Her father said nothing. Then, after a minute or so of now rather painful silence, Queenie-Queenie went on, "And Charlie would like to ask you something."

Isaiah closed his eyes briefly. "There are many questions to be asked," he said.

From somewhere inside the house there came the sound of a door opening. Then, bounding into the room came a large brown dog. Stopping in its tracks when it saw Charlie, the animal bared its teeth.

"Meat!" shouted Queenie-Queenie.

Charlie looked at her in astonishment. "You're giving him meat?"

"No, that's his name. Meat! Down!"

The dog began to crouch, but then rose and walked slowly towards Charlie, its body moving in a curiously sinuous motion.

"Just hold out your hand," said Queenie-Queenie. "He won't bite you."

Watched with unconcealed amusement by Queenie-Queenie's father, Charlie extended a hand. The dog sniffed at it, and then licked it. Its demeanour now was friendly rather than threatening.

Isaiah laughed. "You see? You see—he likes you." He paused. "Meat is a good judge of character, you know."

The dog was now sniffing at Charlie's shoes. Then he lay down at his feet, looking up at him.

"That's amazing," said Isaiah. "Look at that, Queenie! See that? Meat likes your young man."

Queenie-Queenie's pleasure was obvious. "I am happy that he likes him. That is very good, Daddy."

Isaiah was observing Charlie with interest. "Questions," he said abruptly. "We were talking about questions."

Charlie looked down at the dog. There was no reason to be frightened of it; Isaiah was a different matter. He transferred his gaze to Queenie-Queenie, who smiled encouragingly. "We would like to get married, Rra," he blurted out. Then he added, "Soon. Maybe next month."

Queenie-Queenie beamed with pleasure. "You hear that, Daddy?"

Isaiah threw a glance at his daughter before looking back at Charlie. "You say you're a detective. You're not a policeman?"

"Private detective," Queenie-Queenie interjected. "He looks into important questions for private people. It is not crime—it is not that sort of thing."

"Let him talk," snapped Isaiah.

"I am not police," said Charlie. "I am on the civil side."

"The civil side?"

"Yes, business. Private affairs. That sort of thing."

Isaiah nodded. "We are traditional people," he said. "We still follow our Botswana customs."

Queenie-Queenie looked anxious. "Charlie is very traditional," she said. "He respects all the traditions, don't you, Charlie?"

Charlie looked at her pleadingly. He knew exactly why traditions had been raised: this was all about *bogadi,* the bride price.

"It will be some time before Charlie can pay what is needed," Queenie-Queenie said. "There are many people these days who do it that way."

Charlie wanted to add that there were many people who now ignored the custom of bride payment altogether, but that was not traditional, and he had just been described as being traditional.

"I wouldn't rule that out," said Isaiah. "There are many ways of doing it."

Queenie-Queenie clapped her hands together. "That's right, Daddy. There are many ways."

Charlie took a deep breath. "I should get the money quite soon," he said. "There are part-time jobs I can do. Hector has offered me a part-time job, but I am not going to take that one."

Charlie did not see Queenie-Queenie's frantic signal. Isaiah did, though, and he turned sharply to Charlie. "My son, Hector?"

"Yes. He has offered me a job with his firm. But, as I said, I am not going to take it."

Isaiah sat quite still. His voice was lowered. "And what exactly was that job?"

Queenie-Queenie started to say something but was silenced by a look from her father.

"He lends money," said Charlie. "He wanted me to . . ." He hesitated. "He wanted me to help him recover payments. But I won't do it. I am not going to go and wreck their cars. I am not going to do something like that."

Isaiah closed his eyes. Charlie looked miserably towards Queenie-Queenie, who was staring at him with contained fury.

Isaiah opened his eyes. "Queenie, do you know about this?"

Queenie-Queenie sighed. "He has been trying to help Charlie."

"Help put him in prison," shouted Isaiah. "Yes, prison. Prison is what you get for that sort of thing. Same as last time. Same, same." He paused. "He promised me he wouldn't get involved in that sort of thing again. He promised."

Queenie-Queenie sagged. "Maybe he didn't mean it, Daddy. Maybe—"

"Maybe, maybe," snapped Isaiah. "Everything is maybe this, maybe that." He turned to Charlie. "I am very pleased that you said you would not do it. That shows me that you are your own man. That is very good. You have stood up to him."

Charlie acknowledged the compliment with a nod of his head, and Isaiah seemed reassured. The anger in his voice abated.

"You do not need to worry about money," he said. "We do not want any *bogadi*. If you are going to look after my daughter and make her happy, then that will be enough."

Queenie-Queenie's reaction was immediate. Rising from her seat, she rushed over to her father and threw her arms around him. "Now I'm happy, Daddy. I'm happy, happy, happy. And we don't want a big wedding—next week, maybe. Just you and us and maybe the aunties."

"You cannot get married without aunties," said Isaiah.

"Of course not. But we do not need all those big parties and feasts and things. Just a reverend. That's all."

"It's your life," said Isaiah.

Charlie looked at him. "Thank you, Rra. Thank you."

At his feet, Meat stirred. Charlie reached down to pat him on the head. He let out a yelp of pain and surprise. The dog had turned and nipped him. It was not a serious bite, but the skin was broken.

"He is a very bad dog, that one," Isaiah observed, adding, "And you know something, Charlie? If a bad dog tells you he has become a good dog, don't believe him."

CHAPTER FIFTEEN

A MAN WHO SAVES LADIES

IT WAS NOT UNTIL the telephone call from Mma Potokwane that Saturday that Mma Ramotswe remembered the offer her friend had made. It had been mentioned on her last visit to the Orphan Farm, when, after Mma Ramotswe had mentioned her old friend Poppy, and her plight, Mma Potokwane had suggested that she should deal with the preacher who appeared to have taken advantage of his convert. Now, over the telephone, after a few words about other issues of the day, Mma Potokwane had suggested that the two of them pay a visit to the preacher's Sunday meeting the following day.

"I have made some enquiries," said Mma Potokwane. "I have found out that he has a meeting every Sunday near the dam. They have some sort of *braai* there at lunch time and they sing a lot. Apparently, it's quite a show."

Mma Ramotswe had agreed to go. She was keen to see Poppy, whom she had not seen for years, and there was a degree of fascination about charismatic preachers, of which the Reverend Flat Ponto seemed to be a prime example. She believed herself to be impervious to their appeal, but she knew that many people fell for them—as Poppy was said to have done. Mma Ramotswe was a regular church-goer, attending the Anglican Cathedral opposite the hospital, but that was different. The clergy there were real clergy, who had studied for years and knew what they were talking about, rather than somebody who had just decided to become a preacher—just like that. Poor women, she thought: To divest yourself of your financial security to benefit a . . . well, what was he? She thought of the expression her father had used to describe those who hoodwinked others into sup-porting their dubious schemes: hot-air merchant. Yes, the Reverend Flat Ponto, with his strangely named Church of Christ, Mechanic, would undoubtedly be the worst sort of charlatan—one who preyed on vulnerable women and tricked them out of their money. Such people deserved to be stopped, and if Mma Potokwane could do that—using her justly celebrated ability to cut through nonsense of every sort—then Mma Ramotswe would be pleased to see that hap-pen. And it might even take place, she thought, that Sunday, in the midst of whatever trickery the preacher had lined up for his gullible followers.

Mma Ramotswe arranged to collect Mma Potokwane in her white van on Sunday morning. She would arrive in time for her to give a report to Mma Tsepole on Daisy's progress before they set off for the picnic grounds near the dam. Mma Potokwane had been pleased to hear that Daisy had settled in so well, and that the young woman who was looking after her had met with Mma Ramotswe's approval. If all went according to plan, Daisy's more permanent arrangements with her long-term foster parents would be in place in a couple of months. "In the meantime, Mma, I am sure she will be very happy with you."

When she met Mma Tsepole, Mma Ramotswe reassured her that Daisy was eating well, had put on a bit of weight, and seemed to be happy in her new surroundings. "I am sure she's thinking of you, Mma," she said.

Mma Tsepole had given Mma Ramotswe some cake to take back to Daisy. It was carefully wrapped in an old tea-towel, and labelled *For Daisy, from your Old House Mummy, who is thinking of you all the time.*

Mma Ramotswe had looked at this—at the wording that seemed to be so odd, but that was somehow just right. "She will be very happy," she said.

They arrived at the dam at the same time as a number of others. People had travelled out in their cars, although some came in a line of overcrowded minibuses belching diesel fumes. Once they had parked their cars or disembarked from the minibuses, people drifted over towards an area of cleared ground below an outcrop of granite rocks—a small *kopje* of the sort favoured by baboons and dassies, the scurrying rock rabbits that inhabited such terrain. Tables had been set out in this clearing, some under the shade of the one or two acacia trees that had been left standing, others out in the sun. Several fires had been built in the middle of small stone circles and over these there were placed iron grids for the barbecue, the *braai*. Emanating from these fires there was already that smell of roasting that was so characteristic of just about every social gathering in Botswana. Meat was what people expected, and what any attentive host would provide.

There was no sign yet of the Reverend Flat Ponto, although a small group of stewards, wearing white armbands, was gathered at the edge of the parking area, evidently awaiting the arrival of an official party.

"The reception committee," said Mma Ramotswe, pointing this group out to Mma Potokwane.

Mma Potokwane snorted. "I know the smell of this sort of

thing," she muttered. "This is all showmanship, Mma. This is not real religion."

Mma Ramotswe looked about her. How did one tell the difference between the two?, she wondered. She was inclined to agree with Mma Potokwane, in that she felt that there really was a difference between those preachers who had love in their heart and those who had money in the same place. Or power, perhaps, because there were certainly people who wanted only to hold people in thrall, to dominate them and tell them what to do, even if they were not all that interested in separating them from their hard-earned savings. From what she had heard, the Reverend Flat Ponto fell into the latter camp, but then she remembered what Mr. J.L.B. Matekoni had said about him—that he was a mechanic who had been caught up with the enthusiasm of a marching church and had only then founded his own church. That sounded as if it might have been a real seeing of the light—whatever the light might be—rather than part of a cynical plan to take advantage of others. She would see; Clovis Andersen stressed time and time again that one should have an open mind and should not jump to conclusions. It was all right for Mma Potokwane, as matron of an Orphan Farm, to make up her mind on the basis of—of what? Her sense of smell? But she did not have that professional interest in detachment and openness to alternative possibilities that you had if you were the proprietor of a well-known, if small, detective agency.

They drifted over towards one of the barbecue fires. A woman who was preparing meat for the grill greeted them warmly. "You are new, my sisters," she said. "I have not seen you before."

"We've heard of the reverend," said Mma Ramotswe.

"We've heard good things," added Mma Potokwane, catching Mma Ramotswe's eye as she spoke.

The woman wiped her hands on a cloth. "I'm not surprised," she said. "Good news travels fast." She put down the cloth. "Would you like sausages? There is some steak, but that is for the Blessed Ones."

Mma Potokwane raised an eyebrow. "The Blessed Ones, Mma?"

"Yes," the woman replied, "they are the ones who have been particularly helpful to the reverend in his mission." She paused. "They are all ladies."

Mma Ramotswe and Mma Potokwane tried not to look at one another. They were both thinking the same thing, Mma Ramotswe imagined, and it would not do to reveal their suspicions if they wanted to hear more from this woman.

But Mma Ramotswe had an idea. Yes, of course. Poppy would be a Blessed One. If you gave somebody a Mercedes-Benz, that would undoubtedly justify promotion to the ranks of the blessed.

"For example," she said, "Poppy. Do you know that lady, Mma? She is called Poppy and she comes from Francistown."

The woman smiled. "Of course I know her, Mma. And yes, she is a Blessed One." She reached for the cloth again and wiped her hands afresh. "She is here today, you know. She is over there, with those other two ladies."

Mma Ramotswe looked around. The crowd had grown, and people were moving about, greeting each other, engaged in animated conversation. "Where?" she asked.

"Over there," said the woman, pointing. "Under that tree. See? There are three ladies. They are all Blessed Ones." She paused. "I should really take them some steak."

Mma Ramotswe stared at the small group. She should have concealed her surprise—Clovis Andersen was clear about the need to do that—but she could not manage that. She gasped.

"What is it, Mma?" whispered Mma Potokwane.

The woman had turned her attention to the grill, and Mma Ramotswe was able to speak freely.

"I know two of those ladies," she said to Mma Potokwane. "That one on the left is Poppy—the woman I told you about. The old friend I have not seen for many years. That is her."

Mma Potokwane shaded her eyes to get a better view. "And the others?"

"That one standing in the middle is a woman called Mma Boko. She lives in those flats near the university. I spoke to her recently about . . . well, it was another matter entirely."

"Would you like to go over to speak to them?" asked Mma Potokwane. "I assume that we're allowed to speak to Blessed Ones, even if they are very blessed."

Mma Ramotswe smiled at the remark, and was about to answer it with a wry observation of her own, when she was distracted by singing at the edge of the clearing. Somebody had arrived, and people were drifting over towards the new arrivals. It was the Reverend Flat Ponto and a small group of people accompanying him. Mma Ramotswe stared. She turned to Mma Potokwane and pointed.

"What?" asked Mma Potokwane.

Mma Ramotswe opened her mouth to speak, but then shook her head in disbelief.

"What is it, Mma?" Mma Potokwane pressed.

Mma Ramotswe recovered. "That woman there," she said, "is Nametso—she is the one I told you about, Mma, the one who is being unkind to her mother." An old friend who was late, she thought, and who then wasn't. But it would be too difficult to explain that to Mma Potokwane right at that moment, as too much was happening. And more than that—she was thinking, and the thoughts that came to her were so significant that she felt she simply had to sit down, rest her head in her hands, and work the whole thing out.

She closed her eyes. The key to everything was a Mercedes-Benz. Follow the Mercedes-Benz—well, not actually follow it—but work out what role it played. And the role, surely, was central. A Mercedes-Benz, especially a silver one, was not a retiring, obscure sort of car—it would be at the heart of whatever was happening.

And now she knew just what that was. It was only a surmise, of course, but the truth had suddenly come to her, and she needed to speak to Poppy without further delay.

"Mma Potokwane," she said. "I need to talk privately to somebody. Can I leave you here for a moment?"

Mma Potokwane replied that she was perfectly happy to be left to her own devices. She suggested, though, that they should meet after a while and help themselves to sausages. Mma Ramotswe agreed that it would be wise to stake a claim to sausages before they all disappeared and that she would need only half an hour or so for some conversations that she needed to have.

POPPY EMBRACED HER WARMLY, hugging her and laughing with pleasure. Standing beside her, Mma Boko smiled and nodded in recognition towards Mma Ramotswe.

"This is my old, old friend," said Poppy to Mma Boko. "We have not seen each other for many years."

"We were girls back then," said Mma Ramotswe, extricating herself from Poppy's enthusiastic hug. "It is a long time ago."

"We've met," said Mma Boko, offering Mma Ramotswe her hand. "Not long ago."

Mma Ramotswe took Poppy's arm. "Could we talk, Mma?"

"You go ahead," said Mma Boko. "I must go and help some of the sisters."

Mma Ramotswe led Poppy into the shade. "It is good to see you, Mma," she said.

"Yes," said Poppy. "I had heard news of you from time to time, but not very much. You lose touch, don't you? The years pass and you suddenly realise that you haven't seen people, and then you . . ." She shrugged. "I suppose you just lose touch. There are too many things to do and you don't find the time to write a letter. You know how it is."

"Oh, I do," agreed Mma Ramotswe. "But you know who I saw not all that long ago? You remember Calviniah?"

"Of course I do. Is she well, Mma?"

"She is very well," said Mma Ramotswe. She hesitated. She could continue this conversation along these lines, following the well-worn tracks of the old friends' catch-up—the endless questions about who was where and doing what, who had married whom, and so on, but that was not what she needed to do. She needed to ask Poppy a simple question about a Mercedes-Benz.

"I heard something, Mma," she began. "I heard that you had become a very keen member of the Church of . . ."

"The Church of Christ, Mechanic," Poppy prompted. "Yes, Mma. I am a sort of elder now. They call us the Blessed Ones—not that I would boast about such a thing."

"Of course not," said Mma Ramotswe. "But it must be a great honour to be blessed."

Poppy nodded. "Yes, Mma, I think it is."

"And I heard too," Mma Ramotswe continued, "that you have been very good to the reverend. I heard that you gave him a Mercedes-Benz."

Poppy seemed surprised that Mma Ramotswe should know this, but confirmed the fact. "Yes, Mma. I gave him a car to help him in his work." Then she added, "But the reverend has asked me not to talk about it. He doesn't want people discussing it. He is very modest, you see."

"That was very generous of you, Mma." Mma Ramotswe looked

at her old friend's face. People change. Things had happened to that face. The years. "Was it a silver Mercedes-Benz, Mma?"

Poppy smiled. "It was a lovely car, Mma. Yes, it was silver."

Mma Ramotswe pressed ahead. "And so the reverend is driving around in it right now—doing the Lord's work?"

Poppy continued to smile. "He was, but then he sent the car out into the rural areas for his followers out there to do the work. They are using it somewhere else, I think—maybe up in Maun. He has people up there, and they must travel up and down to Gaborone on the Lord's work, I think."

"I see." They were the only words that came to Mma Ramotswe, and yet they were just right. She did see. She saw very well. And now she had to speak to Mma Boko to ascertain whether what she saw was indeed what was there.

SHE FOUND MMA BOKO talking to two women at one of the tables under the trees. They were stacking hymn books and inserting sheets of paper into each.

"These are the reverend's texts for the day," explained Mma Boko, handing one of the sheets to Mma Ramotswe.

"Very interesting," said Mma Ramotswe. "But, Mma, could I have a quiet word with you?"

Mma Boko excused herself from her companion, joining Mma Ramotswe under another tree. The tree was in flower, and tiny flecks of blossom, white and virtually weightless, drifted from its boughs. "What is it, Mma?" she asked. "I must help those ladies."

"Yes, of course," said Mma Ramotswe. "It's just that I wanted to ask you something connected with what we talked about the other day."

"Yes, Mma?"

"That young woman who lives next door. You know she is here?"

Mma Boko gave a start. "Where, Mma? I don't see her."

"She's over there—with the reverend."

Mma Boko looked over in the direction of the knot of people around the Reverend Flat Ponto. She drew in her breath audibly. Mma Ramotswe could see that she was struggling with something— but with what? Jealousy? "I see." Mma Boko composed herself, and her expression now was sweet. "You see, he has helped her in the past, Mma. He sometimes goes to give her texts. He is trying to save her." Her eyes shone. "That is what he does, Mma. He saves people."

Especially ladies, thought Mma Ramotswe. And there were so many ladies to be saved.

"Saves them?" asked Mma Ramotswe.

Mma Boko stared at her. "Of course."

Mma Ramotswe was silent for a moment. It was difficult to judge how one should approach these matters, she thought. You had to be honest, but you had to be careful not to be too brutal.

"You have a special relationship with the reverend, don't you, Mma?"

Mma Boko gave her a searching look. And then the decision was made. Mma Ramotswe was to be trusted. "I believe that he and I will one day become joint agents of the Lord, Mma. I believe that—since you ask."

"You believe that he will marry you?"

"If the Lord approves," said Mma Boko. "Which I think he does. He has already given signs of that approval."

"I see."

"Yes, he approves very firmly, I believe."

Mma Ramotswe steeled herself. The moment could not be put off much longer. "Mma Boko, may I ask you something? Who told you about the businessman who rents the flat for Nametso? Was it the reverend, by any chance?"

The question took Mma Boko by surprise, and she seemed to struggle with something before she answered. But then she said, "Yes, it was. He told me about it. He disapproved very strongly—as you can imagine."

Mma Ramotswe bit her lip. He would; he would.

"Do you see him about the place often?" she asked. "Does he go to save Nametso just about every day?"

Mma Ramotswe noticed that Mma Boko's hands were shaking. She knew. And of course that should not surprise her; a woman would know these things. She was equally convinced, though, that Mma Boko would have denied any knowledge she had of what the Reverend Flat Ponto was up to. She would have known and not known, both at the same time. That was the way people survived in the face of crushing disappointment.

"Oh, Mma," Mma Boko suddenly blurted out. "That girl is a Jezebel. She is leading the reverend astray. He knows that his future must be with me, and yet he is being kind to her because she needs support—and saving. But his heart is not in anything that he does with her, Mma. I know that. I know that very well."

There was nothing more that Mma Ramotswe could say to Mma Boko other than to hold her hand briefly and whisper, "I am sure that he loves you, Mma. But it is good to be careful about loving men back. Think about that, Mma."

SHE LEFT MMA BOKO and began to look for Poppy. The crowd was now quite large, and there were children running around, squealing and yelling and making everything noisier and more chaotic. Eventually she found Poppy talking to an elderly man in a wheelchair. She drew her aside and a young couple came and wheeled the man off to one of the food tables.

"Are you enjoying the picnic?" asked Poppy. "People love these occasions."

"It is all very joyful," said Mma Ramotswe.

"That is the reverend's influence," said Poppy. "He spreads light wherever he goes."

Mma Ramotswe was non-committal. "Well, he's certainly popular." She looked at Poppy. Who, she wondered, did Poppy have to pick up the pieces? Were there children, or siblings, who would provide her with a shoulder to cry on? For a few moments she wondered whether she should do this at all, or whether she should walk away and let these people get on with living their lives as they saw fit. But then she thought, No, I shall not do that—because if I don't do anything there will be more Poppies and more Nametsos and poor Mma Bokos. There were any number of ladies with hearts to break, just looking for a charismatic preacher to break them.

"Mma," began Mma Ramotswe, "I have found out something that makes me very happy."

"Oh yes?" asked Poppy.

"Yes. I have found out that the Mercedes-Benz you gave to the reverend is being put to very good use."

"I know that," said Poppy. "It is doing the work of the Lord up in Maun. Or somewhere up there."

Mma Ramotswe shook her head. "No, Mma, it is doing good work far closer to home. He has given it to a young woman—a very attractive young woman. She is driving round in it right here in Gaborone."

Poppy frowned. "I don't think so, Mma. The reverend told me—it is out in a remote area doing work there."

Mma Ramotswe sighed. "I'm afraid not, Mma. It is being used by that young woman over there. You see her? Right next to the reverend? He is being very kind to her. He visits her most days, I believe—trying to save her, of course—and he has given her the car for her own use. For getting to work and going shopping too, I think. She has some very nice clothes, and she needs to go off and buy those. A silver Mercedes-Benz is ideal for that sort of thing, you know."

Poppy listened to this in silence. She pursed her lips. She looked down at the ground, and then up at the sky. Mma Ramotswe reached out and took her hand—the hand of an old friend.

WHAT HAPPENED NEXT happened rather quickly. Mma Ramotswe found Mma Potokwane helping herself to a plateful of sausages from one of the barbecue pits.

"I am helping myself," explained the matron. "After all, don't they say that the Lord helps those who help themselves?"

"They do," said Mma Ramotswe. "And I think that it is probably true. But, Mma, I have something very important to tell you."

Mma Potokwane listened gravely as Mma Ramotswe outlined her exchanges with Mma Boko and Poppy. As the tale lengthened and its full implications became clear, she looked around for a table on which to put down her plate of untouched sausages. "This is very shocking, Mma," she said, wiping sausage fat from her fingers.

"It is the way the world is," said Mma Ramotswe. "I think this sort of thing is going on all the time."

Mma Potokwane straightened the front of her blouse. It was such a gesture as might be made by one setting out for battle—a girding of the chest, a readiness to carry the banner. "I am ready, Mma Ramotswe. I am going to have a word with the reverend."

"Be careful, Mma," said Mma Ramotswe.

"Ha!" snorted Mma Potokwane.

"He has many admirers here," cautioned Mma Ramotswe.

"Ha!" Mma Potokwane repeated.

Mma Ramotswe watched in fascination as Mma Potokwane strode across the clearing to the place where the reverend was standing, surrounded by a small coterie of ladies. She watched as Mma Potokwane elbowed her way past these women and took the reverend firmly by the arm, leading him away from the circle. Then she watched as the reverend was addressed by Mma Potokwane, who gestured firmly as she spoke, jabbing one index finger into his chest while shaking the other one directly under his nose. The reverend, cowed, took a step backwards, only to be immediately advanced upon by Mma Potokwane. A further step back led to a fresh and even more intrusive advance.

It only took ten minutes, and then Mma Potokwane returned to Mma Ramotswe and her plate of sausages. The matron was smiling broadly.

"Well?" asked Mma Ramotswe.

"Simple," said Mma Potokwane. "All solved."

Mma Ramotswe was wide-eyed.

"Yes," Mma Potokwane said. "He's like many men like that. Lots of hot air and no muscle. No backbone either. One push and they fall to bits."

"And?"

"Well, I told him that we knew what he was up to. I told him that unless he took certain steps right now, today, then I would be clapping my hands and addressing everybody present. I would tell them that the Lord had spoken to me about the Reverend Flat Ponto and instructed me to tell them all about some of his part-time activities."

Mma Ramotswe began to smile.

"Yes," Mma Potokwane went on. "I told him that there were certain things he could do. He could restore to Poppy everything he had taken from her, including the silver Mercedes-Benz. Then he could tell Nametso that he was going back to his wife and that she was to go and see her mother without delay—and be kind to her again, as a daughter should be. I think that young woman will still do anything for that man, and so I suspect she will obey."

Mma Ramotswe wondered whether he would comply.

"Oh, he will, Mma," said Mma Potokwane. "I gave him half an hour to do these things. I also told him that he should watch his step in future, as we would be keeping an eye on him. I told him there was to be no further taking advantage of the members of his church."

"And do you really think he will do that?" asked Mma Ramotswe.

Mma Potokwane thought for a few moments. "I think he will," she said. "There's a reason why that man will do as I ask."

Mma Ramotswe waited to hear it.

"I only realised it today," said Mma Potokwane. "It came back to me. Flat Ponto was one of our children—a long time ago."

Mma Ramotswe expressed amazement. "A graduate of the Orphan Farm?"

"Yes," said Mma Potokwane. "I had forgotten about him, but then I remembered. And so I am sure that he will do as I tell him, Mma. And anyway, he was very ashamed when he saw it was me."

"I can imagine," said Mma Ramotswe.

"I think he might behave better in future," Mma Potokwane concluded. "I have seen something today."

"And what was that, Mma?" asked Mma Ramotswe.

Mma Potokwane pointed to a group of women standing under a tree. "There is a woman over there who has lost her husband. I happen to know about her—she lives in Tlokweng."

Mma Ramotswe waited. "That woman over there, Mma? The thin one?"

"That's her, Mma. And I saw him with her a short while ago. I saw how kind he was being to her. He went over to speak to her, and

I watched him reach into his pocket and give her money. That woman is very poor, Mma. He gave her some money—I saw it happen."

"So he is a kind man, Mma?"

Mma Potokwane smiled. "I think he is. And that's the biggest thing in my view, Mma Ramotswe—kindness. He's a kind man who is also a bit weak . . . But then, what men aren't a bit weak, Mma Ramotswe?"

"You're right, Mma," said Mma Ramotswe. "It is not always easy for men."

"No, it isn't," agreed Mma Potokwane. "Flat's problem is simply a problem that many men have—and reverends are obviously no exception."

"Ah," said Mma Ramotswe. She knew about that problem—the problem that so many men experienced. It was all to do with women and the effect that women had on them. Some men simply could not resist. It was not really their fault, she felt—it was a sort of design flaw in men. But they would have to try, and if Mma Potokwane, or her like, was around to help them try, then that might make it a bit easier for them. Poor men.

Mma Ramotswe's gaze shifted to Mma Potokwane's plate of sausages.

"You have these," said Mma Potokwane magnanimously. "I will get some more for myself."

Mma Ramotswe thanked her, and took the plate. Then she thought: of course, these sausages are now cold. The next plate of sausages would be warm.

"No, Mma," she said, handing the plate back to Mma Potokwane. "You are too generous, far too generous. I shall go and get some for myself—it is no bother."

ON MONDAY MORNING, Mma Ramotswe collected the mail on her way in to the office and had already opened and perused it by the time Mma Makutsi arrived. Mma Makutsi viewed the pile of letters on Mma Ramotswe's desk with an inquisitive eye. "There are many people writing to *us*, Mma," she said. The *us* was stressed because Mma Makutsi preferred to open everything herself, even if she immediately passed it on to Mma Ramotswe: this ensured that she saw everything, even those letters marked *personal* or *confidential*.

There was one letter in particular that Mma Ramotswe had set aside from the rest—a mixed bag of bills, advertisements, and rambling missives from members of the public who wrote, out of the blue, for information on family history, unsolved crimes, and ancient rural jealousies.

"There is a letter I think you should see," said Mma Ramotswe. "It is from Mma Mogorosi."

Mma Makutsi sat down at her desk, adjusted her spectacles, and began to read the letter that Mma Ramotswe had handed her. After she finished, she laid it down and sighed. "Why did he go to all that trouble?" she asked. "Just to impress people?"

Mma Ramotswe said, "Forgiveness is good, Mma. If she can forgive him, then that is a good outcome. And remember, Mma, he is a man—and a man of a certain age. When men get to that age, they sometimes do foolish things—they forget themselves—because they are . . . well, they become anxious that ladies no longer find them attractive. It is called insecurity, Mma."

Mma Makutsi snorted. "Men are very fortunate that women are so understanding." She paused, and smiled with a certain air of satisfaction. "So I was almost right, Mma. I said that man must be up to something—and he was. It's just that it wasn't quite the thing I thought he was up to. I did not think that he would just pretend to be having an affair with that mathematics teacher."

"Who was entirely innocent," Mma Ramotswe added. She paused as she contemplated innocence. She had suspected Mma Mogorosi of having an affair herself, having seen her with that man in the supermarket, allowing him to pinch her. But if she had been, then why would she have written that note to the teacher? Jealousy perhaps lay behind that, or double standards. She might have expected her husband to remain faithful while she herself had a dalliance with somebody else. Or the man in the supermarket was, indeed, a member of her family and not a lover at all. Or the husband was not making it up—he *was* having an affair and she was misleading them in saying that it was imaginary on his part. She might do that if she felt guilty about her own conduct and wanted to present him in a better light. That was possible.

Mma Ramotswe sighed. You had to sigh sometimes, because life was so complicated or impenetrable; or because people behaved in a messy way; or because there was simply no ready solution to a human mix-up. What did Clovis Andersen say about it? Anything? Did he not say that you should not expect a resolution of everything because some details in any picture were simply not there, and never would be? Did he not say that—that great man from Muncie, Indiana, who gave the world that singular gift of *The Principles of Private Detection*? It came back to her. *Don't think you can explain everything*, Clovis Andersen wrote, *because you can't.*

Mma Makutsi shook her head in wonderment at the foibles of people. "Sometimes you really have to ask yourself: Why do people do the things they do, Mma? That is what you ask yourself."

"Because they are people," said Mma Ramotswe. "I think that is the answer to that."

The door opened. It was Charlie. He looked at the two women. He smiled. "I have an announcement to make," he said. "Next Saturday, two o'clock sharp—I am getting married. It will be a small wedding because there is not much time, but you are both invited. And Phuti. And Mr. J.L.B. Matekoni."

Mma Ramotswe stood up. She held her arms open, and Charlie rushed headlong into them. She hugged him to her. He said, "Oh, Mma, oh, Mma . . . ," and he began to cry.

Mma Makutsi came out from behind her desk. She too opened her arms. "Dear Charlie," she said. "This is very good news."

Mma Ramotswe released Charlie, wiping at his tears of joy with the sleeve of her blouse. He turned to Mma Makutsi and she embraced him. Her glasses scraped the bridge of his nose. That did not matter.

Mma Makutsi made tea. They drank it while seated in a circle. They talked about what they would wear and about what Charlie should wear. Mma Makutsi said that Phuti had a suit that was a little bit too small for him but that should fit Charlie perfectly. It was made of a sort of shiny black fabric that was very fashionable these days, she said. Charlie said that he would love to try it. "Even if it is a bit tight, I can hold my stomach in," he said.

Not much work was done that morning, but there was not much work to do. At midday, Mma Ramotswe suggested that Charlie should take the afternoon off. Mma Makutsi said that he could come with her to her house and try on Phuti's suit. For her part, Mma Ramotswe had a lunch appointment, on the verandah of the President Hotel, where she was due to meet Poppy and Calviniah and talk about the old days in Mochudi.

They did just that. They talked. And at the end, Mma Ramotswe looked with fondness at her two old friends. Calviniah was happy because her daughter had returned to her; Poppy was relieved because she had been anxious about what she had done even before

Mma Potokwane resolved the situation for her. Her car had been returned, along with other property she had parted with. "I was very foolish," she said. "It went to my head, I'm afraid."

"We are all foolish at some time or another," said Mma Ramotswe. "There is no shame in that."

After their meal they went their separate ways. Mma Ramotswe started to drive back to the office, but thought better of it and made her way back to her house on Zebra Drive. She would spend some time in her garden, she decided, getting it ready for the rain that people said was forecast for the following day—the life-giving rain, the rain they had awaited for so long. And she would think about all the good things she had had in her life—good things given to her by her father, by her friends, by her country, Botswana, that dear and good place—and the good things she still had, which were so many; so numerous, in fact, that it would take far too long to count them.

afrika
afrika afrika
afrika afrika afrika
afrika afrika
afrika